Evolution's Child – Earthman
Republic of Luna

November 2092

I0546388

Charles Lee Lesher

"Where knowledge ends, religion begins."

Benjamin Disraeli (1804-1881)

Republic of Luna

This is a work of fiction. All characters, places or events portrayed in this book are fictitious and any resemblance to real people or events is purely coincidental. The author reserves the right to modify, change, add or subtract to this work in its entirety without notification or restriction.

File Compilation: 2015
Print ISBN 978-1-938586-06-4
eBook ISBN 978-1-938586-01-9

Shadow War Trilogy

Republic of Luna

Book 1: Evolution's Child - Earthman

Some Things About Chuck

Preamble

In a century filled with strife, the dogs of war are gathering once more. By late 2092, climate change and war have devastated the planet. Even thinned by bloodshed, famine, and disease, Earth's population exceeds 10 billion. Food and water are in short supply, refugee's number in the hundreds of millions and lawlessness abounds. Humanity is in turmoil.

Religious zealots exploit this despair, claiming it's God's punishment for man's misdeeds. Within the North American Federation, Christian theocracy displaced democracy, plunging once proud America into a Dark Age. On the other side of the planet, the Islamic Brotherhood controls a third of the world from Indonesia, across Asia and the Middle East and well onto the African continent, India the only holdout. China, the leading space faring nation on Earth, allies with the Brotherhood providing them with science and technology for a price. Only within the European Union is there still a semblance of individual freedom. The nations of the world align along sectarian lines as global violence escalates.

In sharp contrast, the Republic of Luna is a technocratic society where information flows freely and nothing is secret, a place governed by humanism and the laws of science. Out of necessity, life on an airless world burrows deep underground and to stay alive, Lunarians unlock nature's deepest secrets, gaining mastery over the genetic foundations of life itself. In doing so, they become the first true extraterrestrials.

From Washington to Rome to Mecca, when Earth's theists learn of the Lunarians meddling in human genetics, they denounce them as abominations. Prince Ahmed Mohammed Al Zarqowi, Caliph of the Islamic Brotherhood, believes he can hide behind this turmoil to attack Luna with impunity and create humanity's first multi-planet empire. To the Caliph this is simply the next step in a plan to bring an unbelieving world under Islamic Law. He unleashes forces intent on destroying the Republic before it's a half-century-old.

The Players

Quan Kiai

» Captain Kitajima Osaka
» Master Sergeant Susan Hackling
» Doctor Howard Grady
» Lieutenant Tempel Dugan
» Lieutenant Tatiana Tushar
» Sergeant Consuela Navarro
» Sergeant John Kipper
» S.I.T. Angel Lopez
» S.I.T. Samantha Odegaard
» Officer Lei Cheung
» Officer Brice Guyart
» Officer Marcel Piqualow
» Officer Karl Svensson
» Officer Corazon Montano
» Officer Karyl Stormberg
» Officer Zoey Tanaka
» Officer Alonzo Tushar

Major Players

❈ Analyst Lazarus Sheffield
❈ Captain Lindsey Marquest
❈ Pilot Nell Goddard
❈ Councilor Abigail O'Neil Dugan
❈ Security Chief Corso Dugan
❈ Officer Cristobal Calatrava
❈ Magi

Islamic Brotherhood

☪ Mohammed Basayev
☪ Imam Nassah Bakr
☪ Commander Ghafour
☪ Major General Abdel Salam Arif
☪ Minister Hasin bin Aunker
☪ Captain Mustafa Malik
☪ Havildar Anwar Jafa
☪ Dalal

Minor Players

☼ Isaac Crenshaw
☼ Constance Haig
☼ Tara Dugan
☼ Mallory Higgins
☼ Lee Chin
☼ Justine Harman
☼ Nicole Dugan
☼ Elizabeth Dugan
☼ Krystin Dugan
☼ Skylor Dugan
☼ Jordan Dugan
☼ Jamie Dugan
☼ Ben Dugan
☼ Zachary Taylor
☼ Yang Lee
☼ Chen Zhi
☼ Odessa Simpson
☼ Zechariah Hargrove

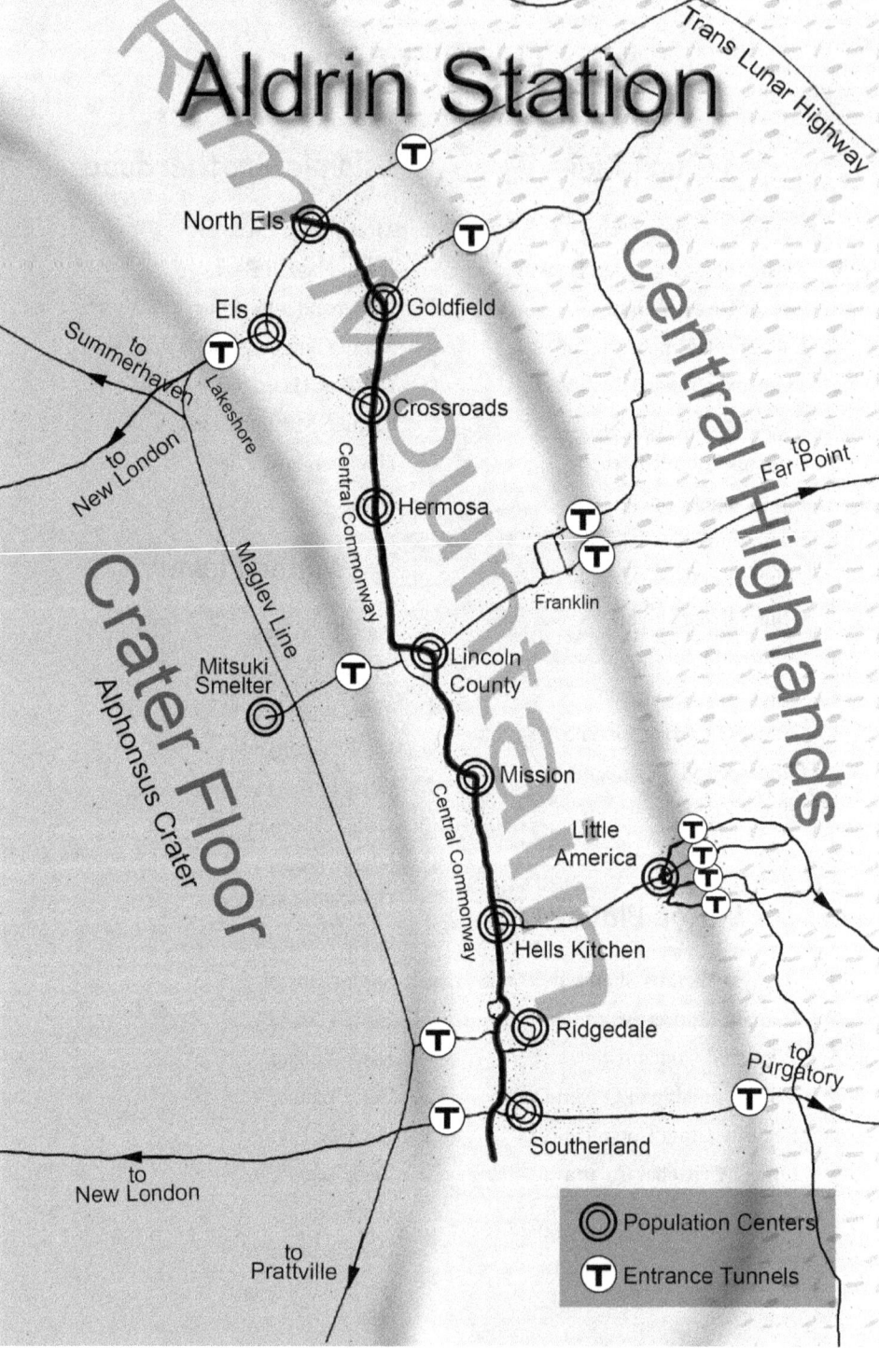

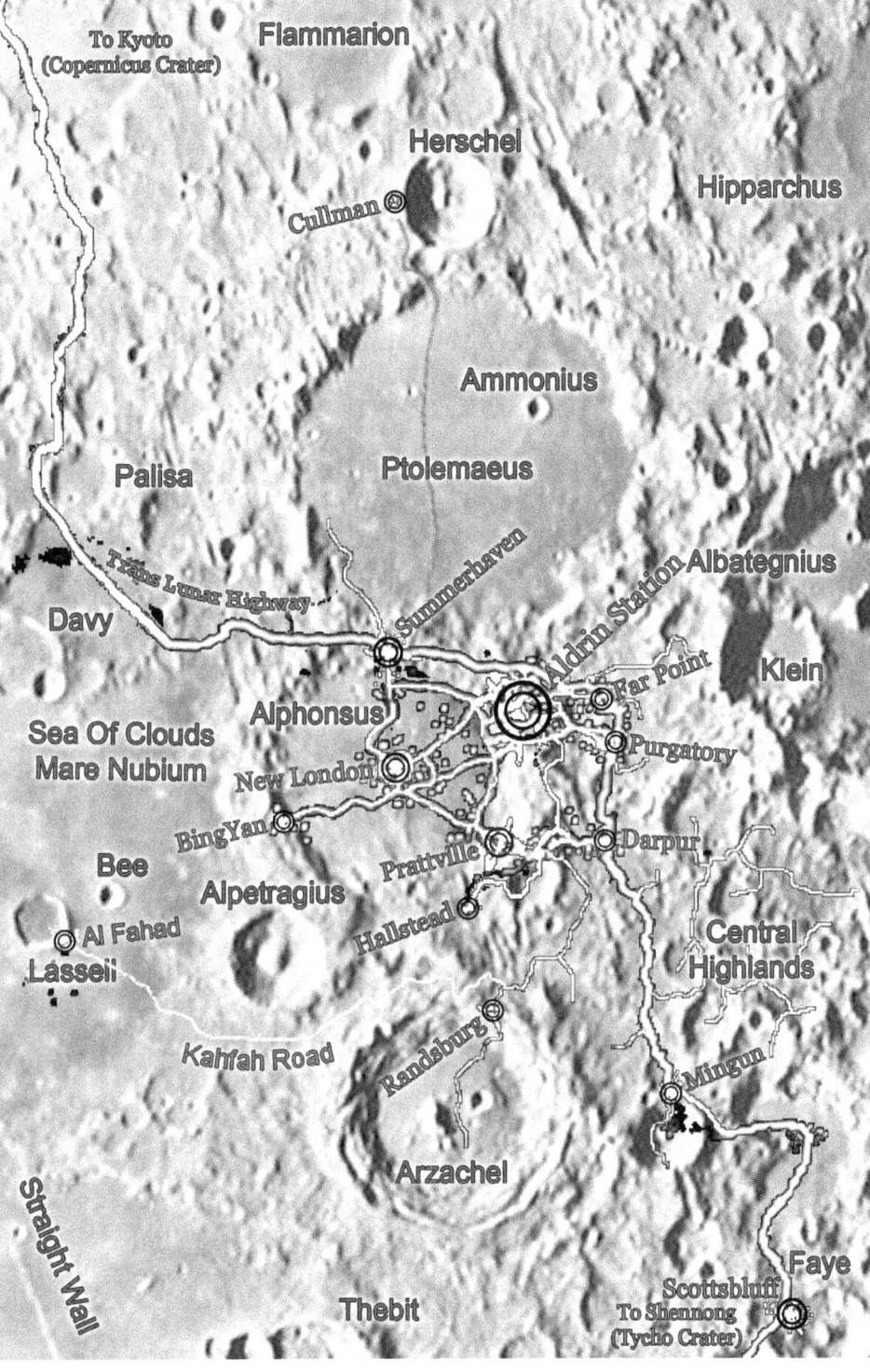

21st Century Timeline

Historical Detail	Year	Historical Detail
Abigail Katee O'Neil 10/15/99	1999	World population tops 6 billion
USS Cole attack kills 17	2000	India's population tops 1 billion
Pres: George Bush	2001	9/11/01 WTC destroyed kills 2996
Planetoid Quaoar is discovered	2002	US invades Afghanistan
1st full human genetic sequence	2003	US invades Iraq
France closes their last coal mine	2004	Asian Tsunami kills >225,000
Genetic therapy improves	2005	Hurricane Katrina kills >1300
Tree of Life project begins	2006	North Korea tests long-range missile
Human Epigenome Project	2007	Global climate change hotly debated
World economy plunges; Cloned organs	2008	Pres. Barack Obama (1st black president)
Iceland declares bankruptcy	2009	Iran launches first satalite
DNA Base Sequencer (DBS)	2010	Drought devastates southern US
Western Space Command	2011	ISS is militarized; Coalition of Christian Citizens
Orbital Nonproliferation Treaty	2012	World population tops 7 billion
Pope Francis	2013	Boston Bomding (3)
Type 3 superconductors discovered	2014	Trial of the Century
First magnetoplasma thruster	2015	EU invades South Africa
China est. Shennong	2016	Pres. Hillary Clinton (1st woman president)
9/11 Houston nuked kills >4 million	2017	Clinton signs North American Free Trade Pact
Powersat beams energy to Earth	2018	Rising sea levels top 30 cm
Longbow Mass Driver operational	2019	North American Federation formed (NAF)
NAF/EU/Japan Lagrange One (L1)	2020	American Church of the Trinity (ACT)
Japan est. Kyoto, Luna	2021	ACT rally 1.5M anti-genetics
S Korea est. Hyundai (L4)	2022	NAF outlaws all genetic research
Meteor kills 19 in Kyoto	2023	George Farcain becomes a Deacon in ACT
NAF/EU/China est. Aldrin Station	2024	Pres. Jesus Martinez (1st Latino president)
India est. Kundara	2025	EU occupies New London, Luna
NAF and EU establish Taurus (L5)	2026	NAF builds orbital battlestation
China est. Far Point Mine	2027	Rising sea levels top 75 cm
EU est. Johanson	2028	China, EU build battlestations
Japan est. Ishikawajima	2029	Great Exodus begins, Luna population grows
Shennong absorbs Ishikawajima	2030	NAF outlaws all biotronic research
Japan builds battlestation	2031	EU restricts biotronic research
India est. Darpur Mine	2032	Pres George Farcain AKA, The Pope
EU est. Purgatory Deep Hole	2033	United Nations bans human genetics

Historical Detail	Year	Historical Detail
Shennong absorbs Kundara	2034	British hospital bombed (117)
China est. Mingun Mine	2035	NAF outlaws football, boxing
Calconn presented to the world	2036	Chinese Unification; NAF absorbs Mexico
Mingun Mine, Central Highlands	2037	President Farcain assassinated; VP John Paul takes office
Expeditions to Mars and Asteroids	2038	John Paul is elected President at age 42
Paradise asteroid discovered	2039	NAF hospital bombed (53); NAF absorbs Cuba
Rising sea levels top 2 meters	2040	Japan admits to UN violations
Israel builds battlestation	2041	Japanese genetic clinic bombed (21)
After 40 yrs NAF leaves Middle East	2042	Islamic Brotherhood (IB) forms, JP reelected (46)
Lindsey Marquest 10/12/43	2043	President John Paul forms Reformation Party
Shennong absorbs Johanson	2044	ACT joins Reformation Party
China begins selling arms to the IB	2045	Japanese Hospital bombed (191)
Egypt sells weapons to South Africa	2046	IB attacks Israel and is rebuffed; JP reelected (50)
World condemns IB	2047	China brokers the Saudi Accord
R.W. McCoy first multi-trillionare	2048	Rising sea levels top 4.5 meters; US revises the Bill of Rights
India lays keel for the ISS Shakti	2049	Venice is abandoned; Presidential term limits abolished
1st Lunarian visor mass produced	2050	IB builds Mogadishu spaceport; JP reelected (54)
Miami is abandoned	2051	IB buys battlestation from Hyundai
Lunarians produce first Zettasphere	2052	Protests grow over Constitutional Issue
Fair Access becomes world law	2053	Boston Massacre (56 dead)
First permanent Mars colony	2054	IB annexes Sudan; JP reelected for life (at age 58)
Luna complains to the UN	2055	Holland is abandoned
Manhattan is abandoned	2056	Korean biotronic program exposed
PR Dugan killed at Far Point	2057	Universal Nanotech, Hyundai Shipyards
Dreadnought tragedy kills 312	2058	IB invades Ethiopia
First asteroid colony	2059	South Korean president assassinated
April 1 - Luna Independence Day	2060	North and South Korea become one
IB establishes Al Fahad on Luna	2061	Reformationists restrict Earthnet
Tokyo abandoned/Calconn Disaster	2062	Federation's Great Revival begins
Lunarian Treaty of Independence	2063	Rising sea levels top 9 meters
Al Fahad population passes 10,000	2064	Farcain establishes the Home Guard
Paradise asteroid swings past Earth	2065	World drought kills tens of millions
Hampton Bay collapse	2066	Scientific research stops in NAF

Historical Detail	Year	Historical Detail
First fusion plant operational	2067	IB annexes Libya and Algeria
Republic establishes Summerhaven	2068	Riots in Mexico kill hundreds
Trans Lunar Highway completed	2069	NAF rejects UN assistance
Tau Ceti probe begins its journey	2070	Turkey withdraws EU, joins IB
Martian microbial worms discovered	2071	NAF opens first reeducation camp
Tempel Dugan 10/31/72	2072	Rising sea levels top 13 meters
Luna's genetic program exposed	2073	Korea allies with IB
Religious radicals call for Luna's death	2074	Ivory Coast pirates seize EU ship
Republic establishes Prattville	2075	Canada votes to withdraw from the NAF
Luna Councilor Chi Lin assassinated	2076	US/Canada 10 Day War kills 1100
Cardinals win Super Bowl	2077	NAF declares martial law
Republic establishes Scottsbluff	2078	Water shortages across Middle East
ISS Shakti discovers life on Titan	2079	IB declares war on India (Food war)
Bombings begin all across Luna	2080	Rising sea levels top 17 meters
First bomb destroys a Lunarian farm (0)	2081	China allies with IB against India
Abby survives assassination attempt	2082	Australian government collapses
3 bombings in Shennong (19)	2083	Imam Bakr arrives buys SMT
Mine sabotage in Darpur (3)	2084	Kahfah Road completed
6 bombs, June 15, Black Friday (255)	2085	Incident at Salvation Rock
1st Highland convoy hijacked (6)	2086	Al Fahad exceeds 250,000
3 bombings during the year (26)	2087	SMT begins modifying convoys
Prattville water reservoir poisoned	2088	Pres. John Paul declares marshal law
7 bombings during the year (102)	2089	World refugees top 1 billion
2 bombings during the year (12)	2090	Rising sea levels top 20 meters
3 bombings during the year (46)	2091	Kashmir Agreement ends India war
4 bombings (39) and LCH (451)	2092	Al Fahad exceeds 500,000

	NAF President	Term
44	George Bush	2000-2008
45	Barack Obama	2008-2016
46	Elizabeth Ann Warren	2016-2024
47	Jesus Martinez	2024-2032
48	George Farcain	2032-2037
49	John Paul	2037-current

Lagrange Points

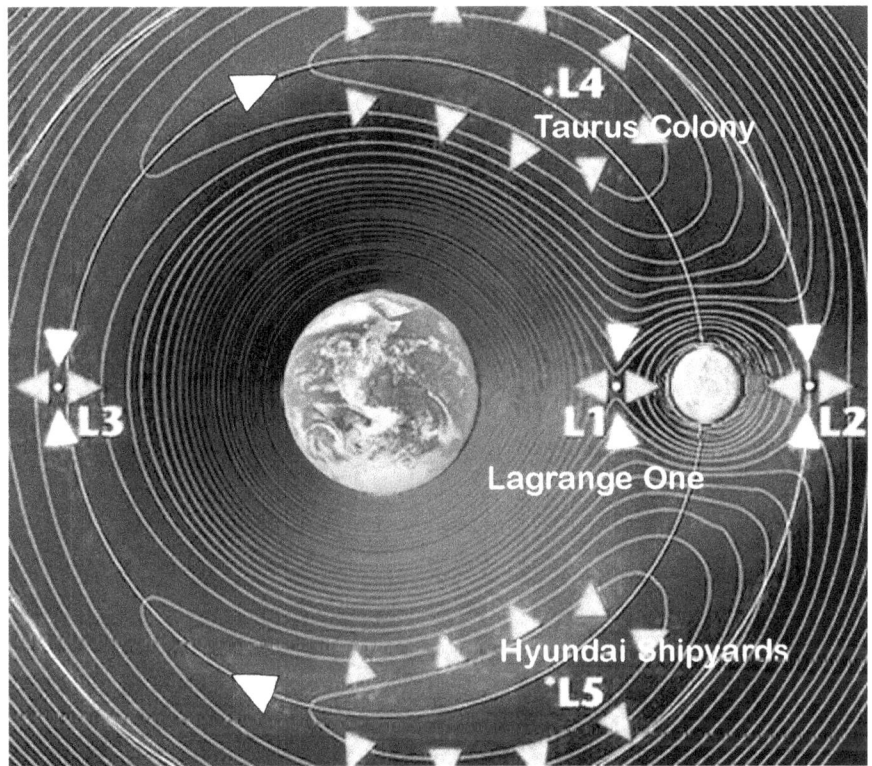

Lagrange Points are the gravitational eddies around any two massive objects such as the Earth and Luna. There are five positions in space where a third body, of comparatively negligible mass, can be placed which would then maintain its position relative to the two massive bodies. The gravitational fields of the two massive bodies combined with the centrifugal force are in balance at the Lagrange Points, allowing a third body to remain stationary with respect to the first two bodies. They all lie on the Earth/Luna orbital plane and share the same period as the moon. L1, L2, and L3 are quasi-stable and require station keeping to maintain long-term occupation. L4 and L5 are stable regions that naturally entrap dust and other small bodies.

Book 1: Evolution's Child – Earthman

"My earlier views of the unsoundness of the Christian scheme of salvation and the human origin of the scriptures have become clearer and stronger with advancing years, and I see no reason for thinking I shall ever change them."

Abraham Lincoln *in a letter to Judge J.S. Wakefield, 1862*

North American Federation

"It is always better to have no ideas than false ones; to believe nothing, than to believe what is wrong."

Thomas Jefferson (1757-1820)

The semi is full of lettuce, radishes, and onions on their way to market. The driver doesn't think twice about barreling through the green light at full speed. He never sees the white sedan, hitting it square in the side.

With a terrible sound of rending metal and breaking glass, the impact obliterates the little car, sending it spinning wildly across the intersection to wrap around a metal pole.

Lazarus sprints towards the wreckage but no matter how fast he runs, he can't make any headway. The smashed car bursts into flames. He throws up his hands protecting his face from the intensity. No one

1

could survive the inferno.

"Rachel," Lazarus cries out. A child screams. Lazarus falls to his knees, tears streaming down his face.

"You can't help them now," a man's voice said from somewhere behind him. "God have mercy on their souls."

ℛℒ

The woman entered the bedroom. "Lazarus… Wake up."

The man in the bed groaned and pulled the sheet over his head. "Rise and shine." The voice pulled him out of his nightmare but cannot purge it from his mind. The horror of it sticks with him.

"Lazarus, you're sweating. Are you ill?" The voice almost sounds like Rachel but it's not. Rachel's been gone two years yet the pain of her death has never dimmed thanks in part to this damn machine.

He moved into Hayden's Crossing right after his wife and little girl died in a horrific traffic accident. He never even had to pack. The Regional Director of Homeland Security, his boss, John Dempsey, ordered everything moved even before informing Lazarus of the tragedy. The director was thoughtful that way and Lazarus appreciated the personal attention at the time. He never had to go back inside the house that he and Rachel had shared with Courtney.

The surrogate arrived a few weeks later. The director had volunteered Lazarus for a study to determine if using surrogates could alleviate a person's grief. Lazarus couldn't believe it when they first introduced it to him, a machine that looked like Rachel. It smiled, laughed, and agreed with him on everything. It may look like Rachel, but it wasn't.

The study doctors insisted that he treat her just as he had treated Rachel, including sex. They even had a pastor come and talk to him. The man of god assured Lazarus that having sex with a machine did not constitute fornication and he spoke for the church.

Still, Lazarus resisted for several weeks but finally succumbed after dinner one night. Two bottles of wine, good food and a massage wore him down. After all, the surrogate did look and feel like Rachel. It was easy and he was human. He learned fast that the surrogate couldn't refuse him anything.

Lazarus throws off the sweat-soaked sheets and sits up pushing his unruly mass of hair out of his eyes. "I'm fine," he said evenly. It wouldn't be good to attract any undue attention on this of all days.

"Good, because today we are going on a vacation. Vacations are fun," the surrogate said cheerfully.

"How would you know?" He couldn't resist baiting it.

The machine looks at him for a moment, smiles and said, "I must have read it somewhere." She smiles even broader. "We are going to have so much fun." The machine claps her hands in front of her face like a little girl anticipating a new doll. It was something Rachel had done on occasion and it sent a jolt through Lazarus.

Lazarus gathers himself before responding, "You're right. We're going to have a great time."

Director Dempsey insisted Lazarus take the surrogate on his vacation. Lazarus tried to convince him that he needed a break from it but no one argues with the director for long.

Lazarus stands and moves past the surrogate pulling the heavy drapes aside letting in the early morning light. He'll miss the view from his ninth floor apartment. Directly below is manicured grass and concrete with Tempe Town Lake along one side. A tall wrought iron fence surrounds the complex. Opposite the lake, a road cuts into the hillside past a large sports stadium southeast of the apartments. The huge structure was a remnant of a bygone age and falling apart. It was the unobstructed view of the Superstitions due east that he enjoyed most. This morning, towering dark clouds beautifully backlit by the rising sun hang heavy over the mountains.

He turns away and goes to the kitchen, the surrogate following a few steps behind. Pouring a steaming cup of black coffee, he heads for the shower.

"Fix me toast with orange marmalade and a small glass of juice."

"Yes Lazarus," the machine watches him leave.

He and Rachel had dreamed up the Athens vacation two years ago. They had wanted to wait until Courtney was old enough to appreciate it. That dream ended on a dark Scottsdale intersection, a single lapse of judgment snuffing out their lives in an instant.

A few months after the accident, Lazarus considered canceling the vacation, and went as far as to broach the subject with a representative from the agency. The man had politely informed him that his travel arrangements were nonrefundable. It was all in the contract.

Just as well. The truth is, planning this trip was the last big thing he and Rachel had done together and fortunately, he couldn't work up the enthusiasm to fight them. It was easy to let things ride.

Emerging from the bath, Lazarus begins to dress. "Turn on *Good Morning Lord.*"

"Yes Lazarus," the surrogate didn't need the remote.

"…and read with me at First Corinthians 11:14…. *Doth not even nature itself teach you, that if a man have long hair, it is a shame unto Him?* Can it be any plainer than that? God doesn't want men to have long hair. It shames Him. Pray with me and support my bill with your votes and together we shall right this ungodliness."

As one of the leading fundamentalists within the Reformation Party, South Carolina Senator Elijah Hanley is a vocal advocate for a more literal interpretation of the bible. This morning he's on the Federation's most popular early show.

Senator Hanley is a short pudgy man, mostly bald with a ghost of white hair around three sides of his head and a neatly trimmed beard. He glows with the energy and vitality of a man much younger. The Senator is wearing his usual white shirt, black tie, and black greatcoat.

He chuckles when reporters call him Modern Moses, but never corrects them.

"I tell you my brothers and sisters, the increase in violence in our cities, the crop failures all across the Midwest, rising sea levels and hurricanes pounding our shores, are all signs of **His** displeasure. We are falling away from **God** and must find our way back before it's **too late**." The Senator waves a fat index finger at the camera.

Screw you Senator. I will keep my hair. Lazarus also keeps his true feelings to himself. He shoves a stray strand back behind his ear.

Lazarus has planned for weeks what to take. In his bag are his bible and a well-worn copy of Robert Heinlein's *Time Enough for Love*, the only thing he has that belonged to his father. So far, the 120-year-old novel has escaped the Morality Commission's black list, but it's only a matter of time. Tucked into Heinlein's novel are several photos and a packet of aging longhand letters, fading ink on brittle paper.

Munching on a piece of toast, he adds a hygiene kit, a new Achilles soccer cap, his hair brush, and an antiquated VR headset, the only device he could get approved by Homeland Security to take out of country. He doesn't bother packing clothing, preferring to buy new instead of lugging the old around.

The man that followed Senator Hanley on the show is a pencil necked geek wearing a buttoned down blue business suit at least two sizes too large and a bright orange tie. His beak-like nose overshadows a lipless mouth, thin mustache, and receding chin. Narrow eyes dart about restlessly under greasy black hair.

"The North American Federation don't need to get involved with the length of hair of its citizens." His shrill voice grates on Lazarus. "For too long, we have stood by and watched our freedoms slip away, one little bit after another until they're practically gone. We don't need the government making laws about how long our hair should be. Some things are better left up to individu..."

The Earthnet mediator interrupts the smarmy little man. "Thank you Professor Gladstone and thank you Senator Hanley for taking your valuable time this morning to join us in the No Spin Zone, the only place you get all the truth and nothing but the truth, so help me God… I now invite all of you to do your patriotic duty and cast your vote. This is, as always, an unofficial poll, but rest assured, Washington is listening."

Lazarus laughs, a strange mirthless sound, devoid of joy. The surrogate joins in.

"What are you laughing at?" Lazarus asks.

"I'm laughing with you," the surrogate said cheerfully.

Lazarus uses the remote to cast his vote. He looks around the apartment one last time. How superficial his life had become. There's nothing here he gave a damn about.

"Call us a cab."

"Yes Lazarus," the surrogate said sweetly and follows him out the door.

They are alone on the elevator ride down. It's early for the residents of Hayden's Crossing. They're still in bed or having breakfast. Walking across the lobby, Lazarus waves impatiently as the attendant opens and holds the door for them.

"Have a great day, Mr. Sheffield. Rachel…"

"Henry, I've asked you not to do that." Lazarus shoots a hard glance his way. He wants to scream *'that's not Rachel,'* but instead said, "I'm fully capable of opening the door myself."

"I don't mind, Mr. Sheffield," the man smiles pleasantly. That too is part of his job.

Arizona in late October is beautiful. Even though the sun is well above the horizon, the chill is still in the air when Lazarus emerges. Outside is a courtyard surrounded by more tall buildings identical to his. The main drive encircles a small pond with a single jet of water rising a few meters straight up. The circle drive has a canopied stop in front of each building.

Lazarus is oblivious to the splendor as he walks to the cab.

The side of the vehicle has a sketch of an empty cross on top of Calvary hill with the words **Christian Cab Company** below. Lazarus hears the car unlock as they approach. The rear door on their side swings open and Lazarus climbs in. The surrogate follows.

"Where to?" the cabbie asks over his shoulder.

"Gateway Airport, Global Airlines," Lazarus replies settling back on the worn bench seat. The cab is neat and clean but at least ten years old, a lifetime for a vehicle in its occupation.

"Shouldn't be much traffic this early in the morning…" The cabbie said and proceeds to tell him all about rush hour and the horror he endures every day. Lazarus tunes him out, staring at the passing city without hearing a word the man said, lost in his own thoughts.

They navigate out of the neighborhood and onto a six lane surface street. This is an older section of the city, many of the buildings need paint and the roadway is full of potholes. Lazarus watches the shabby shops and fading strip malls go by and his stomach knots up. *Am I doing the right thing?* He takes a deep breath and runs his hand through his hair like a comb. It's his only choice.

He misses Rachel. This damned machine at his side has done nothing to ease the pain of her death. In fact, it made it much harder. Every time he looks at it, it reminds him of her, the real Rachel. It's an open wound that's been festering for almost two years.

God Damn. He misses Rachel. When he closes his eyes, he can feel her presence. His heart aches even as his destination instills a sense of adventure. Did the Pilgrims feel this way boarding leaky wooden ships and setting sail across the Atlantic, or settlers packing everything they owned into Conestoga wagons and heading west?

"Friday and Saturday's the best, taking home all those drunks whose cars won't start…," the cabbie said.

The cab enters the onramp and accelerates towards Interstate 10. The whine of the electric motor rises in pitch as it comes up to speed. Early morning traffic is light. They are almost alone on the wide ribbon of asphalt. Maintenance crews have the inner lanes segregated using concrete barriers. Trucks and other vehicles share the freeway in near perfect silence.

"You couldn't pay me to trade in my cab on one of those new models…" the cabbie drones on.

Now the scenery flashes by. Lazarus can only get fleeting glimpses of the structures and signage along the industrial corridor between Phoenix and Tucson. Lazarus runs his hand through his hair, pushing it back in place. *Relax, I can pull this off.*

The surrogate reaches out to hold his hand. "What's wrong Lazarus?"

He looks at her, "Oh… you know about me and flying. We don't mix very well."

"Fear of flying?" the cabbie injects. "Let me tell you. You would never get me in one of those machines. No sir. I'm stayin' right here on Mother Earth…"

It's a short trip to the airport. Located at the intersection of Interstate 8 and 10, Gateway International Airport is the Southwest's regional hub and services over a hundred million citizens yearly. Hypnotized by the city flashing by, and with thoughts of Rachel and his little princess filling his head, Lazarus doesn't notice when the cab cuts back across the lanes of traffic and climbs the airport's entrance overpass. He finds himself swinging in a great arc above I-10's sixteen lanes of traffic. Below him, the freeway is a ribbon threading through an endless city as far as he can see. He has a momentary pang, hearing his daughter ask sweetly, *"Daddy, are we up?"*

Descending from the heights of the overpass, the cab eases into traffic. The first checkpoint comes and goes unobtrusively, its MRI scanners poking into every nook and cranny looking for anything out of the ordinary. Comparing the results to the millions of previous scans, it finds nothing of significance.

"Never been outside Arizona myself…" the cabbie keeps talking.

As the vehicle passes through the open spaces surrounding Gateway's main terminal, Lazarus can see arriving planes in the crisp morning sky appearing almost motionless. The road tunnels below all three east-west runways. To his left, a huge Airbus Maximus lumbers through the sky in slow motion, touching down just as his cab dips into the shadowy passage below the runway. By the time they emerge, the giant plane is gone. The road curves away from the tunnel bringing into view the bone-white terminal and the silhouettes of planes clustered around its gates.

"Idiot politicians talkin 'bout puttin' in a second airport…"

The pride of Arizona, the terminal's main construction is an enormous structure that fills the horizon as the cab approaches. It reminds Lazarus of a giant circus tent that drapes and swoops over huge metal supports hundreds of meters tall, each topped with an radiant Christian cross that's visible for many kilometers. The building itself is shaped in a giant cross and when the sun is just right, it can be seen from space.

"Too much vote'n if you ask me…" the cabbie never stops talking.

The main thoroughfare drops incoming travelers along a concrete and glass canyon running through the heart of the airport. The outside lanes on both sides are for unloading passengers, the inner lanes for through traffic. The cab stops a short distance from Global Airline's main entrance.

The cabbie twists about to look at Lazarus, "Total is ninety-six thirty-five. It's already been deducted," the cabbie said when Lazarus reaches into his pocket.

Lazarus gives the man a fifty, "God-be-with-you."

The man beams, "God-be-with-you, and a pleasant journey." It's the best tip he's had in over a year.

Clutching his bag, Lazarus steps out and looks around, half expecting airport security to be waiting. Around him, a steady succession of vehicles squeezes into curb side openings as soon as they become available. As one pulls out, a new one takes its place in a tightly choreographed dance of disembarkation. Farther down, busses disgorge their passengers. The drop-off area seems tiny in the vastness under the canopy.

Lazarus moves through the crowd with the surrogate staying close beside him. They stop in front of a large information screen. Lazarus scans the display until he finds Global Airlines Flight 119. It's on time in Gate 4B. *So far, so good.*

Turning abruptly, Lazarus nearly collides with an old couple. They had stopped behind him to read the screen. Both are wearing typical Federation attire, the man's dressed in a black suit, white shirt and dark tie. His wife's in a plain brown dress that covers her from chin to ankles, her faded red scarf the only real color.

"Forgive me. I need to look where I'm going," Lazarus addresses the man as is proper.

No one notices the exchange. Most people prefer to keep to themselves, their eyes never wandering far from what's right in front of them, wishing nothing more than to remain an indiscriminate particle amidst the homogeneity of humanity. Bright clothing is almost completely absent and the women all wear scarves covering their heads.

Putting his arm around his wife, the man said, "No harm done. God be with you, brother." The old woman smiles at Lazarus and ignores the surrogate. Her dark eyes are full of life putting the lie to the wrinkles surrounding them. She must have been beautiful once.

Lazarus returns the smile. Looking back at the man he said, "And with you, brother," he moves around the couple and heads for the screening area, the surrogate keeping pace.

Federation security personnel in cobalt blue uniforms are the only people within sight wearing Earthnet communication devices. They look like dark sunglasses. Decades earlier, during the Great Revival in '62, pious politicians enacted laws under the Freedom of Information Act forbidding all unauthorized access to Earthnet and giving themselves control of the manufacture, distribution and usage of the devices that provided it. Possessing an unlicensed Earthnet portal became a felony and every good American knows breaking the law's a sin. Consequently, the travelers sharing the terminal with him are barefaced and introverted, avoiding each other and the armed men among them.

He picks the shortest of the lines feeding into airport security. Like his fellow citizens, Lazarus avoids eye contact with the nearby guards. The line moves quickly. He cut the time tight on purpose but that's not what makes him run his fingers through his hair, time after time. He isn't exactly afraid of flying. Flying just makes him jumpy, that's all. Running his hands through his thick hair charges his courage like a capacitor sucking up voltage, a habit he picked up years earlier. Most times, he doesn't even know he's doing it.

The security scanners are contained in tunnels that each passenger must pass through to go deeper into the airport. Upon entering, the bioID embedded in his left hand provides Lazarus Sheffield's complete personal history to the DHS database. Comparing this data with his prerecorded and approved travel plans verifies his current activity. Meanwhile, powerful olfactory sensors identify and categorize substances on him and his clothes down to parts per million, and a bank of MRI scanners sweeps over him many times looking for anything unusual inside his body or belongings. Finding nothing out of the ordinary, he receives authorization to enter the terminal. The entire security process is complete by the halfway point in the tunnel. If DHS lifted his authorization, armed police will be waiting at the far end.

The sides of the tunnel glow with a tranquil green, specially designed by DuPont to calm a troubled psyche. Lazarus walks slowly down its length, convinced this is where his journey ends. Sweat beads up on his forehead. He swipes at it with his sleeve. The automated tracking and surveillance system recognizes his body's nervous signals but attributes them to his documented phobia of flying, something he's counting on. Upon emerging, he moves forward with his fellow travelers.

Just when he thinks he's made it past the checkpoint, a heavyset security guard steps in Lazarus's path, taking him by the arm saying, "Sir, please come with me." He motions to the surrogate, "You too, come with me."

Shock and dismay flash through Lazarus, "Is there a problem officer?" He asked as the guard pulls him away from the stream of passengers, a few of whom glance fearfully at the enfolding scene. Lazarus finds himself staring at the thick black mustache beneath the dark lens of the guard's visor.

Suddenly, a vice clamps around his other arm. He utters a startled yelp. The two guards hustle Lazarus into a waiting area. The surrogate follows smiling pleasantly. The second officer points at a row of chairs lined up against a wall and orders gruffly, "Sit."

Lazarus obeys and the surrogate sits beside him still smiling.

Something's gone terribly wrong. He runs his fingers through his hair. He must maintain a clear head.

He stares at the officer's twitching mustache. The man's talking rapidly with someone online. Nodding, the officer abruptly turns and walks towards Lazarus.

Lazarus convinces himself in those few seconds that he's about to be arrested. Everything he knows about reeducation flashes through his mind.

"Thank you for your cooperation, Mr. Sheffield. It's standard procedure to check the travel permits of any Homeland Security officer leaving the Federation. I hope we didn't delay you too much." The guard's words say one thing but his body language another.

Confused but relieved, Lazarus manages to stammer, "No, not at all." The guard escorts them to the exit and returns his bag.

Lazarus glances back. The guard stands at the checkpoint staring after them as they disappear into the cavernous terminal.

Bewildered but elated, Lazarus follows the signs down several flights of stairs before finding the subway that will take them out to Terminal 4. He stands and waits patiently for the next train, the smiling surrogate at his side. The crowd is so thick by the time the train arrives they have no choice but to move with it as it surges aboard. Neither Lazarus nor the surrogate manages to get a seat. He stands clutching a cold stainless steel rail, his bag slung over his shoulder. The surrogate just stands there.

The acceleration's smooth and almost unnoticeable. Infomercials flash by on the walls outside the cars windows. One is selling a Hawaiian time-share and another is pitching the spiritual insight of Reverend Gausault's newest book, *When Angels Speak.* The passenger's move forward in anticipation as the train comes to a stop. The doors are not fully open when the first traveler squeezes out followed closely by the horde. Lazarus has lived with crowds his entire life and deals with it stoically. He knows nothing else.

While walking up the stairs back to the surface, he can't stop thinking about the incident at the checkpoint. Why did they let him go? The authorities don't move until they're sure they have a person dead to rights. Then they move quickly and decisively.

He's lived under the Federation's eye his whole life but this felt different. *Am I bait?* DHS agents could be following him to identify his contacts, waiting for him to lead them to others before arresting them all. Much more likely but it still didn't make sense. Why alert him by stopping him at security?

He shudders, feeling like the mouse in a game of cat and mouse, a sentiment shared by most Federation citizens at one time or another. *As far as I know, the vacation story's intact.*

The stairs lead up to a large circular room. Around its periphery are a number of airline gates. Gate 4B is bustling with activity as Lazarus and his surrogate approach.

Thirty minutes. He couldn't have timed it better.

He spots a small Old-Mex style citizen's lounge among the terminal's coffee shops and eateries. No telling when he'll have this chance again. "I need a drink…" Lazarus said to the surrogate. "It's good for my nerves." He heads for the cantina.

Inside, men sit on barstools and around the tables. A middle-aged brunette with bored eyes tends the bar. She's appropriately dressed in a formless turtleneck sweater and a scarf. Stepping up to an open section, Lazarus waits for her to acknowledge him and said, "Jack's Hard Cider, three fingers, straight up."

She nods, sets a shot glass on the counter, snatches a black labeled bottle from under the bar, and pours. Sliding it across, she said, "thirty-two-fifty."

Lazarus shakes his head, marveling at the cost of things in the airport, and peels off a hundred. "Bring me a refill in ten minutes and keep the change."

"Ten minutes," the woman said. That was quite a wad of bills. What else can she sell him? As johns go, this one doesn't look bad. She has a cot setup in one of the maintenance closets downstairs to supplement her income on occasion.

Picking up the drink, Lazarus walks over and sits at a table overlooking the terminal. The surrogate comes in and joins him. Bringing the small glass under his nose, he looks across the rim at the surrogate, "To our vacation."

She beams back at him, looking beautiful. "To our vacation." she repeats.

Taking a generous sip, he holds the fluid in his mouth, anticipating the coming fire. It burns all the way down, going off like a bomb at the

14

bottom. He leans back letting the harsh elixir relax him from the inside out.

Several flights arrive at the various gates, disgorging their passengers and collecting more. DHS guards are evident everywhere. There are two at each gate and more walking the floor. No one looks, much less speaks to them. A child squeals loudly and runs from his mother, coming too close to a guard. Reaching out, the guard picks up the boy by the back of his shirt and holds him. Fear replaces glee and all's quiet once more.

The brunette sets his second drink on the table and picks up the empty. She stares at the surrogate wondering when this smiling bitch showed up. All thoughts of getting some extra cash slip away. "Is there anything else I can do for you?"

Lazarus glances up, "No, I'm fine."

"God-be-with-you," she said in the monotony of endless repetition.

"And-with-you," Lazarus replies. He notices something unusual about the man walking past in the terminal. He thinks back and tries to remember where he had seen him, realizing the man has passed at least twice before. Once means nothing, twice understandable, but three times starts the warning bells ringing in his head.

As inconspicuously as he can, Lazarus studies the man, medium build, short brown hair, and clothes that merge him into the surrounding crowd. If he were any more nondescript, he would be invisible. His luggage, pulled along behind him, is virtually identical to hundreds of others. He makes a beeline for the information panel, stopping and looking intently up at it, his back to the cantina. Turning abruptly, the man walks towards Lazarus.

Picking up his drink, Lazarus takes a sip, letting action cover his nervousness. With as little concern as he can muster, Lazarus casually focuses directly on the man. For an instant, their eyes meet and Lazarus is certain that the man is shadowing him. He's seen it done plenty of times and knows the routine almost as well as this field agent, but therein lies the heart of the matter. Lazarus has never actually been to the field. His participation as a DHS Senior Analyst was always early in the process identifying the target or later after the suspect was in custody. He finds it much different to be the target. His heart pounds in his ears.

Instead of arresting Lazarus, the man walks right past him and enters the dim interior of the bar. Now he's behind them. Resisting the temptation to turn, Lazarus pushes his hair back in place and takes a deep breath. He looks around the terminal floor. Field agents are never alone. Teams consist of at least two agents.

With relief, Lazarus hears the announced arrival of Flight 119. He gulps the dregs of the second shot and uses his peripheral vision to check on the man at the bar. Slinging his bag over his shoulder, Lazarus and the surrogate leave. He must stay cool and play the part of a man and his surrogate going on vacation. They walk side by side across the terminal.

If he's right and not just letting his imagination run amok, the normal procedure would be to watch and wait for the quarry to show their hand. Obtaining court evidence is simply a matter of time. Eventually, everyone who has something to hide gives it up. Just keep watching.

On the way to his gate, Lazarus pops a couple of mints designed to mask the smell of cider. A quick glance back at the lounge did not reveal any sign of the agent, but that doesn't make him feel any better.

They end up close to the front of the line. The giant Airbus Maximus is in plain view outside, distinctive with its double row of windows. Double-decker walkways extend out from the terminal servicing both the upper and lower decks of the Airbus. A seemingly endless stream of people exits the colossal aircraft. The big planes can deliver over eight hundred people anywhere on the globe and this one arrived fully loaded.

The disembarkation process is orderly and the flow of humanity finally dwindles and stops. An attendant steps forward and directs the people in the front of his line to proceed to the checkpoint. Again, Lazarus is sure this was as far as he's going to get.

"Please move forward. We have a lot of people to get aboard." The attendant looks bored as she walks up and down the line urging compliance. Some ignore her but most do as asked.

When Lazarus reaches the checkpoint, he passes his left hand over the reader. His seat number and name flash onto the screen.

"Good morning, Mr. and Mrs. Sheffield." The young flight attendant sees his unease. "Is something wrong?" She asked.

"No, nothing's wrong. I don't like flying, that's all. Not to worry. I fly often and it's always this way." Lazarus tried to disarm her concern with a smile.

"Just the same, I'll keep my eye on you," she said.

Lazarus finds their row and shimmies down until he comes to his seat. The surrogate follows and sits beside him, still smiling. A man, his wife, and their child are beyond his and a young man in a business suit takes the seat on the far side of the surrogate. Lazarus buckles the lap belt and lays his head back, listening.

From somewhere behind him a woman complains, "How can this machine possibly get off the ground with this many people. It don't seem natural."

"This is just the top level. There are five hundred more seats below us," a man drawls in response.

"Dear Lord, don't tell me that," she shrieks.

"Calm yourself woman. Put yourself in God's hands and everything'll be just fine," is the man's stern response.

Finally, after everyone's settled, the plane lurches forward. A powerful tug tows them all the way to the takeoff staging area before detaching. In spite of his phobia, Lazarus wishes he had a window seat, but that would be out of character.

Lazarus grips the arms of his seat as the giant plane lumbers down the long runway. He endures the takeoff and the steep climb to altitude. The ride is smooth up here, and quiet. He lays his head back and to his surprise, dozes off.

He awakes as the plane is landing. Athens International Airport is even more crowded than Gateway. Tens of thousands of people share the space under its enormous roof at any given time, day or night. Over a billion tourists pass through this single complex every year and it seems to him that most of them are still here.

As Lazarus and the surrogate move past an information board, he lets his eyes run down the list, careful not to give away what he's really looking for. He finds it. The next flight to Heaven's Gate is on time.

Looking around, he locks eyes with the man from the bar who turns away and disappears into the crowd. Lazarus is stunned. "Come on," he said to the surrogate. "I've got to use the facilities."

Stretching as far as he can see is what appears at first glance to be an ancient market, the facades of shops and stores line both sides in a capitalistic imitation of a 600 BCE Greek city street but much wider. This is the world famous Athena's Marketplace, a tourist trap of mammoth proportions.

The buildings have an ancient look, as if they truly have been here a long time. Tables loaded with merchandise are in front of each establishment and surrounded by shoppers. Down the center of the mall, thousands of people move in both directions. The web of struts and rafters holding up the roof diminishes the affect. Modern signs in several languages hang from the rafters, pointing the way to other gates, ground transport, and luggage carousels, a reminder that this is an airport and not just another mall.

The last big weekend of the fall season sweeps Lazarus along like flotsam on a river of humanity. The predominantly Asian horde paws through the merchandise packed along its banks, gleefully haggling with the locals to get the best price. To his left several small electric trams ease their way through the crowd, their bells dinging warnings for people to clear a path. A thousand different sounds assault his senses.

Lazarus discreetly looks for the agent but fails. The throng is just too thick. Carried along by the crowd, Lazarus spots the entrance to his gate. He keeps going for another hundred meters then stops outside a public bathroom.

"Wait here," he tells the surrogate.

"Yes Lazarus."

Outside the bathroom is a traffic jam. Lazarus moves into this scrum. Once inside, he catches the eye of a young man among a group of young men standing over by the sinks. He gives him a subtle wink and head motion towards the stalls in the back. The youth looks Lazarus over and nods. Without a word, he comes over to stand next to Lazarus. They wait their turn.

Lazarus is first. When a stall comes open, he enters, shuts the door and locks it. Ignoring the smell, he removes his backpack and hangs it from the hook on the inside of the door. Bending down, he slips off his shoes being very careful not to step in the puddles on the floor. In place of socks, he's wearing soft-soled slippers of a style currently popular in Europe with the younger generation. He instantly loses almost eight centimeters of height. His blue jeans are next, exposing a pair of baggy shorts underneath. He transfers his cash money from his pants pocket to the shorts. Unzipping his red jacket, he slips it off revealing a dark blue t-shirt underneath.

Reaching inside his bag, he puts the copy of Heinlein's *Time Enough for Love* into his pocket and removes the hat and headset. He stuffs his shoes, jeans and jacket in beside the bible then hides the backpack behind the toilet.

He hears the toilet flush next door and someone new enter the stall. Lazarus taps his foot under the divider separating the two stalls. A second later, a large bath towel appears on the floor and someone whispers from under the panel. "Com'a mate. We dun got all day."

Lazarus lies down on the towel and slips under the panel with help from the youth. Standing up, Lazarus smiles and shakes his head. He holds up a small roll of bills.

"This will be the easiest three hundred Euros you have ever made. All I want you to do is walk out of here with me like we are together. Make it a good show and there will be another three hundred when we are back in the mall."

The young man stares at Lazarus for a moment, smiles and winks, then reaches out and takes the roll of money. "Whateve' U speak gove'na'. U da boss."

Lazarus puts his hat on backwards before sliding his thirty-year-old headset over it. State-of-the-art when it was new, its low tech is precisely why it's so popular with young Europeans. The lack of advanced features give the wearer a certain amount of anonymity by their very absence, not to mention it completely obscures the top two thirds of his face behind a dark shield. Unlike a modern visor which lazes directly into the wearers eyes, the image Lazarus sees is projected on the inside of the shield.

Lazarus takes several sections from the roll of toilet paper and stuffs it into his mouth. Chewing carefully, he works the paper into a long narrow blob that fits behind his lower lip extending out into his cheeks, breaking up his jaw line, making it difficult for the facial recognition software to identify him. The youth nods approvingly.

They exit the stall, arm in arm. The guy is all over Lazarus, making good on his deal. The two merge with those leaving the bathroom. Outside the exit, they pass within a few meters of the man from the bar. Lazarus doesn't trust himself to look at where he left the surrogate. She might see through his disguise.

Seconds later, they're in the market's main corridor, surrounded by people. In less than a minute, he's changed his height, posture, clothing, hidden his hair and most of his face behind a mask, and added a companion. Lazarus came up with this plan from watching countless

DHS training vids describing in detail the tricks of a terrorist, then added a few twists of his own. He slips another roll of money into the prostitute's hand.

The young man bats his long eyelashes at Lazarus, "Gracias. I hope you get away with whatever you're doing," he said in English with a Latin accent. He speaks a dozen languages including the pigeon talk used in his profession.

Lazarus hugs the lad, whispering in his ear, "Thanks. You might want to be someplace else for a while." The youth nods and they part ways.

Navigating the river of people, Lazarus spots what he's looking for. It's a large statue of the Greek goddess Athena. Armed with spear and shield, she's standing on a column in front of a temple. The goddess is serenely beautiful, gazing forever at the horizon.

Wide steps invite tourists to enter the Temple's inner sanctuary. Hidden speakers play classical Greek music. Outside the entrance, women dressed alluringly in revealing white robes call out to the people as they pass, enticing them to enter the Temple of Athena where they will find only the finest quality of merchandise.

Moving up the stairs, the nearest siren assures Lazarus that he will not be sorry. He stares at the young women, unaccustomed to such bawdy displays of nudity. Upon entering the shop, he glances at the time. If his calculations are correct, the employees of Athena's Temple should be finishing their break soon. He moves through the store picking out shoes, shirt, a pair of pants, and a small overnight bag, blending in perfectly with the tourists that frequent Athens.

He lays his items on the counter. From a rack close by, he picks out a pair of dark sunglasses, a cheap imitation of a Federation visor. He adds them to his pile. The touch panel pops up with the price and a voice informs him, "That will be three-hundred-fifty-one Euros."

"I want to talk to the manager," Lazarus states, knowing he must haggle or risk drawing unwanted attention.

"Certainly. One moment please," the voice answers.

Tourists, most of them Asian, far outnumber store employees who are easy to spot by their flowing Greek robes exposing one tit or the other. He sees several people who might be Federation agents but no one stands out. He must assume his deception has worked.

"Sir, may I help you?"

Lazarus turns and looks down at the bored little woman standing behind the counter. She's wearing a white robe with her left tit exposed and a gold belt drawn tightly about her narrow waist.

"Yes, I hope so. I want to purchase these items but the price seems excessive to me. I think two-hundred-fifty Euros is a fair price," Lazarus states.

"For you it would be, but for me, the Temple would lose money. We cannot stay in business long if I do that," she's clearly bored with a conversation she's had uncountable times.

"You won't stay in business if you don't sell your merchandise either. What about three-hundred even? I think I can stretch that far," Lazarus is acutely aware he's wearing baggy shorts, slippers, and a headset that hides his face like some EU teenager.

The woman knows Lazarus is not what he seems. He's obviously involved in some self-conceived fantasy, not the first to do that. After all, whatever happens in Athens, stays in Athens. "Very well… three-hundred plus tax totals three-hundred-forty-one Euros." She enters the sale before Lazarus can blink. When he still hesitates she adds, "The Union gets its cut. There's nothing I can do about that."

Lazarus shrugs and doles out three-hundred-fifty Euros while the woman puts his items in a bag. "So why is the Goddess of War the mall symbol?"

Amusement flickers across her face. "Athena is not only the Goddess of War and the patron deity of Athens but also the Goddess of weaving, pottery, and crafts."

Picking up a brightly colored cigarette lighter from a countertop basket, He asked, "Then this must fall into crafts?"

"No, that's a fire maker. It falls under the war category," the woman answers.

"Oh," he replies unsure if she's serious. He replaces the lighter and continues, "I'd like to change. Is your dressing room in the back?"

She points, "The door on the left. Someone's using it but they shouldn't be long."

"Thank you," Lazarus accepts his change, picks up the bag and walks deeper into the store. To his right is a second door, obviously not the dressing room. Lazarus busies himself by looking at racks of garments. Minutes later, the person in the dressing room exits and still he waits, feigning interest in a rather frilly shirt. Finally, it happens. Two employees emerge from the second door, laughing about something as they return to work. With his heart racing, Lazarus slips through the open door without even touching it, making sure it clicks shut behind him. This part had worried him greatly and now it was past.

He's in a warehouse. To his right is a paper-strewn desk, a computer touch screen peeking out from the mess. Boxes and racks of clothing fill the rest of the room. Near the large rollup door is a big pile of discarded packing and shipping material. Lazarus breathes a sigh of relief that no one's in sight.

The employee bathroom is a storage closet equipped with a toilet and sink. Lazarus uses his forefinger to clean his mouth of paper. Next, he removes the headset, strips and puts on his new clothing, tucking in the shirt and lacing up the shoes. Using another paper towel, he folds it carefully and wets it in the sink before inserting it into his left upper cheek. A second towel mirrors the first, blurring the outline of his high cheekbones, giving his face a round full appearance. The water soaked paper should escape notice in the MRI scans he will encounter, at least for a while.

He transfers everything he wants to keep into the new overnighter. Everything else goes into the empty shopping bag, which he hides among the boxes destined for recycle. Slinging the new bag over his shoulder, he completes his second changeover.

Lazarus unlatches the loading dock's rollup door and pulls upward. The rattling shatters the quiet. He looks over his shoulder at the mall door uneasily, half expecting someone to walk in.

Perched precariously on a narrow ledge a meter above the pavement, Lazarus pulls the door back down. Outside the massive building, he can see trucks backed up to various loading docks. Here and there, people and machinery move about keeping Athena's Marketplace stocked with goods.

Lazarus jumps off the ledge and begins walking along the backside of the mall.

Oil and tire rubber stain the concrete in front of each dock. Avoiding the worst of the mess, Lazarus moves as fast as he dares, passing under several of the giant rigs, their drivers too busy to take notice. Finally, he decides he's come far enough. Approaching the next trailer, he cautiously peeks into the gap between it and the storage room beyond.

A man and a woman are working inside unloading the delivery. Lazarus listens for a few minutes, keeping well out of sight. The woman is recording the items using a handheld scanner as the man expertly wheels them off the truck. On each trip, the pile grows in the center of her floor. Lazarus can't understand what they're saying, but it's obvious the two know each other.

He leans against the wall until it becomes quiet inside. Waiting patiently for several more minutes, Lazarus pokes his head into the room. Seeing nothing, he hoists himself up and moves behind the newly stacked boxes. Only then does he hear them. From behind the door to his left comes the unmistakable sound of two human beings in the throes of passion, the woman being particularly enthusiastic. Seems they know each other pretty well.

Lazarus walks down a short hallway, stopping to listen at the door. He concentrates, categorizing what he hears. This is another crucial moment where something unexpected can ruin everything. He doesn't know what's on the other side. Taking a deep breath, he squares his shoulders, opens the door, and moves through as if he belongs.

It's a gift shop. The shopper closest to the door has her back to him and the only person that notices him looks up but turns away. Lazarus walks through the store doing his best to look like just another tourist. No one pays him the slightest heed.

Lazarus picks up a miniature Parthenon as it would have looked in 400 BCE and marvels at the detail in the piece of colored plastic. Putting it back, he casually meanders his way back into the crowded mall. A few minutes later, Lazarus passes the restroom where he had made his first change of clothing. He spots the agent talking to a woman, slight with dark hair and pastel clothing, her features unremarkable, a perfect match for the man. Lazarus memorizes their faces as best he can.

As he watches, the woman shrugs and the man swears in frustration, unheard from this distance but intense. He grins, thinking about the trouble they'll be in when they finally admit they lost him. He's counting on them delaying until they're sure he's gone. Just thirty minutes more is all he needs. In the Federation, they would scan for his bioID to pinpoint his location. That's not possible in Athens where human rights have placed restrictions on the government's right to know where you are at all times.

Moments later, Lazarus is beyond sight of the agents. Athena's Marketplace was built almost thirty years ago and is considered one of the great wonders of the modern world. In a land of ancient learning and humanity's first democracy, this is but a hollow reminder of what once was. He pities the travelers who fly into Athens and never make it beyond this tourist trap. Lazarus shakes his head with regret when he realizes he's one.

He takes the corridor leading to his gate. Lazarus goes directly to the ticket console and places his left hand on the pad.

The image on the screen looks like someone's grandmother, kind, compassionate, and wise. Caring brown eyes and welcoming smile draws him in.

"Greetings, Mr. Sheffield. My name is Margaret. How may I assist you this morning?" She has perfect inflection and looks human in every way but she's not. AI's have been doing this type of work for many years and most people don't even realize they're talking to one, but Lazarus knows.

"I want to purchase a round trip ticket to Heaven's Gate, outbound on Frontier Flight 701 and returning in three days on Flight 1205."

"I'm sorry sir, but Flight 701 is full. May I offer you some alternatives?"

"No. I'm invoking DHS591 Section 9, Paragraph 34B of the International War on Terror. Use account number 119186722." His voice rings hollow and fraudulent in his own ears.

"Very well, please hold…" A mountain stream replaces grandma, its sights and sounds intended to be soothing.

As the seconds drag on, he stares blankly at the screen without seeing it. Lazarus succumbs to the temptation to worry about things he has no control over. His position within DHS authorizes him to make the purchase, and the number is for an offshore account that should not attract attention until he's well away. There should be just enough in it to cover the ticket and the penalty for bumping someone off a flight, unless DHS has frozen the account. Sweat trickles down his back and he wipes damp hands on his pants. At that moment, his plans seem foolish and transparent. From somewhere deep within grows the conviction that this will never work. Each second an eternity, he runs his fingers through his hair and stares at the screen.

Abruptly the AI reappears and said, "I have debited your account eight-thousand-four-hundred-fifty-eight Euros. Is there anything else I can do for you?"

AI's aren't curious. They run their programs and if he stays within certain parameters, nothing will happen. So far, Lazarus has only done what agents of the Federation, the European Union, China, and even the Islamic Brotherhood have been doing for decades. By the time anyone notices, he'll be gone.

"No," he said hoarsely, "That'll be all," not bothering to make nice. What would be the point? It's just a program.

With his boarding pass secured, he goes to the waiting area. The newly arrived Stratoliner empties quickly in comparison to the Airbus. Lazarus notes the strained faces and laborious movements as they pass just a few meters away. It must be the sudden immersion back into high gravity.

As his line begins to move, he avoids any thought he's going to make it. Nothing could jinx him faster than overconfidence. Running his hand through his hair for the hundredth time, he keeps a tight rein on his emotions, managing a weak smile for the young flight attendant at the boarding checkpoint. He's come too far to blow it at this late stage. *I'm going on a vacation, something to enjoy, not dread.*

As the line advances, he hears an angry voice back at the checkpoint, "What do you mean, my seat's been taken?"

"I'm sorry sir. There's another flight this evening and I'm sure you can get on it."

"Why can't I take this one? Fifteen minutes ago, I had a seat and now I don't? What gives?" The man asks irritably.

Lazarus glances back, sincerely hoping his little maneuver will not cause too much trouble. Besides, it's not as if he had a choice. The man is still arguing as he moves out of earshot.

It's a short walk down the tunnel to the Stratoliner. All he's leaving with is an out-of-print novel and an out-of-date headset. *I came into this world with nothing and I'm leaving it the same way.* At least he's not naked. He allows himself a smile.

Lazarus runs his fingers through his hair and walks right by the flight attendant, wiping away sweat from his upper lip with the back of his hand as he shuffles past. She thinks nothing of it, accustomed to people being nervous boarding her flights. After all, they're on their way to space, many for the first time. Lazarus finds his seat and stows his meager belongings.

Leaning down as though looking for something beneath his seat, Lazarus pulls the paper out of his cheeks, stuffing the soggy mass into a hollow. Straightening, he buckles in, fumbling with the unfamiliar four-point harness. He runs his hand through his hair dividing his attention between observing the activity outside his window and watching the stream of people entering the Stratoliner.

Near the end of the procession, Lazarus is stunned. No. It can't be. It was the surrogate. In total shock, he watched the woman nod pleasantly to the flight attendant and turn towards him. There was nowhere to run, nowhere to hide, but the closer she came, the more he realized, that's not the surrogate. Removing his sunglasses, he stared incredulously at the face under the bright blue scarf. It's Rachel's. A little older but it's Rachel.

She moves purposefully down the aisle, glancing at row markers, flashing her bright smile and quick wit along the way. Her movements, her smile, her connection with others, it's Rachel. She reached up and swept her long hair back in place sending memories cascading through long abandoned regions of his brain.

The thumping in his chest thundered in his ears. Lazarus can't take his eyes off her. The coal black hair held in check by a bright blue scarf, the tilt of her head, her radiant smile, it's Rachel and the closer she gets, the more surreal it becomes. Lazarus stares, his mind swirling in a million different directions as memories of his beloved wife overwhelm his senses. His vision narrows until all he can see is her, the chatter inside the Stratoliner recedes to the bottom of a well.

The woman stopped at his row, and looked down at Lazarus with a puzzled expression, "I believe this is my seat."

The spell shatters. Lazarus gasps and turns away, his senses reeling as they snap back to reality. Clearly, the lady is very attractive but she's definitely not Rachel. How could he think even for a moment that she was?

"Please forgive me. I thought you were someone else," Lazarus stammered.

"No worry... I rather like having that affect on a man." She flashed her smile at him.

It was an image Lazarus would never forget.

Heaven's Gate

"All our science, measured against reality, is primitive and childlike - and yet it is all we have."

Albert Einstein (1879-1955)

The woman settles into her seat and said "Lindsey Marquest."

Lazarus hesitates, "Lazarus."

"Just Lazarus?"

"Lazarus Sheffield."

"Well Lazarus Sheffield, looks like we have a full plane today." She looks him over. Square jaw... high cheekbones... long hair pushed behind his ears... bushy eyebrows overshadowing intense blue eyes. Not bad looking in a rugged sort of way. He was wearing a wedding band on his finger and a Christian cross hung around his neck on a gold chain.   The man reeked of tension verging on fear, and for that single fleeting moment, a deep sadness had flashed across his face.

"I believe you're right," Lazarus said, licking dry lips. They taste of paper. He watches her adjust the four-point harness around her tits.

Lindsey can sense his interest and puts on a good show. Glancing up, she catches him staring and smiles.

Lazarus grins weakly in return and looks away. When the hull door finally shuts, his worry shifts from the Federation catching him to what lies ahead.

With a lurch, the Stratoliner moves away from the terminal. On cue, the flight attendants spring into action, running through the obligatory safety presentation, pointing out the exit ports, flotation devices, and emergency beacons. Lazarus doesn't pay much attention. It only makes him more nervous to think about useless escape plans while streaking through the sky at seven kilometers per second.

Lazarus wipes sweat from his brow with the back of his hand and wills himself to relax. Lindsey smiles encouragingly.

The powerful tug pulls the Stratoliner in line with the other aircraft waiting for takeoff, shepherding it in time and space towards a very specific launch window. The tug releases it at the far end of a long ribbon of concrete and immediately the pitch of the hydrogen turbojets increase. The spaceplane picks up speed.

Acceleration pushes Lazarus deep into the padded seat and he feels the rotation as the nose rises. Seconds after liftoff, the wheels tuck away with a thud. A rivulet of sweat runs down his cheek.

Lazarus grips both armrests, knuckles turning white, his head hard back against the headrest. He hates heights. His knees grow weak just climbing a ladder, yet his eyes remain locked on the scene enfolding out his window.

Lazarus concentrates on the view, not his perspective, using the incredible detail to control his fear. Athens stretches out before him under the late autumn sun, its roads and structures partially hidden beneath the green canopy of an urban forest. Rising sea levels have blurred the coastline. When dikes and levees proved ineffective, people abandoned many of the world's coastal cities but Athens is relatively unscathed. Along the shore, rooftops stick out of the water. Other buildings are completely submerged. Yet, the majority of the city remains high and dry.

As the spaceplane banks into its trajectory, he catches a fleeting glimpse in the distance of the Acropolis and the Parthenon, influential architecture from the dawn of civilization.

As the avenues and buildings disappear into minutia, the world below becomes a mottled swatch of color bordered by the blue of the Mediterranean along one side and the many shades of browns and greens of the Greek peninsula on the other. The ship shudders and Lazarus feels the brief sensation of weightlessness as the hydrogen turbojets give way to the magnetoplasma thrusters.

Mountain climbers reaching the summit of Mount Everest, almost nine kilometers above sea level, can see the curvature of Earth's limb. It's so slight many think it's an optical illusion. Lazarus watches spellbound as the curvature becomes more and more pronounced.

As Mother Earth dwindles, the first bright pinpricks of stars appear. A sudden pitch change startles Lazarus and marks passage of the sound barrier. Later, a gradual fade to near silence as the outside air pressure drops to zero. Only the low throb of the ships thrusters remain.

Earth's mountains and seas dwindle to a mosaic of browns, greens and blues, and cloud systems become great white smears across the vast landscape. The higher he goes, the more fragile the atmosphere shrouding Mother Earth appears and strange as it seems, the less he fears.

Eight minutes into the flight, a chime softly rings out, "Welcome to space, everyone. We just exceeded one hundred kilometers."

Lazarus feels like cheering but holds his tongue.

The acceleration continues. The long sleek spacecraft keeps its nose pointed up long after the blue-sky morphs into the diamond-studded black-velvet of space.

Twelve minutes into the flight, Mother Earth is a giant globe spread out below him, only partially seen from his window. The sun is behind him and out of view. Before him, the intense points of light from a hundred thousand stars burn brightly, more stars than Lazarus has ever seen on even the clearest desert night.

"Your first time?" his neighbor asks.

Lazarus reluctantly turns away from the window. Lindsey smiles as their eyes meet and his reluctance fades.

"I don't like flying," Lazarus returns the smile. A bead of sweat rolls off his forehead and into an eye causing him to blink and rub.

"There's really nothing to be afraid of. Statistics show space travel is far safer than any ground transport," she replies.

Still shaking his head, "I'm not afraid, just aware. In an automobile, if you have a flat tire or the motor shorts out, you call roadside service. You can't do that out here."

"How far are you going?"

"Heaven's Gate… and you?" Lazarus said.

"Aldrin Station"

"Republic of Luna," Lazarus blurts. "Are you a citizen?"

"Yes," Lindsey nods.

"What do you do?" He asked.

"Up until yesterday afternoon, I worked as an engineer for MetCal, but not anymore."

In an instant, the last whisper of sound disappears and freefall begins. Lazarus feels as if he were falling. As far back as he can remember Lazarus has had serious nightmares about falling. As a child, they terrified him. As he grew older, he came to terms with the dreams but they still haunt him.

Lazarus grips the arms of his seat until his knuckles turn white. His inner ear delivers one message, his eyes another. It feels like his head is getting larger and his sense of time warps. A few seconds later, nausea threatens to bring up the liquor and his breakfast. He grabs an airsickness bag and prepares for the worst.

Lindsey raises her arm, signaling the attendant that her neighbor needs some extra help.

Lazarus accepts the pill offered by the pretty attendant floating above the aisle. He bites down on the nipple of the juice bottle and uselessly tips it back just as he would have done back on Mother Earth. Realizing his mistake, he squeezes the bottle.

The chime sounds again as one of the attendants prepares to address the passengers, "My name is Lee Fong, Sarah is the pretty one. We will be your flight attendants today. On behalf of Frontier Flight 701, let me welcome aboard everyone. We are currently on schedule to dock with Heaven's Gate in 42 minutes, weather permitting." He chuckles at his own joke. "Seriously folks, if Heaven's Gate isn't in your travel plans, you need to let one of us know immediately. We will be glad to help you into a parachute and shove you back out the door."

Lindsey keeps a wary eye on Lazarus, not wanting a surprise if he pukes.

"For those of you staying, we will periodically make orbital corrections, that is, we will turn on the thrusters now and then as we make adjustments on our way to Heaven's Gate. We'll warn you when this is going to happen by turning on the Fasten Seat Belt sign and sounding the acceleration alarm." He demonstrates by blinking the sign a few times and giving the acceleration klaxon a short burst. "Please immediately return to your seats and fasten your seatbelt. Take your time, you'll have about a minute." Lee Fong chuckles again.

"Connecting flight information can be obtained using Frontier Spaceline magazine located in the seat back in front of you or at www. frontier.spaceline.org. Thanks again for selecting Frontier Spaceline, your gateway to the stars."

While the pretty flight attendant, Sarah, is serving refreshments, Lee Fong demonstrates his freefall prowess by soaring from one end of the cabin to the other, snagging a headrest, flipping over and landing smoothly on the forward bulkhead. He receives a mixed reaction from his passengers. A few laugh and applaud, some smile, most simply ignore him.

The little pill works wonders. Lazarus is famished. He turns to the fruit juice and the package of cashews. The juice mixes pleasantly with the rich oiliness of the nuts and lingers on his tongue long after he swallows, savory and delicious.

"I'm not going to eat these. Would you like them?" Lindsey offers.

Lazarus looks into her riveting gray eyes. "Yes, thank you. They're very good."

"Freefall affects taste buds, usually in a good way," Lindsey said, pleased the handsome young man has accepted her hospitality.

"That seems to be the only good thing about freefall." Lazarus shakes his head, eating another nut.

"Oh, believe me, there are loads of fun things to do in freefall," Lindsey said with a wistful grin, staring straight ahead, ignoring Lazarus when he stares inquisitively at her.

"That sounds like the voice of experience," Lazarus comments. When it becomes obvious she's not going to elaborate he continues, "Have you spent a lot of time in freefall?"

"Enough," she replies, "I worked the Hyundai Shipyards for a while." Hyundai Shipyards is an enormous manufacturing facility located at Lagrange Four.

Smart and beautiful. Lazarus is feeling a little out of his league. "I'm a desk jockey. Not very exciting, I'm afraid."

Raising her eyebrows Lindsey said, "Excitement is a human response that has only a weak dependence on physical surroundings. You would be surprised at how many boring people are in unusual and romantic occupations and how many exciting people do the most mundane things." She leans over conspiratorially, her breath hot on his cheek, "My first husband was a taxi cab driver. By far the most exciting man I've ever known."

Lazarus is stunned when she actually winks at him. He can't help smiling, feeling a little more at ease with this beautiful and unusual woman. Her openness and self-confidence is magnetic and those eyes...

"There must be something about being a desk jockey which excites you," she's the very picture of innocence, mouth puckered, head tilted. "Come on, tell me what it is," she insists intimately, pulling the truth out of him.

The religiously correct answer involved God and duty but staring into those gray orbs only centimeters away, he realized this woman was not asking for a recital of the slogans and sound bites that dominate Federation politics.

"You don't mess around, do you?" Lazarus asks.

Her dimples become even more pronounced. "I'm a Lunarian."

He's reluctant to provide any real information, even to so charming an inquisitor. "Well... I guess I just like tilting at windmills." He settles for a vague half-truth, a trick his father had taught him at an early age and one that has worked well throughout his career.

Lindsey laughs and lets him win this minor skirmish, "Oh, a modern day Don Quixote. Or perhaps you are just doing God's work?" Nodding at the cross floating on its chain outside his shirt.

"Perhaps. With God, one never knows," he said removing the chain from his neck and putting them in his pocket.

"What kind of a desk jockey can commandeer a seat on an

international flight?" She watched him intently. The dilation of his eyes and sudden increase in breathing signals she'd hit a nerve. "Mr. Hamlin should be sitting in your seat."

"He's your friend?" Lazarus blurts out, caught off guard yet again by this remarkable woman.

"Friend? No, not really. He's a MetCal employee I worked with on occasion. What you did will cost him money, but don't worry, MetCal pays well. He can afford it," Lindsey states, making Lazarus squirm. "So tell me, what kind of desk jockey can requisition a seat on a Stratoliner at a moment's notice?"

Lazarus bows his head and ignores her question, "I'm sincerely sorry for that. Perhaps you can give me his address and I can send compensation later?"

She shakes her head, "Stop changing the subject and answer the question…" When she realized the man was not going to respond, "Then at least tell me why you're in such a hurry to get to Heaven's Gate?"

Lazarus weighs his options and for some inexplicable reason, tells her the truth, "Actually, Heaven's Gate is not my final destination. I want to go on to Luna."

Lindsey rewards him by hooking her arm under his and pressing her left tit firmly against him. Casually, she lays her other hand on his wrist where she can monitor his pulse. "See, that wasn't so bad… any particular place? Luna contains well over a million citizens," she said, measuring and probing for the slightest sign of falsehood.

"Aldrin Station," Lazarus replies, the only Lunarian city he could think of at that moment. It's an instant decision that will prove to have far-reaching consequences.

"What are you running from?" Lindsey asks, not giving him time to come up with a better story.

"No, it's nothing like that," Lazarus denies much too quickly, "This is strictly a vacation. I simply want to see an underground city with my own eyes and this is the only way I'll ever do it. Homeland Security would never grant my request for a Luna visa."

The best lies have some truth in them but Lindsey lets it drop for now. Looking down at Lazarus's wedding band, "Is your wife going to meet you at Aldrin Station?" She asked. Once again, sweeping changes in his polygraphic indicators tell her she's hit another nerve.

Lazarus sits stiffly, staring straight ahead, wondering how the conversation had gotten here, of all places. He turns back to Lindsey before speaking. "My wife died two years ago," he said twisting at the wedding band, "I wear this just to keep all the women at bay." He grins weakly at his own halfhearted attempt at humor.

"I'm so sorry…" Lindsey said softly. Putting two and two together, she declares, "You thought I was her. When I boarded the plane, you thought I was your wife."

Startled, Lazarus stammers, "Only for a moment." This woman is driving him nuts.

The Earthman actually told her the truth, Lindsey noted. "You must have loved her very much."

Lazarus slides the ring off and stares at it for a moment "Yes, I did," he puts it in the pocket with the cross.

The silence extends uncomfortably long, "You're going to love Aldrin Station," she said.

Lazarus gratefully accepted her change of subject. "What's the Republic of Luna like? I've seen every National Geographic vid, played net games, and read everything I could get my hands on."

The Federation discourages its citizens from reading and by the time the censors finish with a NatGeo vid, it's of little value, depicting Lunarian cities as dark subterranean caverns deprived of sunlight and stripped of humanity, the implication of hell never far from the surface. Without exception, the games are even worse, designed to vilify Lunarians. They are terrible sources of knowledge for anyone seeking truth.

Lindsey shakes her head, "Then you know nothing. Lunarian cities are bubbles of air carved from solid rock containing life in all its diversity. There are forests and meadows complete right down to the bacteria in the soil. Luna is a place of light and life that is diametrically opposite to what the Federation would have you believe."

"What's it like to live in the Republic? We hear so many reports of violence. Do you live in fear?" Lazarus asks.

"To be sure, we are threatened by an enemy not willing to negotiate, but I do *not* live in fear." She frowns and shakes her head, "Over the last decade, necessity has made the Republic of Luna an armed camp with everyone contributing to the common defense, just as Israel has done the last hundred-fifty years and for pretty much the same reasons. It seems there are many who hate us."

"Do not count me among that number. I'm looking forward to my stay on Luna."

The acceleration klaxon blares, sending passengers scurrying back to their seats.

Located in a near perfect circular orbit just over 1600 kilometers above sea level and in the Earth-Luna plane, Heaven's Gate serves mainly as a passenger transfer point. Most outbound cargo rendezvous with freighters in much lower orbits and transfer payloads across the vacuum of space without the need of elaborate orbital structures. Going the other way, earthbound shipments are packaged within heat shields, decelerated by an orbital mass-driver before plunging through the atmosphere in well-established drop zones. Humans, on the other hand, pass through Heaven's Gate, coming and going.

Supporting only a small permanent population, Heaven's Gate contains a hotel and several restaurants in addition to harboring spaceline support personnel. Tourists come here to enjoy freefall and it's somewhat of a honeymoon status symbol. For many Earthmen, this is as far into space as they will ever get.

Lindsey retrieves the Frontier Spaceline magazine from its pocket on the back of the seat in front of them. The magazine is a thin flexible touch screen with a wide variety of flight information available through it. Lindsey accesses a live view of the station as the Stratoliner draws near.

Together, they watch the station grow from a bright spot on the screen into a dull metallic tubular shape hanging motionless in the void of space. From the Stratoliner's direction of approach, the structure appears at an angle. The end facing them is a shallow dome with its edges melding smoothly into the sides of the cylinder making Heaven's Gate look like an over-pressurized aluminum can on the verge of bursting. Stubby appendages protrude from the body of the station at various points like nails driven partway into a log. Antenna and power receptors sprout here and there.

A sense of scale eludes Lazarus until he realizes another Stratoliner is docked to Heaven's Gate, held fast by one of the stubby extensions. It looks like a child's toy airplane, dwarfed by the bulk of the station.

Another quite different spacecraft comes into view during approach. It doesn't have the aerodynamic outlines of an atmospheric craft. It's an open framework of beams and girders enclosing a thick disk. Instead of minimizing the frontal area, this vehicle maximizes it.

"I believe that's our ride," Lindsey said. "The front part is the Lander and the tanks and other stuff is the TLM or TransLunar Module. It will thrust all the way to Luna."

The station grows on the screen. At the last possible moment, the thrusters vibrate to life, bringing the ship almost to a stop in relation to the station. Much more slowly, the sleek atmospheric craft closes with the orbiting station. Outside the window, the stars rotate as the spacecraft positions itself for docking. On the screen, multiple external cameras seamlessly maintain the view of the station.

When Heaven's Gate fills the screen, one of the extensions reaches out and closes around the fuselage of the spaceplane. Lazarus feels a bump and the sound of metal against metal as the electromagnetic grapplers find their place. A whirring vibration fills the cabin as the mechanical safeties screw down, signaling the end of the docking maneuver. The Stratoliner is now physically part of the station.

A soft chime sounds, "Welcome to Heaven's Gate. Please be patient for just a few more minutes while the crew checks everything. We wouldn't want to open the door to vacuum."

Most of the passengers unbuckle, retrieve their luggage, and start moving towards the exit. Many are clumsy, bumping and jostling each other, chuckling at their own inexperience, excited to be here. It's easy to pick out the veterans, they move with grace and skill.

Lindsey puts her hand on his arm stopping Lazarus from unbuckling, "Might as well relax, could be awhile. The first time I was here, they had us waiting for over an hour. Besides, our connecting shuttle isn't scheduled for departure for three hours," Lindsey informs Lazarus. "There's a nice java shop inside. Do you feel up to joining me for a cup?" Lindsey asks smiling.

Lazarus has a fleeting moment of suspicion that evaporates with one look in her gray eyes. "I don't know about the coffee but I would be happy to join you," he said, returning her smile, thrilled that she wants him to stick around.

"Good," she said enthusiastically.

"I need to get my ticket for the shuttle first. Perhaps you could spare the time to accompany me?" Lazarus asks hopefully.

Lindsey laughs, "There isn't a ticket counter or agent. The only way to get a ticket is through Luna Central. You do have a visor, don't you?"

"Yes, of course… in my bag," Lazarus said.

Lindsey unbuckles and floats into the aisle. Hooking her toe under a loop, she opens the overhead and takes down her bag first, and then what must be Lazarus's. She hands it to him and buckles back into her seat.

Lindsey stifles a giggle when he pulls out his antiquated headset. State of the art several decades ago, it still works but just barely. She takes out a visor from her bag and slides it on. It molds itself into her ear channels, and fits snugly across her face completely covering her eyes. This is the first time she's worn her visor since arriving on Mother Earth over six weeks earlier. For her, putting on the visor means she's home.

She tries to link with Lazarus but the old headset is not equipped to handle modern protocols. "Go to lunacentral.rol," she directs him. She watches as his hands flail about.

"Got it," he said triumphantly.

The blurry image of an AI appears before him and asks politely, "How may I be of assistance?"

"List the availability of passage on the next Lunar Shuttle," Lindsey said.

The information appears within their VR as a seating chart.

"You're lucky. There are still seats available…" she selects two together next to a window designating one as hers and the other as being purchased. "Go on. This is where you pay for your passage," Lindsey tells him.

Lazarus nods and with a few jerky hand motions, downloads his financial information into the site.

"I'm sorry Mr. Sheffield, but passage is denied," the AI said.

Lazarus is stunned.

When he remains silent, Lindsey asks, "Why?"

"Federation authorities have indicted him on multiple counts of Earthnet security breach, lying to a police official, and failure to obtain the proper visas. They have requested his return on the next available flight."

Lazarus is horrified. Without knowing what to say, he silently runs his fingers through his hair.

Lindsey seizes the opportunity. "Under the Lunarian constitution, Lazarus can stake claim to Freedom of Movement. He is not a violent criminal and has the right to go where he pleases." She knows what the AI's response will be.

"To do so he must reject his Federation citizenship and apply for Lunarian. Do you, Ms. Marquest, sponsor him in this?"

Lindsey sits back and looks intently at Lazarus. His peculiar headset makes it impossible for her to see the upper half of his face but she knows she has him right where she wants him. "So… what do you think? You want to become a Lunarian?"

Lazarus struggles to control the emotional roller coaster of the last few seconds. In planning his departure, he didn't let himself dwell on the things he had no control over. Being brutally honest, he never believed he would get this far. His comrades in the Department of Homeland Security are just too good at their jobs. When imagining what kind of people he would meet along the way, never in his wildest dreams did it occur to him that a beautiful woman would magically appear to help him.

He wonders briefly why she's doing this, but frankly, he doesn't care.

"You would sponsor me?" Lazarus asks, hardly daring to breathe. "You don't even know me."

"You're running from the Federation. What else do I need to know?" Almost flippantly, Lindsey continues, "It's not that big of a deal for me. On the other hand, for you this is huge. Do you even know what you'll be expected to do?"

"I must pass a test and a physical," Lazarus croaks, his voice harsh with barely contained emotion.

"It's much more important that you never lie to me or any other Lunarian ever again. Can you do that?"

He thinks for a moment and said, "I don't know but I can try."

"That's good. You learn fast. You must also find a freehold that will take you in. Would you accept Dakota hospitality until you decide?" She asked.

There are times in a person's life where a single decision, contemplated for only an instant, completely changes the path of their lives. "Yes, of course, I would be honored." Lazarus said not daring to believe what is happening.

"It's settled then." Lindsey chuckles, "You didn't fool me for a second with that vacation story. I suspect the Federation would skin you alive if they got their hands on you. It only makes sense if you're running… emigrating. With Lunarian citizenship, you may return someday and visit your family. Without it you're dead meat," Lindsey ties the knot firmly about his neck. Addressing the AI she said, "Yes, I will sponsor Mr. Lazarus Sheffield in his application for Lunarian citizenship."

"Your sponsorship has been recorded and Mr. Sheffield has been granted provisional Lunarian citizenship. His passage to Aldrin Station is secure. The shuttle will depart in three hours and fourteen minutes."

Lazarus can hardly believe it. He never imagined it could be this easy or painless. It seems all he had to do was ask. He begins to understand one of the basic tenets of a free society, that it cannot withhold its freedoms from anyone, even those wishing to harm it.

"Lindsey, I can't thank you enough. I will never be able to repay your kindness." His emotions are raw and stressed to the breaking point.

"Like I said, it's no big deal, really. You're the one that will bust your ass getting up to speed. Have you ever been in a vacsuit?"

Lazarus shakes his head, "No, but I have extensive training time in environmental contamination suits and they're similar."

Lindsey chuckles. What desk jockey needs training in environmental contamination suits? "That's debatable but the fact remains, you will need to be qualified in the Lunarian version before you can even take a walk on the surface."

"Oh yes, certainly." Lazarus would agree to just about anything at that moment. Nothing was going to stand in the way of Lunarian citizenship.

With a clank, the Stratoliner's door disengages and swings open. "Be sure to collect all personal items before leaving. Watch your elbows and knees during disembarkation. Do not leave your luggage unsecured while in the station." The message softly repeats, over and over, with a few seconds pause in between.

Lazarus removes and returns his headset to his bag, maneuvers out of the seat, and joins Lindsey in the aisle without mishap, something he hardly notices in the magnitude of the moment. Smiling her congratulations, Lindsey gracefully propels herself towards the exit, leaving Lazarus to admire her behind. To his credit, Lazarus only ricochets once.

He does his best to keep up with Lindsey but finds he's the last to leave. Beyond the Stratoliner's open door stretches a long tubular corridor, its far end clogged with departing passengers. Lazarus manages to keep to the center, more or less, reaching out to brush the walls as he traverses the tunnel.

His mind races and he can't rid himself of the feeling that this is a dream and he will awaken only to find himself alone in his luxury apartment, stuck in a job that no longer holds value, in a culture that makes him hide his true beliefs and live a lie.

Already he's come further than he had dared hope was possible. After all, he's entering Heaven's Gate. Never has a name been more apropos. Moreover, thanks to Lindsey, he will be on his way to Luna in a few hours with the very real possibility of citizenship. He quells the surge of euphoria by reminding himself that provincial status is not full citizenship.

The other passengers are long gone by the time Lazarus emerges from the tunnel. He's in a small sunken alcove, its depth maybe three times his height and its breadth not much bigger than that of the airlock. Netting similar to the climbing rigs found on an old three-mast sailing ship extends out of the alcove and into the station. As most recent arrivals from Mother Earth will do, he orients himself alongside the net. Movement overhead catches his eye.

"Thank you for flying Frontier," the young woman said as he clears the airlock, interrupting his thoughts. Floating effortlessly within easy reach of the net, she's holding out an odd dumbbell shaped item for Lazarus to take.

Seeing his confusion she explains, "This is a Personal Maneuvering Unit or PMU. It will help you get around while you're here." It's something everyone learns about in the mandatory classes that all tourists must take. She glances over at the waiting Lindsey.

"It's an aerosol. Use it when you can't reach something to push against," Lindsey explains turning so he can see the PMU clipped to her belt. "Everyone gets one, not just the shortimers. They would have talked about them in orientation if you had taken it."

"Great," he said clipping the PMU onto his belt. In the process, he releases his bag, which promptly spins away.

"Sir," the attendant exclaims as she retrieves the errant luggage.

Without realizing what he had done, Lazarus is now floating in midair. When the attendant returns his bag, she gives him a slow spin. Reaching out he can't quite touch the net as it passes by repeatedly. Stretching out his leg doesn't bring him any closer. He realizes he has no way to move forward or back, or stop spinning. Just centimeters from the net, he's stuck. He watches helplessly as the world leisurely turns around him.

Lazarus can see them both grinning at him and realizes that she's testing him. Fine. He retrieves the PMU from his belt.

"Think about the physics of what you're doing," the attendant instructs him. "Remember, force equals mass times acceleration. You are just another satellite obeying the same laws as every other body in orbit," she struggles to keep her amusement in check. It happens all too often that people show up with inadequate training, skipping or daydreaming through the classes. Even after only a few months on Heaven's Gate, she can recall more than one Federation visitor who after messing up, prayed for God to save them.

"Why not just grab me?" Lazarus asks irritably, losing his good humor and getting a little peeved at the smirking young lady. He's not in the habit of being the butt of a joke. Worse yet, he can feel the first twinges of space sickness returning.

"That won't help you when you do it again. Everyone goes through this at some point. You would be surprised at how many do it in the first few minutes," she said openly smiling, giving up any pretense that this was not entertaining.

Lazarus ignores the churning of his stomach and concentrates on the PMU. The hourglass shaped device has a small nozzle at one end and padding at the other. In between is a comfortable hand grip with a power dial in easy reach of his thumb. Figuring to curtail his next screw-up, he turns the dial to its lowest setting.

"You trigger the PMU by squeezing," the attendant volunteers.

Glancing out, Lazarus catches Lindsey grinning wickedly. He dredges up the mechanics of motion he studied years ago. For every action, there is an equal but opposite reaction. Referencing the nets, he gauges his plane of rotation as best he can. Extending his arm straight out in that plane, he squeezes. The PMU hisses and he flexes his arm muscles against its force. His rotation slows considerably. A few more seconds proves too long and actually starts him rotating in the opposite direction. He flips the PMU over and gives it another very short burst, coming to a stop, more or less.

"Hey, this isn't so hard," Lazarus proudly exclaims until he looks over at the attendant and sees that he has stopped upside down in relation to her.

She couldn't care less about his orientation. She has lived in Heaven's Gate long enough that she doesn't think about her environment in terms of up and down, recognizing people no matter which way their heads are pointing.

She smiles at Lazarus, "Very good, sir. You'll do fine with a little more practice." Speaking to Lindsey on her way out of the alcove, "Maybe you can stick with him while he's here?" she suggests with a knowing look.

"Maybe," Lindsey said with a grin, "Come on, Mr. Sheffield. Let's go get that coffee."

Still thinking about physics, Lazarus places the PMU against his side just under his rib cage. He squeezes a couple seconds, pleased when he moves, without much rotation, towards the webbing. Grabbing the net with his free hand, he pulls himself towards Lindsey. It reminds him of scuba diving off the coast of Mexico.

"This gadget might actually be fun," he said, returning it to his belt. The two float along within reach of the webbing.

With disconcerting suddenness, they emerge from the confines of the small alcove to openness beyond his wildest imagination. Fear grips him. He's falling into the abyss. In danger of fainting, he gropes for the net, clutching the nearest thing to solid he can find. A whimper escapes his lips.

Lindsey's at his side, "Are you okay?" She asked, real concern etched across her face.

Lazarus focuses on the webbing and by strength of will, begins to regain composure. "Yes, I'm fine," he said gripping the net with both hands, concentrating on its fine weave. "Just give me a minute. I wasn't ready for… this." He manages to bring his fear under control.

Glancing at Lindsey, "You did that on purpose," he accuses her.

Nodding, "You're right. I wanted to see how you handle yourself."

"How'd I do?"

Lindsey shrugs, "At least you didn't pass out." She likes the resilience he demonstrated. It shows courage.

The video in the online magazine did not do Heaven's Gate justice. The station is a huge cylinder with one end dominated by the sun and the other capped like a gigantic tin can. Like a crazy inside out planet, the interior buildings extend inward from the walls. Many buildings are covered in vid projections, sometimes working together to form a single enormous picture, other times they are a chaotic tangle of independent images.

Webbing, similar to what he and Lindsey are using, stretches across the space at strategic locations and at different angles but never intruding far into the central open space. More webs stretch from one end of the station to the other, also staying close to the buildings.

The entire center of the massive cylinder is clear air where hundreds upon hundreds of people are flying using wings in every color, shape and size ranging from the length of an arm to four or five times that. Some are made of fabric, others with artificial feathers, and still more are plastic. Some are utilitarian strap on wings while others are full costumes incorporating a theme. Birds, dragons, insects and even pterodactyls populate the space.

The flyers seem to be everywhere, soaring with joyous abandonment. The large eagle-like wings are the fastest. About ten of them in tight formation are on an oval path the length of the station, their speed astounding and the ability to swoop into a turn thrilling to watch. Lazarus can hear their wings stroke the air as they pass just a few meters away.

Many use small maneuverable wings and dart about like a hummingbird. They fold against the body to reduce drag when not being flapped. Out in the center, a group using these wings is playing a game, twisting and cavorting around a huge ball. All the flyers wear visors of one style or another without exception.

The ambience reminds Lazarus of a bustling ice rink or a busy Colorado ski resort. People come here to play and have brought every gadget and device they could dream up to help them do it. Humanity has finally found a way to fly and is enjoying every minute.

"Is that the sun?" Lazarus asks indicating the brightness at the far end. It lights up the interior of the space station like a giant floodlight.

"Mirrors reflect sunlight into the station. That end is actually pointing away from the sun," she said.

"Incredible. This is better than Las Vegas." Lazarus exclaims in amazement.

She removes her visor and slides it into her pocket careful to fasten the Velcro restraining strap. Lindsey reaches out and pulls him to her, holding him tight with one arm around his waist. He drops his arm about her shoulders just as she weaves her leg past his crotch and hooks her toes on his ankle. She pushes off.

"Relax and let me pilot." Lindsey said. "The first thing we need to do is get you a real visor. That thing you call a headset runs on vacuum tubes, doesn't it?" She asked not expecting an answer. "We can get you a visor over there."

"Do you think I need one?"

"Yes Lazarus, you need one," Lindsey replies. "And that's not all you need."

Lindsey's boldness draws him to her like a fly to honey. Yet, he's sailing in unfamiliar waters and fearing he may be misinterpreting her signals. He would never be so bold as to make sexual advances. Sexual solicitation is a serious offense within the Federation.

"OK, lead the way," Lazarus said.

She grabs the webbing and swings them like a monkey on a branch, sending them soaring across free space towards the shop.

Lazarus shuts his eyes, briefly feeling his stomach churn but maintains control. Lindsey swings her free leg making them rotate with just enough angular velocity to be facing backward when they hit the webbing.

She giggles as he gropes for a handhold. "Relax," she repeats, using the rebound to swing them through the circular front door.

Inside is a world of gadgets. On one wall are wings of every shape and size, hovering in mid air are racks filled with merchandise, another wall is one large vid screen.

"Greetings. Can I help you find something," a disembodied female voice asks.

"Greetings. Yes, we need a visor. Nothing elaborate, just something solid for a new emigrant." Lindsey said.

The lights flicker and dance around a nearby rack. "We keep an assortment of visors here," the velvety voice said.

"Thank you…" Lindsey guides Lazarus to the rack before releasing her hold on him. Looking over the selection, she picks up a silver and black model. "Here, try this on." She hands it to him.

Lazarus takes the device and fits it over his eyes, maneuvering the flexible earpieces deep into his ear canals. At first, it felt all wrong, putting pressure at the most peculiar places. Then it seemed to relax and get better.

"The Razors come with a free fitting," the voice observes.

"Of course. How much?" Lindsey asks.

"Our basic Model CS130 is $2149.99," the silken voice said. "We can also provide you with a CS190 for $8949.99 or a CS160 for $5749.99. Both the CS160 and CS190 cover the standard spectrum. The CS190 uses the latest Archstone interface."

"Let's go with the CS160," Lindsey said.

Lazarus is stunned. That's a huge chunk of his cash.

"Charge it to my account," Lindsey said.

"No." Lazarus blurts, "I can pay for it myself," he said a little more calmly. He pulls his money out of his pocket.

"Put that away. You don't pay until the mods are complete."

"Are you sure I need a visor?" Lazarus asks again.

"Trust me on this, you do," she replies.

The modifications take less than a minute, not even enough time to look around. His new visor emerges from the depths of the display case. He puts it on. The visor molds itself to his face enclosing his eyes completely, creating a perfect blindfold, and the audio inserts fit comfortably into his ear canals blocking all sound. Yet, Lazarus can still see and hear, only now it's filtered through the visor.

"How does it feel?" She asks.

"Fine," Lazarus said. He's not thinking about the clarity of the image or the comfort of the fit. He's oblivious to the technology he uses so casually, clueless about the sophisticated visual sensors providing live video of his surrounding directly onto his retina.

He is however, aware of the young woman standing next to him.

"Oh." He turns awkwardly to face her. "Who are you?"

"My name's Helen. I'll be serving you today." It's the owner of the velvety voice. She has regular features, a head devoid of hair, and clothes pleasantly fashioned for comfort and utility. The woman is totally non-threatening and helpful, the perfect combination for a salesperson.

Lindsey smiles and puts on her visor, "That's better. You're one step closer to becoming Lunarian."

Lazarus retrieves his change from the dispenser and looks at Lindsey. "Didn't you just put your visor on?" He asked.

She chuckles, "I did. The reason you don't see it is that internal sensors pick up my facial expressions and broadcasts this information to other visors, including yours. Your visor simply overlays your live feed with my transmission, effectively making my visor disappear. There isn't any magic here, just a simple set of graphic calculations."

Lazarus swallows hard, "This is better than anything available in the

Federation."

"Better than anything on Mother Earth," Lindsey corrects him, "even the Chinese."

"It's not perfect, though. I can still see your visor when you move your head around."

"That's done on purpose. It lets you know who's wearing visors and who isn't." Lindsey turns her head side to side causing a ghostly outline of her visor to fade in and out. "Don't worry, in a few days you won't even notice. Right now, it's much more important for you to become familiar with using the virtual control panel. If you'll allow me, I'll link to your visor and demonstrate."

"By all means, show me," he said.

Lindsey chuckles, "This is demo mode," she said. "It duplicates my visor settings in yours."

Looking down, he sees Lindsey's hands where his should be. In the virtual world, she's taken control of his visor. She gives him a moment.

"Ok, the first thing to learn is how to turn the control panel on and off. Observe."

Lazarus watches as she rolls her hand counterclockwise in a graceful twisting action. Suddenly, a ring of pictographic icons appears about his waist, flat as if lying on a table. She repeats the movement and the icons vanish. "Now you try it," she said.

Lazarus emulates her motion and the icons reappear.

"The icons you use most frequently are arrayed to your front. All you need to do is look at one and move your hand down. Subtle hand movements will do. No need to go swinging wildly about," she grins. "Or you can touch the icon if you want. That works too… The pictograph of the satellite is your Earthnet portal. Right beside that are the search engine, visor settings and link monitor icons."

"What's a link monitor?" Lazarus asks.

"It shows you how many citizens are linked to your visor."

"It's a number, two. Does that mean there are two other people linked to my visor right now?" Lazarus asks without understanding.

"Sort of… It's you and me. Look, there are over two hundred icons and we have a long flight ahead of us. Let's study the ones you find interesting then." Lindsey suggests.

"Great idea," Lazarus said. "This part is similar to what I've used on Earthnet. I should be able to catch on quickly." What he does not elaborate upon is the clarity of the graphics or their response speed. Far superior to anything in the Federation.

Lindsey files that away with the other information. Very few Federation citizens have access to Earthnet.

"Let's go then," she takes his arm and wraps her left leg inside his right leg pressing her hip against his crotch. She skillfully pushed off, sending them soaring gracefully across the shop and through the entrance portal.

If he would notice, the interior of the station looks different now. The most obvious is he no longer sees any of the visors on the people around him and now when he takes the time to look at them, the advertisements strewn across the interior of Heaven's Gate are more distinct, their sounds clearer, and their colors sharper. In the same way, distances shrink. He can now make out the eagle flyers even at the far end of the station, but only if he stares for a few seconds. The fact is, he's already forgotten he's wearing a visor, so perfectly does it meld to his eyes and ears while supplying him with a flawless reproduction of his physical surroundings. However, exploring this marvelous device will come later. Right now, all he can think about is Lindsey.

"I will never in a hundred years be able to repay your kindness," Lazarus said hoarsely, intensely aware of her tit pressing against his arm and her hip wedged against his bulging crotch.

"You don't owe me anything. I did what any Lunarian would have done. I helped someone who needed help," she said, her leg expertly putting pressure in the most delightful places.

"Do you know what you're doing to me?" Lazarus asks softly, losing the fight against millions of years of evolution.

Batting long eyelashes, she purrs, "Oh… I have a pretty good idea." She did indeed.

Lazarus looks outward at the people flying, trying and failing to use them as objects of distraction.

Pointing at Heaven's Crib, "I stayed there my first time, had some time to kill waiting for my ride." Looking impishly at Lazarus, "That's when I joined the club."

"Joined what club?" Lazarus asks hoarsely, his brain frying under her administrations. He has problems focusing on her words.

"Freefall sex. There's nothing like it on Mother Earth." Lindsey smiles, her gray eyes limpid pools of sexual attraction inviting him to dive in. "Why do you think this place is so popular? It's not the food." Everything about her drove him crazy, her low husky voice, her hot breath on his cheek, her hotter body pressing against his.

He pushes back. Sexual energy from the hard spike between his legs surges through him, pounding his brain like a hurricane lashing the Florida coastline. He can stand it no longer. Lazarus pulls Lindsey into a full embrace, his lips engulfing hers. Her arms encircle his neck and her legs clamp down around his waist, focusing even more pressure on all the right places. His blood boils, matched perfectly by the furnace burning inside of Lindsey.

From somewhere in the vastness of Heaven's Gate a voice calls out, "Get a room."

Lindsey reaches out and grabs the webbing, expertly swinging them towards the Crib's front entrance without even breaking the kiss. She'll take enthusiasm over experience any day.

ℜL

The Data Acquisition and Control Center (DACC) of the FBS Yorktown is a dimly lit cocoon nestled deep inside the battlestation. Exposed braces march down its length like ribs inside a giant whale. Mounted within the braces are sixteen high-G couches containing the bridge crew.

Lieutenant Gilmore is tracking a spacecraft just leaving low earth orbit (LEO). He retrieves its information and runs a preliminary check on its registered flight plan. "Sir, I have an outbound freighter, Evolution's Child, Republic registration. Request permission to interrogate," he said to the watch commander.

"Proceed Lieutenant," Admiral DyGoon replies. The admiral thrives on bridge duty. It keeps him in touch with the inner workings of his battlestation and her place within the fleet.

"Yes Sir."

The lieutenant initiates an encrypted command that cascades through a constellation of seven Forward Observation SATellites, none bigger than a briefcase. The FOSAT closest to the freighter sends a powerful MRI beam sweeping over the spacecraft, the equivalent of a sonar ping in Mother Earth's oceans. The returns are collected and transmitted back to the battlestation then compared with a vast storehouse of other scans, looking for any abnormalities in the data. The entire exercise requires less than thirty seconds.

"Nothing unusual, admiral. Standard heavy-lift freighter, cargo is mining equipment and foodstuffs. Destination is Cullman Outpost, Luna. Only the pilot aboard, no passengers."

The admiral asks, "Where, pray tell, is Cullman?"

The lieutenant does a quick search, "A small mining settlement outside Herschel crater, at the northern edge of the Four Craters Region."

"Very well, Lieutenant, carry on."

The admiral's much more interested in finding the Houris, the Brotherhood's newest battlestation. They have been playing a game of cat and mouse for over a week, each battlestation trying to maneuver her FOSATs to find and maintain track on the other. Freighters half an orbit away don't merit more than a few seconds of the admiral's valuable time.

Evolution's Child continues on to Luna uninterrupted.

Lunar Transit

"Religion belonged to the infancy of the human race; it had been a necessary stage in the transition from childhood to maturity. It had promoted ethical values which were essential to society. Now that humanity has come of age, however, it should be left behind."

Sigmund Freud (1856-1939)

They're early. Human and robotic handlers are still loading supplies onto the shuttle as they approach. Lindsey has Lazarus in the now familiar lovers lock. Neither appears willing to disengage any time soon. Not that he wants her too. In fact, he can't remember the last time he felt so good. Lazarus vows to be worthy of this amazing woman. For the first time in his life, he feels truly free, like a hawk riding desert thermals a thousand meters above the desert.

Even though Lazarus had managed to keep up with Lindsey, it would take months before he could come close to matching her skill in freefall. He remembers her face, framed by coal black hair, hanging over him. Her legs wrapped tightly around him, breasts rippling with every move, gray eyes boring into his as she brought them to a simultaneous climax. He grins. Who knew that sex could be so good?

Lindsey glances at him, "If you keep that up, people will think you're a sex addict."

"Maybe I am," Lazarus said, his smile fading. He can't avoid feeling guilty about making love outside of marriage, an echo of endless lessons that sex is something dirty performed in the dark of night for the sole purpose of procreation and is a sin in any other circumstance. Certainly not just for fun. Sex is a sacred duty within a marriage. Making it cheap entertainment perverts it. At least, that's what the Church and his mother hammered into Lazarus.

Lindsey maneuvers them towards an apparent hole in the skin of the station. Several people float out as they come to a stop. "Are you ready?"

Lazarus nods and Lindsey guides them headfirst into the hole. They emerge outside the hull of Heaven's Gate. Lazarus grits his teeth. Running his free hand through his thick hair, he concentrates on the shuttle a few meters away. It's easier to maintain rather than regain control and being prepared for the experience certainly helped. More likely, it's because Lindsey's there and he would rather die than look weak in front of her.

The shuttle rests at the end of one of the stations many appendages. It's an ugly conglomerated tangle of components. Small free-flying robots scurry about the vessel completing final inspection and detaching lines.

He shifts his gaze to the incredible beauty of the stars framing the shuttle. Even the dimmer ones shine true in uncounted millions. At his back, the immense curving expanse of Heaven's Gate seems so tiny when compared to the vastness of the cosmos.

"You handled that nicely," Lindsey said, impressed with the mental toughness and tenacity she senses within him.

"Thanks... The stars are magnificent." he hasn't yet realized his visor is bringing everything more sharply into focus. Lazarus reaches out, banging his hand into the invisible material of the portal. "What's this?"

"Duraglass, a fully-transparent non-reflective ceramic."

"This would be considered magic by our ancestors," he said.

"It's more likely they would mutter some unintelligible mumbo jumbo and start a new religion. Our ancestors were very inventive when explaining things outside their knowledge."

Lazarus finds her criticism strangely disturbing, "Yes, I suppose you're right. I'm just not used to hearing religion ridiculed."

She looks sharply at him, "I'm not ridiculing the need for ignorant savages to believe in gods, but I am ridiculing modern humans for believing in those same gods in the face of real answers."

"I didn't say I don't agree with you. It will take a little time for me to adjust to things being discussed so..... freely," he said.

It didn't take long for you to set aside the Federation's sexual code of ethics... but she doesn't say that. Instead, she said, "Lunarian society is quite different from the Federation... Are you sure you want to go through with it? There's still time to go back."

Lazarus swallows. "I can't go back. There's nothing for me back there."

"Well then, you better prepare for some rather radical changes in your life." She pulls at his arm, "Listen to me."

They embrace and she wraps her legs and arms around him bringing her face right up to his.

"When things pile up on you I want you to remember you can always come to me... We might even talk once in a while," she purrs seductively, rubbing the tip of her nose on his.

Holding Lindsey so close, feeling her heartbeat next to his, Lazarus doesn't feel alone for the first time in years. He grins. "Did you know that the ancient Greeks believed the Milky Way was actually milk spilled from the tits of the Greek god Hera? The story goes that Zeus, the king of the gods, tricked Hera into nursing Heracles whom she didn't like. Discovering who she was suckling, she pulled him from her tit but a spurt of milk escaped and formed the smear across the sky that we call the Milky Way."

Lindsey chuckles, "In fact, I have heard the story, but where did you learn of it?"

Before he can answer, a lazy drawl interrupts their conversation. "That's gotta be most godforsaken ship ever bolted together. A Winnebago with a thruster up its tailpipe."

Lazarus and Lindsey break their embrace and turn. It's an old man dressed conservatively in a dark gray jumpsuit open at the neck. Close-cropped white hair forms a fringe around his gleaming baldness. A bushy white mustache hangs in a sweeping arch below his nose almost hiding his upper lip and extending down past his chin. With leathery skin covered in wrinkles, he's without doubt, the oldest individual Lazarus has seen since leaving Athens. Despite his obvious age, there's no missing the lively twinkle in his eye. This old man loves life.

"I hesitate to ask what a Winnebago is, but I assure you, this ship is well designed for what she does. There's not one unneeded kilo in her design." Lindsey said with a smile, "Where you see a collection of hardware, I see the fruit of many hours of dedicated labor. There's beauty in simplicity."

"Humph," the old man snorts, "Is that what you engineering types call the KISS principle? Keep It Simple Stupid? Yes….Well… Nothin' beats first class, if you ask me."

"Maybe the shuttle is a little crowded but we'll be comfortable.

Besides," Lindsey continues, "unless you're some big corporate weenie with keys to the company yacht, this is the only way to get to Aldrin Station. Why waste your breath on something you can't change?"

Huffing like an old male lion on the plains of Serengeti, the old man chuckles dryly, "Darlin' I' been do 'in that my whole life… but you're right, why waste energy. It's a freighter and we're the freight… Name is Isaac Crenshaw but you folks can call me Izzy," he said nodding in the customary Lunarian greeting.

"Lindsey Marquest," she said with a nod in return.

"Lazarus Sheffield," he extends his hand. By necessity, handshakes are different in freefall where one simply grasps, squeezes and releases, without actually shaking the other persons hand. That is, if it's done at all.

The wrinkles on the old man's forehead deepen but he accepts the gesture. Lazarus immediately starts to pump, sending them all into motion.

"Whoa." Isaac exclaims.

Lindsey laughs.

"Sorry," Lazarus mutters with embarrassment.

"It's alright. No harm done. So where you folks headed?" Izzy asks. "Don't tell me, let me guess, y'all are emigrating?"

"I'm going home," Lindsey said.

"A citizen. How about you?" Izzy asks Lazarus.

Lazarus feels Lindsey hug him tighter, waiting for him to respond, but in his world, a person does not willingly reveal truth to anyone, let alone strangers. He hesitates, shrugs and said, "I'm waiting to see how the story ends."

"Ain't we all?" Izzy laughs. "What 'bout you sugar, what freehold stakes claim on you?" Izzy asks bluntly, not bothered in the least that these two are not a couple, even though they certainly act like one. Maybe they just didn't realize it yet. It happens.

"Dakota," she replies, finding the old gentleman charming.

"Fine freehold... solid traditions..." Izzy said nodding approvingly. His eyes gleam mischievously, "Y'all ain't gonna believe this but Abby and I go way back." A chuckle erupts from deep in his belly and his eyes glaze over. The old man laughs again, "Hell, who'd forget ol' Izzy?"

The flight announcement sounds, "Passengers are now free to board Trans World Flight L95 bound for Aldrin Station, Luna." The three of them float up and out of the observation portal and head for the gate. They join the gathering throng entering the boarding tunnel. MRI scanners sweep over them, identifying who they are and where they're going, looking for anything out of the ordinary or out of place.

At the end of the tunnel awaits a rather petite flight attendant, "Welcome aboard," she said hovering just outside the shuttle's airlock door. She's wearing a Trans World fight uniform consisting of loose grey slacks and a white blouse with TWS monogrammed across the left pocket. Her brown hair is cut short in what Lazarus concludes is the popular style. After glancing down at something only she can see, she looks back up at Lazarus and smiles, "Mr. Sheffield, you're in 29A. To your right and six rows down. It's the window seat." Looking at Lindsey she adds, "Miss Marquest, you're in 29B, right next to Mr. Sheffield."

Looking around the shuttle Lazarus feels he's entering the proverbial padded cell, only much larger. The seats are in rows like spokes in a wheel and the ceiling is high and roomy.

Lindsey expertly maneuvers them through the shuttle looking for row twenty-nine. She playfully pushes Lazarus into his window seat.

Izzy takes the seat next to Lindsey and a middle-aged woman the seat next to him.

His window faces Heaven's Gate and thus, doesn't afford much of a view but Lazarus can see the portal they had been in a few minutes before, packed with people waiting to see the shuttle depart.

The outer airlock closes with a thump. A moment later the inner door swings shut with a clunk and the male attendant screws down the safeties.

"Good day everyone, on behalf of your crew, let me welcome you aboard Trans World Flight L95. Your attendants on this flight will be Alan and my name is Susan. We will be departing shortly so if your destination isn't Aldrin Station, Luna, now's the time to speak up. We will begin serving as soon as we're underway."

The acceleration klaxon sounds off, followed by a soft whirring that fills the cabin. A clank and a sharp sideways jolt rocks the shuttle as the station releases it, supplying a little push in the process. Lazarus looks out his window and is amazed to see how far the shuttle has already separated from Heaven's Gate. Even as he watches, the station grows smaller. Very gently, almost imperceptibly, the shuttle rotates.

A minute after separation, acceleration pushes Lazarus down into his padded seat. It builds until it reaches one-sixth Earth normal and holds steady. A low throbbing accompanies the acceleration. Lazarus is not sure if he's hearing it or feeling it in the seat of his pants.

"Nice to have a little weight back," Lazarus said with relief.

"You telling me you didn't like freefall?" Lindsey asks lifting her eyebrows inquisitively.

"It has its moments," Lazarus said grinning. "Where's the pilot on one of these?"

"There's no human pilot on a shuttle." Lindsey said.

"Folks don't pilot out here. A computer runs the show and we're just 'long for the ride," Izzy adds.

"So there's no one onboard who can fly?" Lazarus asks looking past Lindsey at the old man. His weathered face looks like it would be more at home on an Arizona ranch than a shuttle on its way to the moon.

"That's a big affirmative. All we have are two flight attendants. A pilot would be dead weight, one more payin' customer left behind." The old man rasps. "Besides, if somethin' went haywire, we'd just sit tight and wait for Luna Control to send a rescue party."

"I would appreciate it if you didn't discuss all the things that could go wrong," said the woman on Izzy's far side.

"Yes ma'am. I'm Izzy Crenshaw and these two love birds are Lindsey and Lazarus."

The woman shakes hands with Izzy, then leans forward to see past him, "Marcy Stephens. Pleased to meet everyone," she said. Marcy looks to be in her mid sixties with a round face and dark eyes. Her collar-length brown hair is fashioned in a serviceable square cut contained under a fine fishnet. Conservatively dressed, Marcy is out of place aboard the shuttle, like a fish out of water.

"I don't mean to be trouble," Marcy continues in an apologetic tone. "It's just that I've never done this before and it makes me bloody nervous to think about what's just outside that window. Better I not think about it."

"What you don't know can kill you out here," Lindsey smiles at Marcy.

"Oh dear," Marcy exclaims in a panic. "I told Christopher I shouldn't come but that boy never listens to me."

"Easy lass." Izzy reaches out and takes Marcy's hand, "Where exactly you goin? Is Christopher your son?"

Marcy shakes her head, "Grandson. He talked me into coming to see him. Said I'll love it. Well, I don't love it." Her lower lip trembles ever so slightly.

"Have you been in an airplane?" Izzy asks her.

"Yes, many times. So don't try telling me it's the same 'cause it's not. There's air outside of airplanes and I can see the ground."

"You're right, space is different," Izzy said rethinking his approach. Is this your first time in space?"

"Oh my yes. I was raised on Ford Farm. Ever here if it? It's a beautiful 14th century farmhouse about eight kilometers east of Plymouth in southwest England. I don't know about all this high technology. I tried to tell him I was too old but he wouldn't hear of it… This last summer was bloody horrible... Lost everything and had nowhere else to go… The farm had been in my family for generations… It's all gone now, under water."

"Tell me about it," Marcy likes to talk and Izzy likes to listen.

Lazarus and Lindsey snuggle ignoring the subdued chatter around them. Lazarus wonders how many fellow travelers would choose to remain at Heaven's Gate if they knew what he knew. He had to admit, he only has suspicions, nothing truly solid. In his line of work, you seldom get solid verifiable facts.

His years in DHS have stripped him of youthful enthusiasm and the belief he was on the side of good. He loves his country but hates what it's become. The greed, the lies, the hypocrisy, and the intolerance made it impossible for him to trust anyone. The final straw was his superiors choosing not to warn the Lunarians of impending disaster, a selfish decision that promises dire consequences for millions of people, perhaps the entire world. His polygraphic indicators reflect the weight of his burden.

"I see the smile's gone," Lindsey said.

He squeezes her hand affectionately. "Please forgive me Lindsey. I was just thinking of the sorry state of affairs back in the Federation."

"Which sorry state is bothering you?" She asked.

Lazarus looks into Lindsey's gray eyes and bows his head breaking eye contact, a frown furrowing his brow.

"What is it?" Lindsey asks again. "Come on, spill it. What's on your mind?"

Lazarus has a brief moment of panic. He's not ready to start talking about the Brotherhood. He searches his mind for something else to say.

"Throughout my life it was pounded into me that sex outside of marriage was a major sin. On my church wall behind the pulpit is a number of biblical passages including one from Matthew 15. *For out of the heart proceed evil thoughts, murders, adulteries, fornications, thefts, false witness, and blasphemies. These are the things which defile a man.* The punishment is death."

"To equate murder with sex is ridiculous," Lindsey said. "Do you think someone deserves to die for having consensual sex?"

"No, of course not..." Looking up in confusion, he hesitantly asks, "Why?" and can go no further.

Lindsey knows instinctively the unspoken details contained in that most-complicated one word question. "Because you needed it," she said. "Are you sorry?" She asked, watching intently for any sign of regret or deceit.

The question hits him like an electric shock. Lazarus looks into her eyes and squeezes her hand almost to the point of hurting her, "Oh my, no. I don't know how but… You hit the nail on the head Lindsey. I needed to break the mold and you did that. I feel hope for the first time in ages. No. What you have given me is much more than just sex."

"Easy tiger. Things are a little different on Luna. Lunarians don't have the same sexual mores as the Federation. Sex is something that brings us together, not something that divides us." Sensing confusion within Lazarus, she adds hastily, "Don't get me wrong. The manner in which a Lunarian conducts their sexual activities is critical but realistically, there's only one rule. As long as everyone concerned is in agreement, then pretty much anything goes."

"Reverend McCarthy claims the Lunarians condone rape, child sex, and incest. Is he right?" Lazarus asks.

Lindsey knows exactly what Lazarus is referring. During this last stay on Mother Earth, she had witnessed a growing animosity within the European Union directed at the Lunarians and fed by government propaganda. Made to look like factual documentaries, they exaggerate the cultural differences and minimize the similarities. Some are subtle, others blatant. The worst of the vids utterly vilify the Lunarians, making them out to be Satan worshipers who have orgies every night. The worst of the worst are the twenty-eight McCarthy videos containing the biggest lies, exaggerated and repeated to the point of absurdity. What's more revealing, Lindsey never heard anyone make a serious rebuttal or challenge the weak evidence put forth. The vids had deeply disturbed Lindsey at the time, a feeling that refuses to subside.

"Rape means at least one party was forced against their will to have sex and child sex means at least one partner was too young to make an informed decision. Either situation could result in the General Council voting for expurgation. What the good reverend calls incest is the fact that Lunarians don't hide sex from their children or fill them with lies. We believe knowledge is the key to making good choices in one's life, not ignorance." Lindsey explains.

Seeing doubt on his face, she changes tack, "Look, Reverend McCarthy is the worst kind of liar, using just enough fact to hook his listeners into believing something hideously wrong. None of his self-described documentaries reflects reality. They're designed to control and manipulate you, not educate you. No Lazarus, completely the opposite is true. If a Lunarian commits rape, the person raped, as well as their family, friends and associates, decides the punishment of the person who did the raping, up to and including expurgation. The laws are really quite simple, letting the people most intimately involved have the most say. The only hard and fast laws in the Republic define how officials collect, analyze and preserve evidence. Everything else is flexible, decided by citizens on a case-by-case basis in open council. Literally any action taken by one party that causes harm to another is subject to adjudication before the General Council." Lindsey said.

"What's expurgation?" he stumbles over the unfamiliar term.

"It's the total wiping of a person's memory. This penalty is only for the most heinous crimes. It's seldom used."

"So someone could get… expurgated… for stealing? That seems a little harsh." Lazarus said.

"Does it?" Lindsey said, "Expurgation requires a supermajority. If that many fellow citizens think you need a total head job, then just maybe you're not a very nice person."

"What about homosexuality? Others besides McCarthy speak of the promiscuousness of the Lunarians," Lazarus points out. "Leviticus 20 verse 13; If *a man also lie with mankind, as he lieth with a woman, both of them have committed an abomination: they shall surely be put to death; their blood shall be upon them.*"

"Again I ask you, do you think someone deserves to die for having sex?" Lindsey asks.

"Well… no…"

"Then how about for blasphemy or speaking ill of the Church?" she presses. "Does someone deserve to die for disbelieving the ridiculous superstitions underlying Christianity?"

"Ah… no…"

"Then you must tell me how a man raised in the heart of the Federation can be so reasonable. I thought they would have ripped out any semblance of logic from you long ago?"

Lazarus sighs and lays his head back. "They tried. I studied the bible every day from kindergarten through college along with everyone else. When I was a kid, I studied the creation story of Adam and Eve, Noah and the Flood, Moses and the Passover and many others. The more I learned, the more confused I became and my teachers didn't help. They didn't like answering questions, not the hard ones anyway. When they bothered at all, their answers were vague and when I pushed for better ones, they kicked my butt."

"Go on," Lindsey encourages him.

"In third grade, I kept asking why God put the tree of knowledge in the middle of the Garden of Eden, told them to not eat its fruit, then left. Was God laying a trap or trying to trick them? Granted, I disrupted the classroom insisting on a reasonable answer, but I really wanted to know. Didn't God realize they would head straight for it once He told them not to? It's what I'd have done. That incident landed me a month's detention…" Lazarus sighs, "Later that same year I asked the schools spiritual advisor why God killed so many innocent people during the Passover. Why didn't God cut out the middleman and just appear before the Egyptian Pharaoh instead of killing the oldest sibling in every family that didn't smear lambs blood on their front door? … And why did God make it rain frogs? None of it made any sense. I was positive that an all-powerful God could have made it perfectly clear to the Pharaoh what He wanted without the need for the ten Egyptian plagues or anybody dying. Well… they didn't see it that way."

"I'll bet they didn't," Lindsey smiles.

"That earned me a trip to the Headpastor's office. Mom and dad had to come to the school. Mom didn't say a word during the entire meeting. She just sat there and stared at me. Total guilt trip. Dad was pissed from the moment he walked through the door. Later I learned the school board fined him a day's wages. They suspended me for a week, gave me another month in detention and two hundred hours of community service under the direct supervision of Pastor Marsh, the history instructor at my school. Needless to say, I learned my lesson…"

"That doesn't explain how you know Greek mythology." Lindsey remembers his story about the Milky Way.

"My real education began that evening when my dad came home from work. The first lesson was all about the mechanics of deception. He told me not to openly question the authority of the Church but to simply say the right things and go through the motions. When he thought I was ready, dad showed me a secret hide-a-way in the floor of the tool shed and explained its use. It wasn't elaborate, nothing but a few loose floor boards with a shoebox space below, but through it passed treasure more precious than gold… Books."

"Books?"

"Yes, but not just any books, outlawed books. If I were caught with them… well, let's just say I'd be in serious trouble."

"So your father put books in this hole?" Lindsey asks incredulously. She can sense he's telling her the truth, but it's so bizarre.

"It wasn't him personally." Lazarus shakes his head, "All I know for sure is a different set of books would appear within days after I finished the last."

"How would they, whoever they are, know when you were done? Or what books should be next?" She asked in wonder.

"I left questions, sometimes several pages of questions. The books that answered them were never far behind, a few weeks at most. I read constantly. Some I even read twice. It was the single most precious gift Thomas Oliver Sheffield ever gave me, and it continued long after he was gone. I never did find out who exchanged the books. Better I not know if caught."

Thomas Oliver Sheffield is his father, a name she can check on later. For now, Lindsey wants to know more about his unusual education, "What authors can you remember?" She asked.

"Oh let's see… There was Twain, Stevenson, Paine, Ingersoll, Plato, Kafka, Bruno, Thoreau, Melville, Darwin, Einstein, Aristotle, Homer, Defoe, Keats, Mann, Steinbeck, Hemingway, Rand, Dickens, Vonnegut, Woolf, Orwell, Jefferson, Faulkner, Fitzgerald, Shakespeare, Asimov, Hawking, Shelly, Lee, Kipling, Sinclair, Machiavelli, Odegaard, Poe, Rousseau, Johanson, Sagan, Wells, and my father's favorite fiction author, Robert Heinlein. There were more, many more, too many to count. In each new set of books was always at least one textbook. I studied astronomy, physics, biology, human psychology and of course, religion. These gave me answers to questions I didn't even know existed before reading them. The more I learned the more I realized just how much there is to know."

"Remarkable." Lindsey said, "Tell me more about your father."

Lazarus sits quietly for almost a minute, "He died when I was ten," he finally said, "KIA… killed in action. I really don't know any more. Believe me, I've tried to find out. Nothing in the official records reveal anything about his mission or his death other than a posthumous medal, Hero of the State. Everything else was marked Top Secret and I didn't need to know."

Another piece of useful information, "I'm sorry for your loss. It must have been hard. Do you have any other family?"

"Two brothers and a sister. I'm the oldest. My mother lives in Portland… After dad died, I shared the gift of books with them. Even though I was cautious, it wasn't enough. When I was a senior in high school, my youngest brother Elijah rebelled against a particularly harsh pastor. He compounded his mistake by quoting a passage out of the Diary of Anne Frank. The school authorities pressed him for two days straight to tell them where he had learned of it. He finally convinced them he had read it on a new not-yet-restricted netsite. Dad wasn't there to stop them, so the school sent Elijah to a camp outside Albuquerque. He came back a total zombie. He couldn't put a sentence together, or play, or even climb a tree… The worst part… his inner fire was gone, totally extinguished. In its place, a child-like zeal for spouting religious platitudes, all his curiosity had been smothered under the oppressive hand of state sponsored truth…" Lazarus said bitterly. "I never again talked with my brother about the secret place or books. For me, Elijah died that day, driving home a very harsh lesson. Never get caught, and I never was."

Lindsey shivers. His tone chills her to the bone. Three decades earlier, she had gotten out just before the Federation became a full-fledged theocracy. What must it have been like to grow up in such a repressive state? She hopes never to find out. "Do you have any kids?"

she can sense him tighten up.

He pauses, "Had… I was married to a wonderful woman I met in college. We had a daughter… they were killed in a traffic accident two years ago..." his voice trails off.

Lindsey squeezes his hand, "I'm so sorry…" Changing the subject She asked, "So tell me, what happened to make you run?"

Lazarus pushes his hair back and wipes away the sweat from his upper lip.

"Relax… I know you must have a very good reason for emigrating. Tell me what it is, beginning with what you did for the Federation." When he still hesitates she continues, "After all, you're going to tell somebody sometime. Do you want it to sound like a first time presentation with no practice at all?"

Lazarus frowns, "I don't feel comfortable discussing this in public."

Lindsey shakes her head, "It's different here. Public and private have different meanings than you're accustomed too."

His frown deepens, "Yes, of course…" but he remains silent.

"Look, you're watched wherever you go in the Federation, right?"

"Sure," he replies thinking of his apartment, work, and social life.

"The Lunarian system is about the same only the data is available to everyone, not just government officials keeping tabs on you, or corporations trying to sell you something. The flow of information goes both ways. The Law of Full Disclosure gives every citizen access to all things public, including all individual, corporate, and governmental dealings. Only agreements made in public are valid under the law. Total visibility. Secrets are not only impolite, they're against the Law. The only exception is when the Republic or someone's life is in jeopardy and even then, it's permissible to maintain secrecy for only a short time. As soon as the crisis is over, all records must again be made public."

"The Law, as I understand it, seems to put everything in public domain, every discussion, every meeting, even conversations between friend's falls into the public domain. Then what is privacy to a Lunarian?" He asked.

"It has the same definition here as it does in the Federation. Privacy is simply the courtesy extended from one citizen to another to leave each other alone, to mind your own business. For instance, our fellow passengers have granted us privacy. Any one of them at any time has the right to watch us, listen to our conversation, and even join in if they are so inclined. But they don't because they have given us privacy…"

"…but this is public transportation," he interrupts.

"When are we not in public?" she retorts. "When we are at work? No. On the street? No. At home? Maybe, but only if you are a hermit totally disconnected from the rest of civilization. Privacy is the state of being apart from others and as such, is more about an individual's pursuit of happiness than a separate constitutional right. Personal privacy suffered a quick death over a century ago in the opening rounds of the Age of Information."

"Not true. Privacy is tightly guarded within the NAF."

"The sheer number of Federation privacy laws is astounding, but it's not your privacy they're protecting. It's the right of State and Corporate organizations to collect facts about you but reveal nothing of themselves to you. Don't you realize you invite corruption when the flow of information is one-way? Those in power use that power to stay in power."

Lazarus feels a sharp pang of guilt. He knows firsthand the power of the federal government, having personally compiled electronic evidence that convicted forty-three men and a woman of information theft. These were the real hard-core offenders, hackers who illegally accessed financial, medical, and corporate data without permission, passing it on to the highest bidder. Now she's telling him this information is openly available to anyone on Luna?

"But shouldn't a company be able to reap the rewards of internal research without fear of competitors riding their shirttails for free?" He asked.

"That's not a privacy issue. That's patent infringement and the Law provides protection for their investment. Again, it's to everyone's advantage if all records are public, everything from raw research to the final marketing plans. How can a company have a right to produce something if they cannot show a logical progression of knowledge? How can a pharmaceutical lab create a finished formula without a history of research and testing? How can a widget maker market a new widget without having records of the designs progression? There must be a litany of meetings, computer data, partnership agreements, and impromptu hallway discussions showing they actually did the work. Because everything is accessible, even a bad solicitor can easily prove who stole the widget design by simply viewing the act of stealing. How can anyone sustain any criminal activity if their every move is public knowledge?"

"I have a lot to learn," Lazarus said.

"More than you know lover…" he blushes and she smiles, a gentle reminder of their relationship. "Now that you understand there can be no secrets, tell me why you're here..." she purrs, her breath hot on his cheek.

He doesn't feel threatened. It's as if he has known her much longer than just a few hours. Sex has a way of doing that. Yet, it seems traitorous to be telling Lindsey any of the things that concern him most. Long years of training are hard to throw off, even with such a beautiful inquisitor as Lindsey.

Through his visor, Lindsey monitors his polygraphic indicators better than an old-fashioned lie detector. It relays heart rate, sweat production, eye movement, and many other observations, making it physically impossible for him to lie. Whatever it is that he thinks he knows, he considers it important enough to turn his back on everything familiar and embrace the unknown, this much she's certain of.

"Ok, let's begin by you telling me your occupational details."

He still hesitates, "I'm a programmer." Lying by omission is still lying.

Lindsey looks intently into his eyes, just a few centimeters from her own, "And?" She watches the last wall crumble.

He sighs and runs his hand across his hair. The lifelong liar realizes he must finally speak the truth and nothing but the truth, "I'm a Senior Analyst for the Department of Homeland Security. My job was to gather and analyze data from a wide assortment of sources and incorporate it into presentations the Director uses to brief the President and the Joint Chiefs."

Well, this is indeed interesting. "What kind of data?" Lindsey asks.

"Pretty much anything pertaining to the War on Terror," Lazarus replies.

"War on Terror. ***Bah.*** The Federation illegally kidnaps foreign citizens and imprisons them for years without trials. They torture and abuse their own people. They reeducate any who dare disagree. To me, that's a War on Sanity." Lindsey said.

"That may be true but if I ever talked that way, I would not only lose my job, I would wake up in a reeducation program myself. Director Dempsey doesn't mess around," Lazarus said.

"My point exactly. So… you're a Senior Analyst working for Director Dempsey. Doesn't that make you an agent?" She asked.

"Not really. I'm more of a technician. I specialize in interviewing suspects and covert data mining. I'm part of a team working towards determining who, what, when, and where the next attack will come from."

The Lunarians have known about this group for some time, but Lazarus is the first defection from its inner circle. In fact, he's the highest-ranking NAF defector in twenty years. Lazarus will answer many questions, a process that has only just begun.

Something substantial must have rattled his cage hard to make him take this drastic step. Now, she's beyond curious. Lindsey snuggles up to him, squeezing his arm, willing him to lock eyes with her, "So tell me, what have you discovered that is worth turning your back on everything?"

Sighing, he runs his fingers through his thick hair before continuing, "Something big is happening within the Brotherhood. People have been falling off the radar until nobody's left. I've never seen this level of participation before."

"What do you mean, falling off the radar?" She asked.

"Homeland tracks thousands of individuals connected with radical fundamentalism within the Brotherhood. We scrutinize their communications, their employment, bank records, who they meet, netsites they use, that sort of thing. Sometimes we had our guys follow them around and even become friendly."

Lindsey nods and motions for him to go on.

"Three months ago these individuals began disappearing without a trace. One day they were there, the next gone. No more network traffic, no more bank expenditures, their apartments empty, their jobs abandoned. They're just gone. Vanished."

"Who are these people? What do they do?"

"They're virtually all male, between the ages of eighteen and forty, and members of at least one fundamentalist splinter group. All of them have received military training at some point. We believe they are the soldiers who will carry out whatever the Minister is up to." Deeply concerned Lazarus continues, "The few thousand we know about is only the tip of the iceberg. It could mean as many as a million men are involved."

"Wait, go back. Who is the Minister?"

"DHS tracks all the upper echelon in the Brotherhood including the important military figures. Most of these remain accounted for but there are a few notable exceptions. In particular, the Defense Minister, Hasin bin Aunker and Major General Abdel Salam Arif are both missing. They are considered high risk and extremely dangerous in the West."

"Go on," she can sense he's not finished.

Lazarus sighs and continues, "It's also a general belief among Homeland agents that the Brotherhood has completed a nuclear program which produced an unknown number of weapons. We haven't the faintest idea where they are, or how many."

"Well… you are just full of good news, aren't you?" Lindsey said. "It doesn't sound like a terrorist attack to me, more like an invasion."

"I totally agree. We picked up indicators the target was off world. Hyundai Shipyard is building the Brotherhood's space fleet and Taurus Colony controls the Brotherhood's electricity. That leaves the Republic. Since the Federation has interests throughout Luna, I managed to convince Director Dempsey to inform the President of my concerns. I thought for sure President John Paul would tell the Lunarians. I was wrong. The prevailing attitude is to stay out of it. Don't get involved…"

"… but they are involved." Lazarus argues with himself, "and not in a good way. Federation media constantly portray Lunarians as villains and monsters. It's not terrorist's people fear anymore. It's Lunarians."

"Relax, don't get yourself all worked up." Lindsey nods in agreement, "But you're right. Even in Europe, I was surprised at the hostility when people found out I was from Luna. I'm glad to be leaving."

"It's just like Hitler's Jewish propaganda leading up to the Second World War." Lazarus said angrily. "Criticize. Demonize. Neutralize."

"I said relax. It doesn't do any good to stress out. How exactly did you plan to tell the Lunarians of this wonderful news?"

"I thought I might speak to a Councilor."

"So you're just going to cold call a Councilor?" she smiles at the hubris of his plan. It just might work.

"Why not?" he replies. "Actually, I never thought I would get this far… I left this part of the plan to ad hoc. Perhaps I should start with the local police department. I just need five minutes with the right person, someone who knows someone, who knows someone. I don't mind going through channels."

"What makes you think the Lunarians will listen?"

Returning her gaze steadily, Lazarus said, "Someone will listen. They must."

She leans back pondering her options. If she helps Lazarus and he turns out to be a quack, she would be embarrassed and possibly labeled unreliable by some. However, if he has information about an imminent attack on the Republic then many Lunarian lives are at stake. Her pride is worth the risk.

"Do you know of Abby Dugan?" She asked.

"Yes, of course," Lazarus said. "She's Luna's most famous Lunarian." What he didn't say was that DHS considers Abigail Dugan a hothead and troublemaker.

"I can't promise anything but I may be able to get you your five minutes. Corso Dugan is her son and he's also Aldrin Station's Security Chief," Lindsey said.

Lazarus is astonished, "You can do this?"

Smiling she said, "Don't look so surprised. I'm a Dakota citizen and have the right to ask. The worst that can happen is they say no."

Something in the way she said it makes Lazarus realize the risk she's taking. "No, Lindsey… The worst is a Lunarian city incinerated by a nuclear bomb… In any case, it looks like I owe you again. Thank you."

"No promises Lazarus. Abby may be too busy to see you herself… For now, settle back and take a nap or go online. I will rejoin you in a few minutes. No matter what, we still have a long flight ahead of us and I plan on sleeping as much as possible."

"I couldn't sleep right now."

"Then read a book," she turns to face front.

"Good idea," Lazarus settles into his seat.

ЯL

Lindsey relishes using her visor again. It's been too long. She routes a call and almost immediately, the seat in front of her disappears. In its place materializes the stately image of Luna's AI. Wisps of gray highlight her dark hair and her broad smile welcomes Lindsey home. The woman radiates acceptance.

"Greetings, Lindsey. It's so good to see you." she said warmly.

Lindsey smiles back, "Greetings, Magi, how are you?"

"I'm fine. Did you enjoy your time on Mother Earth?" The lag as the signal travels to Luna and back is barely noticeable.

"Some, but I'm glad it's over. I'm ready to come home," Lindsey said and Magi nods knowingly, "Is it possible to speak with Abby or Corso right now?"

"Corso is unavailable but I can check with Abby," Magi said. "It may take a few minutes," she smiles and disappears.

Lindsey nods and accesses the Republic's main database. One of Luna's national treasures and an essential component of the Law of Full Disclosure, the Public Records database is dispersed throughout the Republic on a vast array of Zettaspheres.

The size of a grain of rice, Zettaspheres are data storage devices with enormous capacity (zettabyte = 10^{21} bytes). A single Zettasphere can contain all of humanity's written works thousands of times over, store a century's worth of audio/video from a security sensor, or record a person's life as viewed through a visor.

Within these tiny data storage devices resides not only the accumulated knowledge of the human race, but also the historical record of its recent past. For the last half-century, the Lunarians have archived into Public Records every digital recording of any kind. They didn't delete anything. Any citizen can access Public Records to determine what really happened. Everything is recorded somewhere, but you need Magi in order to find anything within the enormous database.

Lindsey occupies herself with catching up on the Republic while she waits. For the last six weeks, she's been getting the news filtered by Earthnet commentators who have only the vaguest notion of Lunarian society. They typically oversimplify the underlying issues if they bother to present them at all. Media hacks carefully screen news items and show only those they can twist into support for their agenda. The interpretations of these snippets are rarely accurate and never questioned by the citizens who view them. This black journalism has become known as foxing a story after an early cable news network called Fox News who perfected the technique almost a century before. Truth has very little to do with power.

For almost a decade, the bombings on Luna have made the news. Graphic images of violence attracts users which sells net time and that's the name of the game. The major networks relish showing the hell suffered by the Lunarians, replaying the bloodiest scenes repeatedly.

Lindsey's shocked by the escalation of violence while she's been gone. She sucks in a breath when she finds the vid of an incident in Hell's Kitchen almost two weeks earlier. A bomb had exploded in a mall killing three, wounding twenty–two. She'd eaten there many times. One of the dead is a young man barely out of puberty and the son of a colleague. The Brotherhood adamantly denied any responsibility and offered compensation to the victims' families who flatly rejected the blood money.

The news vid freezes and shrinks to an icon, replaced by Magi. "Excuse me Lindsey but Abby is ready to see you."

Abigail Dugan takes Magi's place. Abby has her blond hair pulled back in a ponytail. She smiles at Lindsey.

"Greetings Lindsey."

"Greetings Abby."

"How was Mother Earth?" Abby asks.

"Worrisome, I'm afraid. Let's just say I'm looking forward to home and don't intend to leave again for a very long time, but that's not why I called. I met someone on my trip back I believe you should meet. A runner named Lazarus Sheffield. He's a Senior Analyst for the Department of Homeland Security and a member of the Directors inner staff, no less. He claims to know about the Brotherhood's nuclear program and the disappearance of Hasin bin Aunker and Abdel Salam Arif, among others," Lindsey said.

The names got Abby's attention, "Does he know where they are?"

"No, I don't believe so. He said at least four thousand have vanished with them, but it could be as many as a hundred thousand. He wants to talk with a Councilor."

"Why's he running?" Abby asks.

"Mainly because the Federation refused to warn us. Quite admirable, actually. Beyond that, I think you should meet with him because he offers a unique insight into the political situation within the NAF. Worth your time."

Abby raises her eyebrows looking intently at the younger woman for a moment. "OK, I'll meet with him but he's your responsibility."

"My responsibility? You mean until we get to Aldrin Station, right?" Lindsey asks.

"You're the one who's sponsoring him, therefore, you're his mentor. It's highly unusual for the NAF to let such a high-ranking official get away. I want to keep a tight rein on the situation. That means you must stay close to him." Abby pauses, peering intently at Lindsey, "From the look of things back on Heaven's Gate, it seems to me you're already half way there."

Lindsey doesn't even bat an eye, realizing that Abby is reviewing the public data available from Heaven's Gate even while talking with her. "It's traditional to get laid your first time in freefall. Besides, it's not every day I meet such an adorable virgin."

"Um… He reminds me of Robert Pattinson," Abby said.

"Robert Pattinson?"

"Pattinson was a teen heartthrob from my youth… Never mind. I don't expect you to know the name."

"I'm scheduled at the clinic on arrival so someone will need to hold his hand for a few hours," Lindsey said.

"I'll send someone to meet you."

"Who?" Lindsey asks.

Abby shakes her head, "Don't know yet. I'll make it a surprise. I know how much you like surprises." She nods and vanishes.

ЯL

While Lindsey was busy making her call, Lazarus explores the net with his new visor. He starts by requesting a general background check on Lindsey.

Lazarus creates a summary using a familiar program. …born in Oxford, England on Monday morning at 9:05, October 12, 2043… She's forty-nine years old? He would have guessed thirty at most.

Grandmother was the technician who first measured Type 3 superconductivity… Mother was a history professor at a community college when Lindsey was growing up… Mother died of unspecified causes… Father still alive and resides in a retirement community outside London... Her only brother, Harley Marquest, killed in 2062 while serving in the Royal Marines somewhere in the Middle East.

She relinquished her citizenship in June 2062 and immigrated to the Republic of Luna… Received a Bachelor of Science in Mechanical Engineering from the University of New London in 2067 and followed that up with a PhD in Materials Processing from the Albert Einstein

Institute of Technology in 2070… Joined Metcal soon after graduation and stayed with them for twenty-one years. Long list of places, responsibilities and accomplishments attributed to her while with Metcal, all of them off-planet. Wait. What's this? Captain, Lincoln County Police Department, Metro Division?

His gut knots up. She had not mentioned being a police officer. It's ironic that his first instinct is to fear, considering his only job since completing college was with DHS.

Lazarus continues reading the summary, noting that all of her accomplishments are engineering in nature. Near the bottom, he scrolls through a list of articles and professional papers she has written over the years. There is only one general enough for him to try reading. Lindsey had written it for Science Weekly, an EU network magazine devoted to promoting science education among the general population. He touches its icon.

"Please select how you would like it read," Magi said.

"No… that won't be necessary. I will read it for myself," he replies.

"Very well"

How Superconductivity Changed the World appears and he starts reading.

Щx

Lindsey waits until he's finished reading, "I've completed my call."

Lazarus sweeps the document from his virtual desktop and turns to face her, "What did you find out? Will she meet with me?"

"Abby will have someone waiting for us at Aldrin Station when we arrive. Let's take it one-step at a time, ok? If there's one thing I've learned, it's not to push too hard, especially Abby."

"Whatever you say, Captain Lindsey," Lazarus said looking intently into her gray eyes. "I thought you told me you're an engineer."

She returns his stare, "I am, but I'm also a captain in the reserve.

84

What's the problem?"

"No problem. I just don't understand how you can be both?"

"Most able-bodied citizens are also members of their local police reserve and are expected to serve eight weeks out of the year. After you're a citizen, you can join." Lindsey glances at his polygraphic indicators.

"It's mandatory?" He asked.

"No, but why would you not want to participate in your own defense?" She hopes she hasn't made a mistake taking on this project. For all her skills at detecting lies and deception, she cannot see into a man's heart.

"Don't get me wrong, I want to participate. Where I'm from, the government discourages a person from taking an active part in society. They entertain and distract with a wide assortment of venues, church, movies, sports, and politics are the biggies. The less interest people have, the easier it is to keep them in the herd, so to speak. It doesn't matter if they vote and most don't bother. The Reformation Party hasn't lost an election in my lifetime. Do the math. Those in control will not allow anyone to upset the status quo." He shakes his head, "No, far from it, I'm looking forward to being a part of something that I can respect. If joining the reserve is expected, then I will gladly do it."

"Let's just say participation is encouraged. No one is forced to do anything." Lindsey stretches, enjoying the feeling of Luna gravity after so long. "Before I go to sleep there's one more thing."

"What's that?"

"Let me stress once again that you must always be honest and open… with every Lunarian, not just me. Lying is never an option. You've admitted being very good at hiding your true feeling and beliefs, and I can understand why... but you cannot allow that part of your former life to continue. If you hope to meet Abby, don't even think about lying or stretching the truth. That would be disastrous to your chances of citizenship. Lunarians despise the dishonesty of secrets and respect a person for being true to themselves and the world around them."

"To thine own self be true," Lazarus said. "And it must follow, as the night the day, thou cannot be false to any man."

"Hamlet, Act 1, Scene 3," Lindsey said completely caught off guard. "Why am I surprised you know Shakespeare?"

"That's the first time I've dared utter those words. It feels… incredible." he looks at Lindsey and a cloud of worry flashes across his face, "Are there subjects I should avoid?"

She shakes her head, "Freedom doesn't tell you what subjects are permissible. Lunarians will discuss anything at anytime with anyone. Feel free to run your mouth, but let me warn you right now, Lunarians are not shy about expressing their opinions on religion, or the Federation, or the Islamic Brotherhood, or anything else." Lindsey said emphatically. "So, if you think I've been hard on you, let me tell you… you haven't seen anything. You had better be prepared to defend whatever positions you take with facts and not opinions."

"I look forward to it," Lazarus said eagerly.

"I'm sure we all will benefit from your insight, but for now, just stop sticking your hand out. That's bad manners on Luna. You see… the majority of Lunarians have this thing about touching. So until you get a feel for how it works, don't touch anyone unless they offer first. OK?"

"I understand they don't like to shake hands, but you're saying avoid all touching?"

"That's exactly what I'm saying, just until you get to know someone, or they give you permission. Lunarians do so much vid conferencing it's become traditional to avoid all physical contact. For the same reason, it's considered bad manners to remove your visor during meetings." Lindsey pauses and adds, "There will be many things you will not understand at first. Just give it time and keep an open mind. Most of them will make sense eventually."

Lazarus smiles, "If other Lunarians have even a fraction of your kindness, than the Republic of Luna will be a paradise."

Lindsey kisses him gently, "Flattery will get you everywhere."

ℜL

This is round trip one-thousand-thirty-nine for Evolution's Child, christened by her first captain twenty years ago. The ship isn't much to look at. Born in the vacuum of space, it will never feel an atmosphere.

Hyundai Shipyards had just completed a refit that included four new magnetoplasma thrusters. They raise the freighter's payload capacity to almost a million kilos. It seems a crime to have less than thirty thousand aboard for the engines shakedown voyage.

Above the engine section is a large pressurized disk containing over five hundred cubic meters of living space. Known as the pilothouse, it's literally the pilot's house.

Above the pilothouse is the cargo bay. It's almost empty with only a few crates secured by ratchet straps.

Evolution's Child is built rugged, both locomotive and boxcar of the late 21st century, able to pickup and deliver cargo from LEO to the surface of the moon and back. Six massive shock-absorber landing-legs surround the engine compartment and extend up past the roof of the pilothouse, each at an angle avoiding the thruster's exhaust.

Pilot Nell Goddard initiates the link with Luna Central, "This is Evolution's Child. Standby for burn in one minute."

The image of a uniformed police officer appears before her. It's the first time she's seen a police officer working LC. Something's amiss. Nevertheless, she keeps her questions to herself.

The two-second round trip is just long enough to notice but not long enough to be a real nuisance, "Roger, Evolution's Child. You are go for trans-lunar burn. We show you at orbital insertion in T-minus seventy-two hours."

"Roger that, Evolution's Child out," Nell breaks contact. The uniformed controller vanishes, "Emcee, you are free to initiate the burn," she informs the autopilot. Emcee is a primitive AI, but always does what she can to make her pilots life easier.

"You got it Nell," Emcee said.

With a subtle flick of her wrist, Nell takes the movie off pause and settles back. The image grows until it fills her visor, immersing her in one of the Harrison Ford oldies. Nell is a film buff, common for those who sail the vast distances of space. She's looking forward on this trip to viewing the latest additions to her collection, the remixed conversions of some of her favorite flat screen classics.

After years piloting this route, Nell is a veteran spacer. Her mind tunes out the acceleration klaxon and handles the three Gs stoically. Only after the burn is complete does she turn away from the movie to check her position.

Right between the white lines. Nell turns back to Harrison.

Quan Kiai

"When I do good, I feel good; when I do bad, I feel bad. That's my religion."

Abraham Lincoln (1809-1865)

It's Halloween and Club Rio's packed. Three times as long as it is wide, the room is without corners or angles to mar its smoothness. A vid of the universe plays across its domed ceiling in exquisite detail giving the crowd below the illusion of moving through the cosmos at enormous speed. It lights the room with dim flickering luminance that is constantly in motion. Around the periphery, brighter stationary pools of light silhouette the bar and highlight the public entrances at each end. Looking down at the center of the room, the stage is a raised dais that pulses and ripples with every color of the rainbow. The room is alive with people.

On stage, a four-man band in garish skin-tight orange and purple jumpsuits belts out their version of a heavy metal classic. The bands singer leaps high into the air as he wails, twisting and cavorting in Luna's gravity.

The guitarists are both playing Duraglass Gibsons. Only the titanium strings are visible when silent, but with the slightest strum, the body of the instrument infuses with color, running up and down the spectrum in cadence with the music. Sound and vision merge, sometimes harsh and violent, other times smooth and subtle, depending on the musician's slightest whim.

At the geometric center of the stage, the drummer hovers high above the guitarists, his drums floating in a great arc about him. They too pulse with color at each impact, complimenting the guitars with a driving beat of sight and sound.

Around the stage, dancers undulate in total unison like a kelp forest in high seas, their heads tilted back and arms reaching for the ceiling. They fill the dance floor and push out among the tables. The haunting echo of the drums pull the dancers into the music's spell, their closely packed bodies swaying in rhythm.

Above them, the domed display is constantly changing, taking them all on a wild ride, passing galaxies like sand flowing through an hourglass, sweeping past one gigantic swirl only to plunge headlong into the billions of stars contained in the next. The vid slows as it soars past an enormous black hole at the heart of a spiral galaxy, its event horizon defined by thousands of stars torn asunder in a gigantic whirlpool of destruction and creation.

Light marks the clubs main entrances, one at each end. The polished stone bar follows the curve of the wall along its perimeter broken only by the two doors. All along the bar, it's standing room only. A lucky few sit on barstools while most stand, crowding up to the bar. Glass shelves behind the bar display an assortment of alcoholic beverages, more than half from Mother Earth. A single shot of authentic Black Label whisky imported from Tennessee or Smirnoff vodka from Moscow will cost a miner a half days pay.

Behind a row of room dividers, several low-G snooker tables are the center of attention. Laughter and the sharp crack of ball-to-ball contact occasionally penetrate the music.

Tables and booths make up the majority of the club's main floor. They're packed with the young and not so young of Aldrin Station. The overhead projection casts a flickering light over intimate conversations deciding the nights sleeping arrangements or some juicy bit of gossip, a human close-order-drill evolved over many generations.

Without exception, everyone in the room is wearing visors. Although Lunarian visors come in many shapes and sizes, most of these are standard Razors, a silver and gold bar that extends from ear to ear with vertical segments along its length. Regardless of the model, visors have one unifying feature, they all have sensors that pick up the wearers underlying facial expression and broadcast this information to other visors thereby rendering themselves invisible.

In the midst of the merriment, a server skillfully weaves through the crowd. She's showing a lot of skin in a tight fawn-colored costume with a large white fluff-ball attached at the base of her spine above a shapely set of butt checks. On her head is a pair of rabbit ears and she's wearing an old-fashioned bow tie.

Arriving with a smile, the server places the full tray on the table and leans down, showing the tab and more than a little cleavage to the young man sitting closest to the end.

"Outstanding costume Sue," Tempel smiles at her. Their visors make it possible to hold a conversation over the music.

"Thanks," Sue replies, "I'm a Playboy Bunny."

"I don't know what that is," Tempel said, "but I like it." He glances at the total and passes his left hand across the scanner embedded in the ticket.

"Where's your costume? You guys are not getting with the program," Sue scolds. Many in the club are wearing standard issue off duty police uniforms including everyone at this table. The only difference is the small blue shield over their heart.

"We decided to come here at the last minute," Sam said reaching for a piece of deep fried soymeat from the tray, getting sauce all over her fingers. Tempel and Samantha have known each other for all of their young lives and their families go all the way back to the founding of Aldrin Station. For twenty years, they have shared classrooms and teachers, friends and family, they even wear each other's clothing on occasion.

"All of Luna is celebrating Tempel's birthday. Didn't you know?" Sam said licking her fingers.

"You don't say. And I thought it was Halloween or something." Turning back to Tempel, she smiles. "How old are you?"

Tempel grins wickedly and said, "Old enough."

"He's twenty," Sam replies for Tempel.

"Twenty is a good age, but so is forty-eight. Let me know if you need anything else." Sue winks and eases back into the crowd, bunny tail swishing in time with the beat.

Their booth is one of many in the nightclub. Its raised position gives them an excellent view of the dancers and stage.

Around them, off-duty officers sip their beverage of choice and unwind. Men and women alike have short-cropped hair or no hair at all and most are over two meters in height.

Brice and Odessa are down at the far end trying to tickle each other's tonsils with their tongues. Oblivious to everything except each other, Odessa is running her hand inside his shirt. Next to her, Marcel is earnestly talking with Consuela, who is doing her best to look interested but not succeeding. Beyond them, Kipper leans forward snagging two beers, handing one to Karyl before taking a swig of his. He makes a big production of laying his arm across the back of the seat behind her before snuggling close. Corazon and Tatiana have their heads together in deep conversation, the newly arrived food and drink ignored for the moment. Tatiana's twin brother Alonzo is exchanging smiles with a dark haired shortimer several booths over.

Sam leans against Tempel, firmly pressing a tit into his arm. "Happy Birthday," Her lips brush his ear, her breath smells of barbeque. Tempel playfully licks a smear of sauce from the corner of her mouth.

Alonzo slips out of their booth, heading for the dark haired girl. Sam nudges Tempel and nods towards Alonzo.

"Lover boy's at it again," she said playfully. Her warm breath caresses his cheek.

The girl smiles as Alonzo approaches. He leans over and said something causing her to laugh. She slides over making room.

Tempel grins, taking another pull off his beer and nuzzles Sam's ear, "Who is she?"

"A shortimer working out at Far Point. Tatiana has met her. Don't know her name." She ends the conversation with a kiss.

When used by a Lunarian, shortimer is a rather derogatory term referring to the people sent up from Mother Earth for a month or a year. Most shortimers tend to keep to themselves but there isn't any law against them being here on a Saturday night but it's unusual.

Tempel's intensely aware of Sam's supple body pressed tightly against his. Time slips by.

ЯL

The two men enter the club by the east entrance. Their clothing marks them as shortimers.

"Excuse me, weapons must be checked in at the bar," the clubs doorman calls out.

The men ignore the command and continue to walk deeper into the room. The volume near the entrance is not much louder than elevator music. Unless they're deaf, they heard.

The doorman signals for help and several bouncers armed only with non-lethal tasers converge on the men before they can get far. "Stop immediately…" Mac addresses them from behind, his hand resting on the butt of his stunner. "You must check your weapons or leave." Several bartenders pause, resting their hands on more firepower stashed under the bar.

"We will be here only a short time," growls the older man.

"That's fine but you will still need to check your weapons."

The younger of the two has continued to look about inside the club and has fixated on the dance floor. He leans over and whispers something in an unknown language to his companion who said with a single syllable grunt.

Turning away from the bouncers, the older man walks to the bar. Sliding his sidearm out of its holster, he lays it on the countertop.

"Left hand please," a female bartender said. "We need to establish ownership."

He stares intently at the woman before placing his left hand on the bar beside his weapon.

She ignores him. "Mustafa Malik, welcome to Club Rio. You can pick this up on your way out. Can I get you a drink, compliments of the house?" She stares back at him.

Without responding, Malik turns away, motioning for his companion to take his place.

The younger man does not attempt to hide his contempt, pulling his weapon from its holster in a show of quick-draw prowess. The bartender steps back and reaches for her stunner.

Malik growls, "Anwar."

The young man laughs, flips his weapon end for end, and lays it on the surface of the bar. With exaggerated slowness, he splays his left hand next to it, palm down.

The bartender, clearly not amused by the maneuver, nevertheless, does her job, "Anwar Jafa, welcome to Club Rio," she said stiffly as the sidearm disappears under the bar. "You can pick it up on your way out. The first drink's on the house."

"Later," Jafa replies. He flashes white teeth, turns, and follows Malik deeper into the nightclub. It was just as Malik foretold. The sound near the entrance is not very loud, but as they penetrate the infidel's lair, the volume soars upward dramatically until it overwhelms any chance to talk normally. Jafa steels himself against its power. *Allah be praised, this is not music.*

ℛ𝕃

A few minutes later, feeling safe within Club Rio, distracted by each other and the alcohol, no one at the table sees the fight start. The bands sudden silence causes Tempel and Sam to break their kiss. Out on the dance floor, people scramble to give the combatants room.

Alonzo is flat on his back, his visor hanging from one ear, with a stranger sitting on his chest slamming his head repeatedly against the stone floor. The dark-haired girl is just beyond them, excitement twisting her pretty face.

No one among the onlooking Lunarians know what the fight is about, but even so, many of them are starting to press forward demanding loudly that the attack stop.

Tempel doesn't wait. In a flash, he's out of the booth and heading for the dance floor. Moving with speed and power, the young Lunarian launches himself and plants his shoulder into the side of the man attacking Alonzo. The impact sends them rolling in a tangle across the

95

floor. By the time they stop, Tempel has the man in a death grip, one twist and he could separate his spinal column between the 4th and 5th cervical vertebra.

The man struggles but soon realizes he's in big trouble. He gasps trying vainly to hold his own even as his face turns crimson.

Just as suddenly as it started, the club bouncers put a stop to the fracas. "Tempel. Let him go," Mac said laying his hand on the young warrior's shoulder.

Surprised by how quickly he became willing to kill, Tempel relaxes his hold and rises to his feet.

The shortimer gasps as the blood surges into his brain, rubbing his neck and only beginning to feel the oncoming headache.

"What's going on?" Mac demands.

Tempel shrugs and growls, "Ask him," without taking his eyes off the shortimer.

Instead, Mac turns to the older man and said, "Malik, you have worn out your welcome. Gather up your comrade and leave."

Malik looks strangely pleased as he observes the group spread out behind Tempel. Sam and Tatiana are kneeling beside Alonzo who is telling them he's fine, to stop babying him, all the while blood continues to flow from a nasty cut on the back of his head. Young Jafa stands glaring at Tempel.

"Cheryl, give these gentleman back their guns… empty," Mac said. "Then I will walk you to the door."

Malik couldn't care less that they are ejecting him from Club Rio and when Jafa starts to speak, he raises his hand stopping him. "Anwar, see to Dalal while I retrieve our weapons." He walks to the bar where Cheryl has placed the two empty guns. He slides one into his holster. Returning, he hands the other to Jafa. "Peace be upon you," he bows, then leads them out the way they had come. The girl follows a few steps behind, her head down.

Once well out of Club Rio, Jafa turns to Malik, *"The one they call Tempel must be one of them. Only Djinn could do that to me."* He speaks in the ancient Aramaic dialect of Nabataean, a language seldom heard since the seventh century. They are reasonably sure the infidels have not translated it but they are cautious, speaking seldom and even then, using special code phrases to increase the confusion.

"Indeed," he motions for the girl to walk beside him. *"Tell me Dalal, what have you learned?"*

"I agree with Jafa. The man I danced with is Djinn and the one who attacked Jafa is a leader. The others I am not sure but I believe they are Djinn as well." In Islam, Djinn is an evil supernatural creature. According to the Qur'an, God created Djinn out of 'smokeless fire' and created man out of clay.

The fear has evaporated from the young woman but subservience remains. She knows dancing with the infidel pushed the boundaries even for an undercover operative, but it was all for Allah. *"They call themselves Quan Kiai,"* she said.

"Quan Kiai..." Malik mused. *"Allah may yet smile upon us..."* He has heard mention of special police units but never anything concrete, just disturbing rumors of advanced technology. As Malik mulls this over, they emerge onto Brooklyn Mall's North Courtyard and are once again among the infidels.

"Come, let us stop and have a cup of fine Lunarian coffee," Malik said in English. He changes direction leading them towards a small cafe. An ad hoc plan is forming. He switches back to Aramaic, *"Let us see what Allah has in store for us."*

They approach *La Bruschetta*, an old-world style sidewalk café. Set in a stone façade, a heavy wooden beam spans the door and both windows, the cafés name prominent upon it. An old-fashioned menu displays in the left window, an arrangement of nuts, cheese and chocolate is in the other. Two replica oil lamps grace the stonework, one on each side of the entrance. A bright red awning tops everything.

Outside the front door, rough-hewn cobblestones and a series of planters define the extent the sidewalk café intrudes on the main plaza. Small round tables with matching red tablecloths are scattered across the patio. A small pot overflowing with live flowers adorns the center of each table. More oil lamps glimmer atop metal posts adding to the old-world ambiance of the café.

Malik selects a chair that puts his back against the wall with a clear view of the courtyard.

Magi makes note of the exchange, placing the conversation in its entirety into a growing database in an effort to decipher this new language. Without a proper cross reference, she stands little chance.

ℛ𝕃

Mac glances at Tempel after the three shortimers have left, "That was some tackle. Where did you learn that?"

"Captain Osaka," he replies, still shaking off the adrenal effects of the encounter.

Mac chuckles, "I should've known."

Tempel kneels beside Alonzo. Tatiana has managed to stop the blood using a bar towel but Alonzo still looks in bad shape. He had suffered several hard blows.

"How you doing?" He asked his friend.

"Never better," Alonzo said. Reaching for Tempel's arm, "Give me a hand," and begins pulling himself up.

"I don't think that's such a good idea…" Tatiana said even as the young man stands, holding the towel against his head. Others see for the first time the extent of blood that has soaked the back of his shirt and stained the floor beneath him.

Mac frowns and orders "Lay back down Alonzo… Emergency Response, report immediately to Club Rio."

Despite his repeated assurance that he's fine and a steadfast refusal to lie down, they finally persuade the young warrior to sit. Quan Kiai gathers around him.

A club patron steps forward to offer assistance. She's an off duty ER medico. "Let me take a peek at that," the woman said as she moves around behind Alonzo. Looking under the bloody towel, "The bleeding's stopped but you will need a surgeon to close it properly." She moves back around, pulling down his cheeks, gazing into his eyes, "You're suffering from a mild concussion. If you take it easy, you should be fine."

"So… was she worth it?" Corazon asks after reviewing the start of the fight as recorded from Alonzo's visor.

Alonzo glares at him.

"I can't believe you let a pretty shortimer set you up for a sucker punch." Corazon grins at Alonzo then shrugs. "Facts are facts."

"On the up side, at least she was pretty. Most of them look like they shaved their ass and walk backward," Brice chuckles at his own crude joke.

Upon receiving a call, Consuela turns away and heads towards the nearby exit. Only Marcel notices.

Tempel listens to the banter and watches a cleanup disk scurry across the dance floor collecting the blood and other biomaterials. Before it's finished, the band starts playing again and things begin returning to normal. Would it have been the same if Alonzo had died? Tempel pushes these dark thoughts aside. "It's been a long day. After Alonzo is taken care of, I'm going to catch a bite, then get some sleep."

"Mind if I join you?" Sam purrs.

Tempel grins and nods knowing he wouldn't get much sleep.

"Not me. I want to party." Brice declares, "SuperNovA has a new game I want to check out. Who's with me?" Brice looks around the group. SuperNovA is nightclub that's glitz and bright lights instead of hard rock and star light.

Turning to Tatiana, Corazon asks, "What about you?"

"I think I will go with Alonzo then hook up with Karl. I'll see you tomorrow at roll call," she said, shutting the door on anything more. She and Karl have become hot items recently, cutting down on the time spent with other friends.

"Tell that big Swede he's the luckiest man alive," Corazon said with a grin. He's not surprised. He turns back to Brice and said, "I'm in." Corazon never lets one rejection spoil his entire night and SuperNovA is one of his favorite hotspots. He never sleeps alone.

Brice snuggles up to Odessa, "An hour or so at the tables, then my place?"

She grins and nods. "Sure, why not. I love kicking your ass right before I kiss it and make it all better," she coos.

Kipper and Karyl both shake their heads when Brice looks at them, "Sorry, something has come up that needs tending." Karyl grins mischievously, tightening her hold on Kipper.

"I'll tag along," Marcel said, suddenly wanting to get shit-faced drunk.

"Great." Brice exclaims and asks Tempel, "Why not eat at Lucifer's Diner? You and Sam can walk with us on our way to SuperNovA."

Tempel looks at Sam and shrugs.

"Sure, why not," Sam imitates Odessa perfectly.

The arrival of ER interrupts them. Without any fanfare, the medicos walk the injured man out to the waiting ambulance, Tatiana at his side. They already know the story and the extent of his injuries and waste no time in getting him on his way to the hospital. By morning, he will be good as new without even a scar to show for his carelessness.

ЯL

Emerging from Steinway Avenue, the group starts across the North Courtyard. Two teen girls are sitting on the edge of the fountain dangling their feet in its water. Other young people move about the courtyard, laughing and enjoying each other's company. Only the three shortimers sitting at the café pay them any attention.

Swinging wide of the tall three-level fountain, they make a beeline for the eatery on the other side of the square. It has a striking holographic sign on its roof just above the entrance featuring a red devil complete with horns and a forked tail. Every so often, he points towards the sign with his pitchfork, *Lucifer's Diner, Fine Dining with a Flare*. The apparition turns to look down upon those passing by, eyes flaring briefly as he flashes a fang-filled smile. Then it turns back, stabbing once more at the message. The basic sequence repeats for every citizen, but never twice in the exact same way.

Tempel and Sam walk towards the diner's entrance and Brice, Odessa, Marcel and Corazon wave and continue, disappearing into the mall beyond.

The interior of the diner is long and narrow with a counter on one side and a row of booths on the other. The booths are next to windows that look out upon the courtyard. Beyond the counter is the kitchen. The booths and stools are bright red imitation-leather upholstery. Everything else is chrome.

"Greetings Sam, Tempel. What can I get for you?" The man behind the counter asks as they come in.

Sliding onto a stool, Tempel replies without bothering to look at a menu, "Greetings Lou, chili and a beer and don't be stingy with the onions."

The man smiles, Tempel always orders chili and a beer. "You got it. And for you, Sam?"

"The same," she replies. The aroma of fresh corn bread wafts from the kitchen. "And a slice of corn bread."

Lou smiles and nods, turns and calls out, "Lucy, two chilies hold the peppers, extra onions and corn bread." He picks up a tall glass and places it at an angle beneath the tap before pulling back on the slender handle. Beer slides in smoothly, building up a fine head. He sits it down and repeats the process, placing the two beers in front of his customers. Reaching under the counter he adds a squirt bottle filled with honey and a platter of butter. Nothing beats fresh baked corn bread smothered in butter and honey.

Behind them, beyond the windows of the diner and across the courtyard, the three shortimers pay their tab and leave the sidewalk café, heading directly towards the diner.

"Tempel, Sam, you have company coming in from across the courtyard. The same people that attacked Alonzo." Magi said. "I have notified the closest police patrol but they will not arrive in time. I have told Brice, Odessa, Corazon and Marcel to return at best speed."

Tempel links to the diner's outside sensors and watch the three shortimers come across the courtyard. He follows Sam to the door,

"Keep that chili hot, Lou. We'll be right back."

Outside the diner, Tempel steps away from Sam giving them both a clear field of fire.

As the two shortimers draw near, they too separate putting a few meters between them. Jafa, the younger of the two, locks on Tempel, hate for this particular infidel boiling to the surface. Malik confronts Sam.

Tempel senses the arrival of Odessa, Brice, Marcel, and Corazon but keeps his focus on the man across from him, the one who wants to kill him.

"We got your back." Brice said scanning the courtyard.

"Prepare to meet Allah." Jafa exclaims.

"If it's death you seek, you came to the right place," Tempel growls back.

Jafa's anger grows until he cannot contain himself a moment longer. He draws and dies an instant later. He never had a chance.

The sharp crack of Tempel's laser burning its way through air and flesh echoes harshly across the courtyard. None of them will forget the smell.

A split second after Tempel fires, Malik throws his hands up and backs away.

The girl rushes over throwing herself on the fallen man. "Jafa." She wails. "Jafa." Looking up at Tempel, she screams. "*Murderer.*"

"Murderer." Malik repeats. He's looking down the business end of Sam's pistol so he's very careful not to let his hand get near his own. However, he has what he needs. He would have preferred that Jafa kill the infidel but this will serve just as well.

"The vid will verify that he drew first and I defended myself," Tempel said. It's shaping up to be a long night but not in the way he had imagined.

⅃

The locker-room is loud and boisterous as LCPD prepares for shift change. Steam rolls out of the empty showers and the sound of hundreds of lockers closing signal it's time for roll call. Quan Kiai is but a small portion of this organized mayhem.

Men and women dressed in Lunarian Police uniforms exit the room and move up the ramp. The bright blue patch on Tempel's right shoulder further identifies him as a member of Lincoln County's 22nd Metro Division, and the clenched fist puts him in Quan Kiai platoon. Named by its founder, Captain Kitajima Osaka, Quan is a Chinese martial arts term meaning, *"fist"*, and Kiai is Japanese meaning, *"fighting spirit."*

Emerging onto the parade grounds, Tempel falls in line with his squad and starts counting heads. It's the job of the Senior Lieutenant to make sure everyone's present or accounted for.

"Sam, where are you?" He asked.

"I've been called to a meeting with Abby. I'll see you after roll call," she said. They don't bother casting an image to each other, staying with audio only for this brief conversation.

Several times, other young officers approach Tempel and congratulate him on his victory the night before. His own troops bask in the reflected glory until he puts a stop to it.

"At ease. I don't want to hear another word. I took someone's life. I didn't win a race." Tempel snaps. They left him alone after that.

Right on time, Captain Kitajima emerges from battalion offices onto the parade ground with the other platoon leaders.

"Quan Kiai present or accounted for. Sergeant Odegaard is absent but accounted for," Tempel reports.

"Thank you Lieutenant." Kitajima studies him a moment. It's not every day one of his warriors kill someone in a gunfight.

The platoon leaders bring the assembly to parade rest, hands locked behind their backs, feet shoulder-width apart, sidearms holstered and eyes straight ahead. Following ancient tradition, the eerie sounds of a bugle echo across the subterranean cavern.

Before the last note fades into silence, Commander House's adjutant calls forth across the parade ground, "Attennnnn*TION*." The sound of four hundred boots striking stone explodes in a thunderclap that reverberates up and down the man-made stone cavern, putting vivid punctuation to the buglers' call.

Roll call sounds along the line of companies, "Quan Kiai, all present and accounted for." Captain Osaka calls out in turn.

A few minutes later it's finished, more of a formality than necessity. The platoons begin their assigned duties.

Keeping Quan Kiai at attention, Kitajima does a sharp about face, "Column Left. Harh.... By Twos, Forward.... Harh."

The squads move out with Master Sergeant Hackling calling cadence from a position near the rear. Kitajima stays alongside, marching the company off the parade ground and through a corridor to the practice field. Here is where the battalion conducts most of its training, everything from target practice to combat maneuvers.

"Double time... Harh." The column begins a long winding run along a track around the huge space, each officer leaning forward, balancing traction with acceleration. Kitajima sets an unusually strenuous pace even for lunar gravity, challenging them to stay in formation while maintaining speed. Although the officers of Quan Kiai are physically fit, they are soon covered in sweat.

Thirty minutes later, "Company... Harh." The formation slows to a walk, all of them gasping for breath. Kitajima leads them off the track to a grouping of tables used as a classroom.

"Company... Halt." Kitajima barks, "Fall out and find a seat."

Kitajima walks past the tables, turns and faces the platoon. "At Ease. A few hours ago, Lieutenant Dugan and several of your comrades risked your mission. When faced with a life and death situation, they blinked. They're lucky they're alive."

"Excuse me Captain but Tempel won in a fair fight," Brice said.

"Who in hell wants a fair fight? I don't and you shouldn't." Kitajima has trained these young people for over two years and feels that he knows them well. "I fear that until you experience combat, you will not fully appreciate the point I'm making."

Kitajima stops in front of Brice, glaring down at him. "When you deployed at North Courtyard you faced outward. Why?"

Brice looks out of the corner of his eye at Marcel.

"Don't look at him, just answer the damn question. Why did you face outward and put your backs to Malik and Jafa?"

"We didn't know if there were any others in North Courtyard or out on the arboretum that would back them up," Brice said.

"Besides, we had two against two," Marcel adds.

"That's my point." Kitajima bores in, "When you come up against any enemy you must threaten them with everything you've got and be willing to back it up. There's no place on a battlefield for sportsmanship. That line of thinking will get you killed."

Kitajima looks down at Corazon, "If you can get behind them, do it." He moves on to Marcel, "If you can shoot first, do it. Find a weakness and exploit it with overwhelming force. It's the only way to stay alive. Work as a team. Together you are strong. But if you voluntarily split your forces you weaken yourselves, inviting disaster."

Kitajima stops in front of Consuela, "You're less likely to need to kill someone once they come to the conclusion that any aggression on their part would be suicide. I'm talking about taking the situation far beyond mutual assured destruction. Make the confrontation as lopsided in your favor as physically possible. By leaving the front door even slightly ajar, you're inviting them to kick it in. You must treat anyone threatening to harm you or your comrades with extreme prejudice. Failure to do so will eventually cost you your life, and those of your comrades. Look around you. Quan Kiai depends on you for support and mutual protection. If you're dead, you can't fulfill that duty." He turns and moves back to center stage, "Am I making myself *CLEAR*."

"*AYE.*"

Kitajima glares around the assemblage of Luna's finest young men and women, and slowly nods. "I sincerely hope that it is, but I doubt it. Knowledge of this type must be paid in blood." His gaze passes from one officer to the next, wondering who will be the first that pays. The thought saddens him.

"Excuse me Captain, but we do have a kill to our name," Brice said.

The captain looks intently at him and then at Tempel, "Yes, I guess we do. I'm proud of the way you've handled yourself during this entire incident. You have my full support."

Tempel nods.

They have absorbed the lesson as best he can teach it. Turning away, "Next order of business, we have a new mission," Kitajima announces in a much calmer voice.

Special Weapons and Advanced Technology is one of the choice assignments within any police department. These officers train with the latest gear and techniques. Quan Kiai is one of several SWAT platoons in Lincoln County's Metro Division. Platoons consist of two squads each containing a lieutenant, a sergeant, a sergeant-in-training and four Special Forces officers.

"Squad One will deploy outside along Cannery Row alternating every two hours with Squad Two. Your job will be to clear personnel and cargo coming off the tin cans before it enters the city." A few groans greet the announcement. No frontline unit likes customs duty and these young Lunarians see themselves as the tip of the spear, even if they have no real combat experience. Kitajima doesn't bother sugar coating the assignment, he doesn't like it much either. "Tempel, you're excused from this assignment. As for the rest of you, I want you to keep your eyes open and your mind on business. This latest rash of bombings could be the start of something bigger. So look sharp."

"Captain?"

"What is it Brice?"

"Can we wear ghost suits?"

"Negative, standard vacsuits only. Any more questions… Lieutenant Dugan, keep your seat. The rest of you, we reform at 0900 on the parade ground. Dismissed."

Tempel watches his comrades leave. A few look curiously at him as they pass. Several link so they can listen in.

Kitajima comes and stands next to Tempel who raises his eyebrows. "Magi, what have you got for him."

Having waited for them to initiate the conversation, Magi appears standing a few meters away.

The AI could present itself using virtually any appearance, but from the beginning, Magi has used the results of morphing a group of female elders into a single entity, a visual average that makes her quite beautiful in a very grandmotherly way. Citizens recognize and trust her instantly.

"Abby wants you and Sam to report to Hawking Spaceport for escort duty. You're meeting a Federation defector, a Mr. Lazarus Sheffield. Lindsey Marquest is bringing him in and will hand off to you. They're arriving on Trans World Flight L95 at eleven-ten. Not only is he the first Federation runner in over a decade, he is a Senior Analyst in the Department of Homeland Security," Magi said.

Escort duty? This is a first. "What are we to do with him?" Tempel asks.

"You and Sam are to take Mr. Sheffield out to lunch. Abby wants you to use your own judgment as to what questions to ask. Just keep him talking. Depending on his answers, Abby has tentatively scheduled a meeting with him at 1300."

Tempel shakes his head as if to clear it, "Wait a minute, Sam and I are taking this guy out to lunch?"

"Aye," Magi said cheerfully. "Sam will meet you at the terminal."

Kitajima shrugs, "I'm sure Abby has her reasons for giving you point on this. Don't let her down."

"I won't."

Aldrin Station

"This is the time when humans have begun to sail the sea of space."

Carl Sagan (1934-1996)

MRI satellites track Trans World Flight L95 from the moment it separates from Heaven's Gate. They sweep the craft many times as it crosses the void between Mother Earth and Luna, probing for the slightest abnormality. Six hours into the flight, Lazarus sleeps through a brief freefall as the thrusters shut down and the shuttle flips 180°, decelerating at standard one-sixth G the rest of the way to lunar orbit. Luna Central oversees the shuttle's orbital insertion, the undocking from the Translunar Transfer Vehicle and the subsequent deorbit of the Lunar Lander.

Lindsey gently shakes him, "Lazarus, wake up. We're preparing to land."

Lazarus claws his way to consciousness. He yawns and stretches, "Thanks. I must have fallen asleep."

"You did… almost twelve hours ago. I've never seen someone sleep so hard."

The descent is quiet and smooth right up to the point the AI cranks up the Lander's main thrusters twenty minutes out of Aldrin Station. Sound builds to a deep resonant throb, felt more than heard. The flight trajectory never exceeds three Gs but to Lazarus it seems like more, much more, pushing his stomach down around his ankles. He grips his armrests watching the stark lunar landscape whirl by outside his window.

Luna Central flight controllers and the defensive cannon emplacements strung out along the top of Rim Mountain monitor the shuttle when it appears over the horizon. Powerful scanners sweep the craft time after time, while the cannons keep their cross-hairs on the spacecraft. Finding no anomalies, the shuttle continues its descent undisturbed. Duty officers in three different command centers relax, letting their systems reset to standard recon mode.

The vibration reaches a crescendo as the AI brings the ship smoothly down to the ground. With the slightest of bumps, the shuttle comes to rest and the thrusters fall silent.

Lazarus slowly releases his grip on the armrests and relaxes, not realizing until that moment how tense he had become the last few minutes.

I made it. I'm on the moon.

Lazarus retrieves his small bag from under the seat and looks at Lindsey in triumph. "I can't believe I'm really here."

Lindsey smiles, "Believe it."

Most of the shuttle's passengers are out of their seats and heading towards the exit. Both flight attendants wait next to the airlock door for the ground transport. Lazarus and Lindsey are content to remain in their seat.

Izzy and Marcy collect their baggage and other items. Before leaving, Izzy turns and said, "Tell Abby I said hi."

"I will," Lazarus said. Turning to Lindsey, "Are you sure you can't tell me who's meeting us?" He asked for the third time, running his fingers through his hair.

"I told you, I don't know who Abby's sending. But you can be sure it will be someone you can trust." Taking pity on this Earthman so far from anything familiar, she continues, "Relax," she pats his arm reassuringly, "as long as you're truthful, you will be treated with respect."

"You keep saying that."

"And for good reason. It's the single most important thing for you to remember. Nothing will sink your bid to become a citizen faster than a lie. Even just one," she replies.

"OK. I get the message and will do my best. But there's one thing I want you to remember, Lindsey. Whatever happens, I want you to know how much I appreciate everything you've done." He smiles, thinking again about the hours they had spent together in freefall. "I will never be able to repay you for the generous way you have helped me. I'm forever in your debt."

Lindsey returns his smile, "There you go again, with that debt crap. Get it through your head. You don't owe me anything."

A sharp bump and the clatter of metal ringing against metal announce the arrival of ground transport. The light over the airlock changes from red to green.

The male flight attendant unlocks the inner airlock and swings it open. Stepping into the chamber and out of sight, he unlatches the outer door. An attractive young woman accompanies him back into the shuttle, "Welcome to Aldrin Station. Please proceed to the back of the transport." She moves aside and welcomes each passenger to Aldrin Station as they move past.

Lindsey leads Lazarus from the shuttle, nodding pleasantly to the flight attendant as she passes. She picks an empty pair of seats leaving the window for Lazarus.

More MRI scanners sweep across the passengers and their baggage before the surface transport begins to move. There isn't much to see from the small window but Lazarus has his nose pressed close nonetheless. Rim Mountain dominates the horizon. Above it, bright pinpoints of stars are set in the blackness of airless space. He can see part of Mother Earth directly upward but not well enough to recognize a landmass. The spaceports main airlock looks like a giant culvert protruding out of the mountain and onto the craters floor. It's just large enough to accommodate the transport. The vehicle slows to a stop just inside. He can see the sides of the airlock from his window. A moment later atmosphere explosively fills the small volume around the transport bringing sound with it. The passengers can hear the inside airlock door open with a clank. The transport jerks into motion and accelerates out of the chamber. Everything out his window becomes an indiscriminate blur.

"How far do we go in this tunnel?" Lazarus asks.

"It's about a half kilometer, I would guess," Lindsey said.

He shakes his head. "That puts, what, a kilometer of rock over our heads?"

"Something like that, but don't forget. Everything, including the mountains, weighs only twenty percent of what they would on Mother Earth," she said.

"Why doesn't that comfort me?" Lazarus states dryly "Twenty percent of ginormous is still enormous," he points out with a grin.

The passengers are not even aware of the transport going through more airlocks, each opening just long enough to let the moving vehicle pass before rapidly closing behind. The system never has more than one door open at any given time. The last opens out onto the expansive main floor of the Stephen Hawking Interplanetary Spaceport.

The attendant glances at the green light over the airlock door before opening it, "Please follow the yellow markings on the floor to customs. Thank you for flying Trans World Spaceline."

As they exit down the ramp, Lindsey links her arm with Lazarus. Initially his feet slip as though he were on ice, his weight insufficient to give him his usual traction on the polished stone floor.

"We must get you some proper deck shoes ASAP," Lindsey said. "They're designed to grip the stone. Until then, do this…"

Lindsey shows him the Luna shuffle, more hopping than walking. Lazarus learns a small amount of grace and large dose of humility by the time they cover the fifty meters to customs.

The terminal doesn't seem that different from the airports he's been in, an open space stretching several hundred meters on its long side and less than half that in width, counters and offices arranged throughout in an open design. People move about at a leisurely pace. It's downright calm compared with Athens or Gateway. The thing that's strangest to Lazarus is the ceiling. It glows blue and creates the illusion he's standing beneath a cloudless desert sky. It's a little unnerving but beautiful.

Falling in line, they wait their turn to go through customs. Lindsey then Lazarus pass their left hand over the reader. Excitement surges through Lazarus, He's officially on the moon.

Lindsey maintains her hold on his arm as they exit customs. He glances nervously at the nearby police officer, his visor letting him see the young woman's face. She doesn't look old enough to be packing a pistol.

A handsome young police officer is waiting for them as they emerge from customs. "Greetings Tempel. It's so good to see you." Lindsey said, nodding pleasantly. The man is taller than Lazarus but probably weighs less, despite his broad shoulders. His close-cropped hair appears to be the dominant Lunarian style for both men and women. Tempel's movements are fluid and powerful which Lazarus attributes to being born here.

"Greetings Lindsey. Welcome back," he nods in response.

Turning she said, "Lazarus Sheffield, let me introduce you to Senior Lieutenant Tempel Dugan."

Lazarus starts to extend his hand, recovers and nods his head in a clumsy imitation of the Lunarian custom, "Very pleased to meet you Lieutenant. Please, call me Lazarus."

"Greetings," Tempel nods coldly. "Grandma Abby asked me to meet you and take you to lunch but don't think it's going to become a habit. I've never met a shortimer I liked."

"Tempel," Lindsey said. "Give him a chance."

"It's all right Lindsey. I understand. He's speaking truthfully." Lazarus shrugs, "Isn't that what you told me, always tell the truth?"

Lindsey smiles, "Exactly."

Lazarus stares. Coming up behind Tempel is the most sensuous young woman he's ever seen. Her beauty is extraordinary. She has piercing light blue eyes, skin the color of honey, high cheekbones, and full lips. Shaped in the perfect hourglass, she's wearing a pair of white skin-tight pants and a white low-cut pullover. Her unrestrained tits sway hypnotically and nipples, hardened by rubbing against the fabric, dare him not to stare. Nearly half a head taller than Lazarus, her hair is not much more than blond fuzz across the dome of her head. A holster rides low on her wide hips, the butt of a weapon clearly visible. As a lawman, Lazarus has learned to both rely on, and be skeptical of, first impressions, but the effect this woman has on him is immediate and overwhelming.

"Lazarus Sheffield, meet Sergeant Samantha Odegaard," Lindsey said.

"Greetings, Mr. Sheffield. It's truly a privilege to meet you," she smiles. Then much to everyone's amazement, she offers her hand.

Delighted and instantly at ease, Lazarus smiles back and accepts, "I assure you, the pleasure's mine… Sergeant…"

Samantha laughs, "Please, call me Sam," turning to Lindsey, "Greetings Lindsey. I hear you're glad to be home."

Nodding, Lindsey said, "The next time I feel Mother Earth's gravity will be too soon."

"Are you going to join us for lunch?" Sam asks her.

"No, I have some things I need to take care of. I'll leave Lazarus in your capable hands. He's something important to tell." Lindsey said.

"Wonderful. I can't wait to hear all about it." Sam turns back to

Tempel and asks, "Have you decided on where to eat?"

Tempel shakes his head, "Not really."

"What's your favorite restaurant Lindsey?" Lazarus asks, wanting very much for her to stay.

"Depends on what you want to eat. Breakfast is excellent at Milligan's Café. Lunch… either Mighty Macs or Lucifer's Diner. Savannah's serves a mean soysteak but if you want a view, nothing beats the Surface Cafe," Lindsey said. She loves Lunarian food and has long since tried all that Aldrin Station has to offer.

"Which one's closer?" Lazarus asks hoping to lure Lindsey to stay by making it fast.

"Are we hungry?" Sam laughs a sultry feminine sound that caresses his ears. "Lucifer's Diner is closest, right next door. We can be there in minutes. Mighty Macs isn't much further. What do you want to eat, burgers at Macs or chili at Lucifer's."

"Take him to Macs and show him Brooklyn Mall. He'll love it." Lindsey suggests.

"A burger sounds good." Lazarus said looking intently at Lindsey, "Are you sure you can't join us?"

"I'm sorry Lazarus…" her eyes look past him and her voice trails off. Annoyance flashes across her face.

Lazarus turns to see a tall young man approaching.

"Lindsey darling, I wanted to be waiting when you got off the transport but was held up. Please forgive me." He brushes past Lazarus to embrace her, his lips targeting hers.

Lindsey halfheartedly returns the embrace, turning her cheek to his lips, "Greetings Dwayne. You shouldn't have bothered."

Dwayne laughs and said, "How quickly we forget." Turning to Tempel and Sam he said, "I told Abby that I would be more than happy to meet Lindsey and our guest but she insisted that you do it."

"You know why," Tempel said.

Dwayne laughs too loudly. He turns to Lazarus, "You must be the shortimer everyone is talking about."

Lazarus is miffed but unruffled. "Lazarus Sheffield… and you are?"

Again, the man laughs for no apparent reason, "Dwayne Taylor, grandson of Councilor Zachary Taylor," he said with a flourish.

"I have no idea who that is," Lazarus said. In those few seconds, Lazarus learns as much as he wants about Dwayne Taylor, grandson of Councilor Zachary Taylor. This guy's familiarity with Lindsey troubles him deeply. *Things are different here*, he reminds himself.

"Zachary Taylor was the first Lunarian." Dwayne said.

"I thought Armstrong and Aldrin were the first Lunarians?" Lazarus said. He can't stop himself. Dwayne rubs Lazarus the wrong way.

It's Lindsey and Sam's turn to laugh.

Dwayne stares intently at Lazarus for a moment. "You have much to learn."

"As do we all," Lindsey said sharply. "DT, I have personal business and Lazarus is having lunch with Tempel and Sam. So if you will excuse us…"

Her dismissal cut through his friendliness and his expression hardens. "As you wish… I have a few things to discuss with you." He returns her stare. "Call me at your convenience." Without another word, he turns on his heel and departs the same way he came.

"Well that was… unpleasant," Sam said looking at Lindsey.

"Don't look at me that way. He has a charming side," Lindsey said. "Or at least he did."

"So does a crocodile if you can avoid his teeth," Tempel chuckles softly, "I still can't figure what you saw in him."

Ignoring Tempel, Lindsey steps close to Lazarus and said quietly, "Don't sweat it. Tempel and Sam will take good care of you and I will see you later," she gives him another short but firm kiss that lingers long after their lips part. Her actions speak louder than words how she feels and for whom.

Lindsey nods to the others and walks away. Lazarus stares after her, feeling very alone. Taking a deep breath he turns and smiles, "She's quite remarkable."

Tempel looks disgusted but Sam smiles and said, "Yes, Lindsey is special. How did you happen to meet?"

Looking up at the beautiful Lunarian, Lazarus thinks back. It seems so long ago. Can it be only yesterday? "She had the seat next to mine on the Stratoliner coming out of Athens."

Sam smiles, "Love at first sight. How romantic." Before Tempel has time to inject a cynical remark she continues, "Well, come on. Let's go get some food in you," she said taking Lazarus by the arm much as Lindsey had done, but Sam is fifteen centimeters taller than Lazarus making him tilt his head back just to look at her. He didn't mind a bit.

Tempel, Sam, and Lazarus exit the terminal and pass through a series of corridors. Lazarus is getting better at the lunar shuffle but occasionally he stumbles. Each time Sam grips him tightly preventing him from falling. She said, "Don't worry. You'll get the hang of it."

"He won't as long as you're holding him up," Tempel said.

"Is this your first time off-planet?" Sam inquires, ignoring Tempel.

"Yes," Lazarus replies.

They emerge into a beautiful courtyard with a magnificent colonial style fountain at its center. Its water flows in slow motion, as though it were molasses, something only a shortimer would notice. Yet, its sound is comforting to him in ways he cannot explain.

Along the three sides of the courtyard are various shops and eateries. To his left is a small storefront dedicated to selling visors and other network devices. Beyond is the wood and stone façade of a sidewalk café, its patio filled with tables and chairs. To his immediate right is a vacsuit retail outlet, beyond that a microbrewery, a bakery, and some kind of general store. Music, laughter, and flashing lights spill from a kid's gaming area across the way.

Against the far wall is a familiar type of eating establishment, a diner. There's a devil on its roof pointing a pitchfork at a sign, *Lucifer's Diner, Fine Dining with a Flare.* Lazarus is startled when Lucifer turns and looks directly at him, the eyes flashing as though possessed by his namesake. Lazarus grins, appreciating the irony of its existence in this place as only a Federation citizen can.

Here and there among the shops are more corridors leading to places he cannot imagine but eager to explore. Lazarus breathes in the humid air, fragrant from an assortment of neatly manicured flower gardens. Past the courtyard is an expanse of grass where young people are playing a game, jumping high into the air, testing themselves against their friends. Their calls echo across the distance. Beyond the courtyard and the game is a forest.

Lazarus could never have imagined a place so beautiful and full of life. Craning his neck to catch a glimpse of what lies ahead, he stumbles as Sam changes course to avoid a fast moving covey of laughing children, none more than five or six years of age.

"Is this the mall?" Lazarus asks.

"This is the North Courtyard. It's just a small part of Brooklyn Mall," Sam leads him out of the courtyard and onto the grass giving the ball players plenty of leeway. She stops at a low wall overlooking the most amazing vista Lazarus has ever seen.

Brooklyn Mall is a massive vaulted cathedral sheltering a Lunarian paradise. Before him lies acre upon acre of mid-latitude hardwood forest, manicured and maintained in perfect condition. It extends farther than he can see. From this elevated vantage point, Lazarus looks down upon a picturesque valley of gently rolling hills without any flat ground in sight. It's relatively narrow where he is, widening considerably as it falls away and curves to the right concealing what lies beyond.

Here too, the upper surface of the habitat glows in perfect imitation of a blue sky on a summer afternoon. The luminosity fades as it extends down from the ceiling disappearing entirely about twenty meters up. It's hard to believe this is a subterranean city on the moon.

Massive trees dot the landscape, their leaves shimmering and rustling in a very earth-like breeze. Birds flitter about. Not far below is a small pond under two large trees. A stream runs from the pond, its path marked by boulders and thickets of flowering shrubs, bushes, and reeds.

Squirrels chatter and cavort in the treetops and rabbits hop about the grass. A rain shower had just finished and the humid air smells fresh with just a hint of fragrance. Lazarus cannot see far, prevented by architecture designed to provide mystery to the vista, playing on his imagination like a maestro directing an orchestra.

To his right more shops and restaurants extend another fifty meters along the wall, their roofs covered in lush grass and flower gardens. As with all Lunarian architecture, there is not a straight-line or sharp corner in sight. Everything is curves, one element flowing smoothly to the next, carved from a single block of stone.

Paths lead down the valley to an assortment of benches and tables. One area is swampy and choked with cattails. Another has a pond with a single massive jet of water dancing fifty meters high. Further away through a gap in the trees, Lazarus spots a gazebo silhouetted on the crest of a hill. The beauty is breathtaking.

"Tempel, why don't you go ahead and get the burgers?" Sam suggests.

"Aye," the young Lunarian said gruffly, glad to be away from this shortimer if only for a moment.

"Totally awesome." Lazarus blurts. Looking up, "I can feel the sun on my face… How's that possible?"

"The lighting is natural sunlight minus the more deadly frequencies," she said.

"Amazing."

Sam guides him down the terrace past several shops towards a small food court. Tucked under the branches of an enormous tree are burnished stone tables.

"Is this ok?" Sam asks.

Lazarus pulls out one of the stone chairs, amazed that he can move something so massive so easily. "This is marvelous."

Sam, amused by the Earthman's quaint manners, smiles and sits down. No one has ever done that for her. She likes it.

"Lunarians use stone like we use wood and metal on Earth," Lazarus observes, running his hand over the glassy smooth surface of the tabletop.

"The quarrying process polishes and seals the surface. The beauty inside the stone can be stunning," Sam slides her finger along a scarlet slash of color running the length of the tabletop. "This is a metal-bearing ore and the color depends on the metal. Needless to say, it makes beautiful furniture and habitats excavated from it are highly prized," Sam said. "My family works HE excavators and makes furniture on the side."

"How do you make a chair out of stone?" Lazarus asks.

"The same way you make a chair out of wood, very carefully," Sam smiles. "Stone is best for tables, benches, and counter tops, but as you can see, it makes a great looking chair too."

"So you must know a lot about excavating?" Lazarus asks.

"Not as much as Tempel. If you have technical questions, he's your guy," Sam states.

"I'm fascinated with Lunarian habitats. Nothing like them has ever been created in the long history of man." Lazarus' eyes sparkle with excitement.

"You're not going to call us cavemen or Neanderthals?"

"No. Definitely not." he exclaims. He looks up as Tempel sets a tray heaped with food on the table.

Tempel raises an eyebrow, "I wouldn't say man has a long history, at least not in any true sense of geological time. All two hundred thousand years is nothing but an instant in the four and a half billion years of Mother Earth's history. You do believe that Mother Earth is old, right? Not that crazy talk about it being created a few thousand years ago?"

"Of course not but I must admit, there's much I don't understand, especially concerning Earth history and evolution. It wasn't taught in school while I was growing up and books about it are banned," Lazarus said, taking a bite.

Sam frowns and wipes her mouth with a napkin. "Citizens allow this?" She asked incredulously.

Lazarus swallows and nods. "They vote on which books to ban, as well as the punishment for those caught reading banned books."

"I find that hard to believe. The government must rig it. Why would anyone choose ignorance over knowledge?" Sam cannot understand. To her, raised from infancy to respect the principles behind science and humanity's quest to understand the cosmos, it's inconceivable that someone would reject ideas simply because they don't fit some preconceived dogma. Ideas are to be examined closely and only set aside if they are found lacking merit. Suppressing an idea because it fails to fit into a religious or political system is unthinkable.

"No one chooses ignorance. Federation citizens are told what beliefs are acceptable."

"Are you not among these citizens? Don't you profess the same beliefs?" Tempel asks.

Lazarus swallows and reminds himself once again he must drop any deception and be utterly honest. It's hard to set aside something that's been such a major part of his life. He licks dry lips before answering, "No... I don't... I searched for it as a kid but all I found were broken shards of clay where there should have been diamonds."

"That's... sad," Sam said softly.

Tempel glances at her with exasperation then turns back to Lazarus,

"What's that supposed to mean?"

"It means that even as a child I questioned religion and the crazy stuff they wanted me to believe." Lazarus wipes away a bead of sweat rolling down his cheek.

"Then how did you become a Senior Analyst?" Tempel asks.

Lazarus looked up from his plate and locks eyes with the young Lunarian, "By being a good liar."

His answer startles Sam and disgusts Tempel.

"Which books are banned?" Sam asks.

Tempel and Lazarus stare at each other for a moment longer, then Lazarus said, "It would be easier to tell you which books are allowed. The banned list is enormous. I think the authorities can find something wrong with any book if they look hard enough."

"What punishment is given for reading them?" Sam asks. Over the last thirty years, there has been a dearth of Federation emigrants limiting her exposure to these strange ideas.

"Depends on what book and who catches you. Best case is a fine, but worst case is a nice long vacation at a reeducation facility."

"That doesn't sound so bad," Sam said.

Lazarus stares at her for a moment, "I would withhold judgment if I were you. I've spent a significant amount of time inside them and it isn't pretty." Lazarus turns away, ashamed in that instant of the number of reeducations he had personally instigated. "As a Senior Analyst, I interrogated suspects… Sometimes that included physical discomfort, sometimes drugs… Specialists would come in and do… other things… When we were finished, we released the suspect for reeducation. When they come out… they're another person… they've been reeducated…"

Sam puts her burger down. Her horrified look drives a dagger into Lazarus.

"You tortured them?" Sam asks.

"We called it enhanced interrogation," Lazarus said.

"You tortured them." Tempel said. It's hard to generate any sympathy for Federation citizens. They made their bed and now must sleep in it.

"What happened to them inside the room?" Sam asks.

Lazarus shakes his head, "I didn't need to know…"

After a moment, Sam asks, "Why would you be a part of that?"

"It seemed like the right thing to do in the beginning, but it changed. At first, the suspects were limited to terrorists or violent criminals, but in recent years, I participated in more and more cases involving citizens whose crimes were more political in nature. Many of them were only guilty of not reporting for the draft. They didn't want to do their six years. Others simply questioned the government or the religious patriotism promoted by the government… I grew to hate my job…"

His voice trails off and they eat in silence. He no longer tastes the meal, thinking about what he had done, thinking about his brother. He blames himself for so many things.

"Why didn't you quit?" Sam asks.

"No one quits DHS…" he said without looking up.

"You did," Tempel said.

"That's right, I did," Lazarus said. "But I had to leave the planet to do it." He sighs and lays his napkin on his plate, "Very tasty. Now I understand why Lindsey likes Mac's."

Sam nods and asks, "Lazarus is an unusual name. Where does it come from?"

"Lazarus is the name of two people in the bible, the man Jesus raised from the dead and a character in one of his parables. My mom named my brothers Saul and Elijah, and my sister Mary, so it makes sense that my name is also biblical. Dad, on the other hand, said I was named after the hero in a science fiction novel written in the mid twentieth century." Lazarus said. "I like that better."

"Whatever the reason, it's charming." Sam said.

"What's an agent for Homeland Security doing here?" Tempel asks, closely monitoring his polygraphic indicators, looking for the slightest appearance of deception.

"I'm not an agent, only an analyst …" Lazarus pauses and sighs deeply, running his hand over his head, "The situation became intolerable for me. I no longer believe in my government, my job, or my life… The Federation has information indicating the Republic of Luna is in grave danger. Since sending troops or an envoy is out of the question, I'm the next best thing," Lazarus smiles.

"Whose idea was that?" Tempel asks.

"Mine," Lazarus said. "Totally mine. You see… I believe the Brotherhood is about to attack the Republic."

"So? Tell me something I don't know," Tempel declares. "Why do you think we need your help? The Republic can take care of itself."

Despite the amazing architecture they're sitting in, life is harsh on the moon and always has been. A Lunarian grows up fast or dies trying. In the beginning, before deep rock excavations were possible, the kids suffered the highest mortality rate of any group. Living in a vacuum is a very unforgiving place to raise a family.

The group currently holding that distinction can't be classified by age, gender, or occupation. Their deaths are the result of sectarian violence. Most Earthmen tolerate Lunarians but some consider them evil. Rumors of bounties and contract killings abound, gunfights are commonplace and people simply disappear.

Born into this situation, the Dugan children began handling weapons as soon as they could hold one steady. Tempel was nine when he recorded his first perfect score in the family's gun range. By the time he was eleven, he could outdraw his brothers, sisters, and cousins, all except Ben.

Patrick Dugan taught his children that carrying a gun is a responsibility, not a toy or an adventure, and if he ever caught one of them playing loose with it, he'd take off their backside with his belt.

None of his kids ever lost any hide. Patrick drilled into them early and often that gunplay was a last resort, but when necessary, done with precision and skill. Tempel often wonders what his father would make of the current state of affairs. He believes in his heart that if his father were alive, he would approve of his youngest son being a Special Forces lieutenant in the police department, a leader of warriors.

"I'm sure you can take care of yourself, but there will be serious consequences if even the tiniest mistake is made," Lazarus said. "You see… there's reason to believe the Brotherhood's going to detonate a thermonuclear device somewhere on Luna."

"I know. I reviewed your conversations with Lindsey," Tempel said.

"You really think they'll nuke us?" Sam asks.

Lazarus shrugs and said, "Yes, I do."

A cold silence falls over the table. Samantha sits and stares numbly at Lazarus, trying in vain to make sense of something that defies logic. "Why would anybody do such a horrible thing? I don't understand why they want to hurt us. What have we done to them to make them hate us so much?" Sam whispers.

Lazarus frowns, "You won't find any reason in their madness. Fundamentalism, whether it's religious or political, displays amazing tunnel vision."

"You still haven't explained why they want to kill us," Sam insists.

"The Holy Qur'ân tells them it's their duty to either convert nonbelievers or destroy them. I believe the phrase used by Islam's leading clerics and imams was that… *all Lunarians are godless infidels*. That places you at the top of the list of nonbelievers to be dealt with," Lazarus said.

"But the citizens don't take them seriously… do they?" Sam asks.

Lazarus bows his head and fiddles with his napkin, "I quote from the Holy Qur'ân 47:4. *When you meet in battle those who disbelieve strike off their heads after you have bound them fast in fetters.* The average

Muslim believes that genetic science has soiled all Lunarians, which means conversion is impossible in this life. They believe that for God to pass judgment on you, they must kill you. It's their way of calling court in session. And if they should be killed while doing the work of Allah, they're promised paradise in heaven for all eternity… Mohammed's version of paradise reflects his sixth century bias and includes plenty of wine, food, and sex with beautiful little girls and boys. 78:31 *As for those who guarded against evil there awaits them a triumph, orchards and vineyards; and blooming young maidens… 76:19… Sons of perpetual bloom shall go round waiting upon the believers…* Blooming young maidens refers to little virgin girls and sons of perpetual bloom are little virgin boys. I'm sure I don't need to explain why children are included in paradise. The Hadith expands the pedophile promise that includes a sex market where these children are on display for the believer to choose from."

"Regardless of why they want us dead, nothing comes or goes in Aldrin without passing through heavy security. A cockroach couldn't get by. Let alone a nuke." Tempel's like the rest of Luna, he believes that Magi and her multitude of MRI scanners preclude this possibility.

"Aren't the reports of bombs getting through accurate?" Lazarus hopes this was a fabrication of the government-controlled media. It would not be the first time.

Tempel stares at the Earthman for a moment, "Lunarians must be helping them," he finally admits.

"I don't know much about Lunarians but I do know the Brotherhood. They're in the final stages of something big. I just don't know the what, when, or where," Lazarus said.

"Do you have any supportive evidence or must we simply take your word for it?" Tempel asks harshly.

"I couldn't bring anything with me for obvious reasons but some of the evidence can be regenerated." Lazarus leans his forearms onto the beautiful tabletop and looks intently at Tempel. "I will help your network people as much as I can."

"Point us in the right direction, so to speak," Tempel said sarcastically, suspicious of anything Lazarus may direct them to. Even if he's sincere, Tempel's skeptical this shortimer can teach Jamie and Jordan anything about hacking Earthnet.

"I'm not a politician, Tempel. What I know is that over the last three months Homeland Security acquired overwhelming evidence of something big coming down, encrypted emails, Earthnet conversations, and security tapes on more than a few suspects. The Brotherhood's Defense Minister, Hasin bin Aunker and Major General Abdel Salam Arif are missing. Do you know who they are?" Lazarus asks.

Sam's face turns ashen and she glances at Tempel whose expression remains stiff and unchanging. "We've heard of them," she acknowledges.

"Don't expect any help from the Federation. They will not honor the Treaty of Independence. The most you can expect is neutrality. They will stay out of it," Lazarus said.

"That's all we ask. If the Brotherhood wants more martyrs, then we will accommodate them," Tempel snarls.

Sam senses Tempel's outburst disturbs Lazarus. She decides to change the subject. "As I understand it, you requested a meeting with Abby? Why Abby?" Sam asks raising her eyebrows.

"Lindsey helped me, but Abigail Dugan is famous even in Arizona." Lazarus looks at her puzzled, "It's not like you have a central government. I can't ask to speak with your President. You don't have one."

"The will of the citizens is the only government we need," Tempel said.

"But a government provides for the common defense and the Republic doesn't even have a military," Lazarus states.

"A standing militia of any kind is prohibited under the Treaty," Sam said.

"Then who decides what needs to be done and enforces the decisions?" Lazarus asks.

Sam sighs, "We all do. The freeholds conform to the majority rulings voluntarily. To defy the Council guarantees sanctions by the rest of Luna. If it's one thing we have a good grip on, it's that nobody survives on Luna without help. Isolation means death."

"*No man is an island*," Lazarus said. He loves the fact he can now say these things in normal conversation.

"Exactly as Mr. Donne intended…" Sam said.

"I don't understand freeholds. What is a freehold?" Lazarus asks.

"A half-century ago, my ancestors determined the only real security they could expect was from their own hand. That meant bringing every aspect of their existence under tight control, right down to the air they breathe. A freehold consolidates these resources for efficiency and security purposes. The freehold is the core unit in the Republic of Luna. I think it's similar to a corporation in the Federation."

"So the Republic is pure capitalistic?" Lazarus asks.

"No true democracy can be pure capitalism or pure socialism. There must be a balance between the two ideas. The Republic of Luna votes on everything and provides an economy based on Gross Percentage Taxation. Voting and paying taxes are responsibilities every citizen takes seriously, even the kids. We don't have a single billionaire, but we also don't have any poverty. We are all middle class."

"What about the non-Lunarian settlements?" Lazarus asks.

Sam shakes her head, "Non-Lunarian politics are even more complicated. Four Earth nations have military stationed on Luna and over one hundred and fifty corporations maintain private security forces. The Law of Full Disclosure applies only within our holdings. Little America and the various facilities of other nations are not part of Luna's network. We have very little control over what they do." When Lazarus looks lost she continues, "Little America is a shortimer enclave east of Hell's Kitchen on the outer edge of Aldrin Station. It's off limits to us. We don't know what goes on in there."

"So a large crate could be delivered to Little America and would not pass through a Lunarian inspection point?" Lazarus asks.

Sam's face clouds over.

Tempel frowns and stands, "Highly unlikely… Come, we should go." He leads them along the edge of a babbling brook cutting its way through the forest. The enormous trees seem small in the huge space, and they but ants scurrying beneath.

"The trees are magnificent," Lazarus said with an awed shake of his head.

"We have taken great care in selecting the best genetic strains and they grow fast in Luna's gravity," Sam said.

"What kind are they?" Lazarus asks.

"These are Ash trees native to Europe," Sam said. "According to Norse legend, Igdrasil is the Ash Tree of Existence with its roots in hell and limbs spreading across the universe. At its base is the Kingdom of Death where the Three Fates live, the Past, the Present, and the Future. Seasonal changes represent various events, things suffered, things done, catastrophes, stretching through all lands and times. As the story goes, an eagle rests on the highest branch of Igdrasil to observe all that passes in the world, whilst a squirrel constantly runs up and down its trunk to report those things the eagle may not have seen. Serpents twine round its limbs and from its roots flow two streams, the knowledge of things past and the knowledge of things to come. According to the legend, man himself was formed from the wood of this sacred Ash tree."

"That makes about as much sense as the biblical version of creation," Lazarus said.

The valley widens considerably as they move downhill and around the curve. A tall cliff face comes into view ahead of them. It's bare stone, craggy and irregular with horizontal striations sculpted into its face. Predominantly pastel red, it's mottled with browns, pinks, and many other earth tones. Lazarus soon realizes it's not simply a cliff, but a massive column that extends to the ceiling far above.

They follow the small stream downhill and the canyon flattens into a broad plain with the column at its center. The trees here are further apart with knee-high prairie grass instead of the manicured bluegrass found in the upper reaches of North Canyon. Around the base of the column, before the floor slopes up to meet the vertical face, are more shops and a picnic area with a decent sized swimming lake. People are everywhere, but it's far from being crowded. Lazarus estimates only a couple hundred are within his sight. If this were in the Federation, that number would be in the tens of thousands. To him, this place is empty.

From the rock face high above, a waterfall begins its descent towards a pool at the base of the cliff. A stream connects it to the lake. A fog shrouds the pool and half the lake. Even from this distance, he hears splashing and peals of laughter.

Several dogs run across the open meadow in great bounds, disappearing into the tall grass only to reappear as they leap again. They flush out several large animals. Lazarus can hardly believe his eyes when a dozen deer break cover, white tails flashing.

"What is this place?" Lazarus asks in a whisper.

"This is Brooklyn Mall," Sam said.

"How big is it?" He asked. The column is so large, he has trouble judging its scale.

"At its peak, the mall is six hundred meters high and contains just over six square kilometers." Tempel answers.

Looking up in awe, Lazarus said, "Six hundred meters. No wonder I feel small. Are all habitats like this?" He asked.

Sam shakes her head, "This is a mall. It's about having fun."

"Malls are designed to give us a little headroom. Grandma Abby said they remind us we came from a planet," Tempel adds.

A screech overhead draws his attention, "Is that a hawk?" Lazarus asks.

Sam glances up, "Peregrine Falcon."

"There are predators here?" Lazarus asks.

"Some. Don't worry, there isn't any big enough for you to worry about," she said.

Shaking his head in disbelief, he said, "Luna is full of surprises. Why's the mall shaped this way? Can I assume the butte in the center is holding up the roof?"

"It's structural if that's what you mean. All habitat geometry is designed to withstand enormous pressure," Tempel said.

"It's quite remarkable," Lazarus said. To his left and right are two more valleys. He can't see very far down either because both curve, but one appears to go uphill and the other downhill.

"I must keep reminding myself that all of this is man-made. The plants, the insects, the animals, they're all selected by you. How do you manage all of this?"

Sam chuckles and leads Lazarus towards a covered picnic table not far from the base of the column. "Let's get under cover before it rains."

They reach the canopy just as a warm rain begins to fall.

Lazarus runs his fingers through his hair. "Everything is so clean, no smog, no pollution of any kind." Lazarus remains standing, gazing up the valley they had just come from, its distance hazed by the rain shower. The air is fresh and sweet, full of the smell of damp foliage. A rainbow graces the distance. "Why not use a sphere? It's been known for millennia that the most efficient use of space is a sphere."

"The rock pressure would crush it. It simply couldn't hold up. By narrowing the classic sphere down to a disk, we are using the arch to hold up the ceiling. You can see the inward curve in the vertical walls," Tempel explains, pointing and gesturing for emphasis. "It's the same design the ancient Egyptians used when they built the chambers under their pyramids."

"I don't understand," Lazarus said.

"The deepest chambers and passageways used a step or terraced design to withstand the tremendous overhead compressive loads. Each successive block layer extended inward a few centimeters until the two sides finally joined high overhead, in effect, creating an arched ceiling. We use the same shape only ours is smooth, not stepped."

"That's amazing. How do you decide where the habitats should go? How big they can be?" Lazarus asks.

"The size, orientation and distribution of all excavations are obviously interrelated and must be controlled," Tempel lectures. "Any miscalculation weakens the city and could cause a collapse."

"I seem to remember that's happened before," Lazarus said, raising one eyebrow.

"Sure it has," is Tempel 's quick response. "We study all the major and minor incidents in school. The Hampton Bay collapse was the largest; it killed over two hundred people. What's your point?"

"You needn't worry," Sam said. "There hasn't been a collapse in over forty years."

"Hampton forced a re-write of the design simulation. Every known factor's incorporated. Not only does the outer envelope maximize support, but the inner structure as well. The floors, ceilings, walls and ramps inside the habitats distribute the load. It's much safer now."

"Is there a master plan for the entire city?" Lazarus asks.

"Of course there is… DREMS incorporates the shape of habitats, transportation and utility corridors, even plumbing. The mountain itself undergoes extensive SQUID evaluation looking for fractures or fault lines…" Sensing his ignorance, "S-Q-U-I-D stands for Superconducting Quantum Interference Device. It maps variations in the mountains magnetic field to identify mini-cracks and stress risers before they fail… The point is, all of these influences are factored into any proposed new excavation no matter how small," Tempel said.

"Dreams?" Lazarus asks.

"D-R-E-M-S stands for Deep Rock Excavation and Maintenance Simulation," he answers.

"Can you show me or is it classified?" Lazarus asks.

"Classified? DREMS is on the public net. Everybody has access to it." Tempel glances at Sam and shakes his head before linking with Lazarus. In a rapid series of hand movements, he brings up a three-dimensional image floating in the air between them.

Lazarus stares in total fascination at the multicolored model. In exquisitely fine detail, it shows the section of Rim Mountain that contains the city. Most of the residential habitats, and their interconnecting commonways, lie within a central region roughly the same elevation as the Central Highlands outside the crater.

A half kilometer below the residential habitats, at the elevation of the crater floor, is another region containing far fewer constructs but with a complex network of tunnels.

Above the residential habitats is a third region. Lazarus stares at one of the largest constructs until his visor identifies it as a reservoir.

Tunnels connect the three levels, some large and well defined, others are wispy threads almost invisible at this scale.

The quality of the graphics astounds Lazarus. As a Senior Analyst, he had access to the best simulations the Federation had to offer but this is far better than anything he's ever seen or imagined possible.

"The upper level is our water reservoirs and some agricultural habitats. The central level is where we live and the lower level is waste recovery and bulk transportation. Currently, there are 1173 habitats, over 125 kilometers of commonways and almost 500 kilometers of primary and secondary service tunnels below the city. The sewer system alone has 1600 kilometers of ancillary tunnels, some big enough to walk in but most are smaller than your fist." A bright pinprick appears within the central level. Tempel points, "Here's where we are."

Tempel circles a group of habitats, his finger leaving behind a glowing trail that fades away, "This is Dakota warren."

"Please define a warren for me," Lazarus asks.

"A warren is a group of habitats that share the mechanicals needed to keep us eating and breathing. Usually they have a short interconnect corridor between the individual habitats but sometimes they butt up rim to rim. A big warren, like Dakota, has habitats spread out vertically and horizontally," Tempel said.

Reaching out, Tempel pulls the image, magnifying it to take a closer look at Brooklyn Mall.

Lazarus staggers. He's no longer standing in the mall but instead he's soaring high above it.

"Take it easy Tempel. He isn't accustomed to using our net." Sam puts her arm around Lazarus to steady him.

Tempel slows and brings him to a stop over Brooklyn Mall's Central Commons. Below them are three individuals standing next to a covered park bench. The rain soaked grass catches the light, like millions of diamonds sprinkled across the lawn.

Lazarus suppresses his fear of heights by repeatedly telling himself… *this is not real*. He isn't actually hovering in midair a hundred meters up looking down at these people. He realizes who they are. He hesitantly waves his arm out in front like a blind man looking for obstacles. The figure below does the same. He resists the urge to look up.

Sam recognizes his discomfort, "Tempel's integrating the mall's sensors with DREMS."

Lazarus had grown up around computers and electronics, yet he realized long ago that one of the sacrifices his country made, as they clung ever tighter to Christian religious beliefs, was that of change. No new technology has developed within the Federation for over fifty years. Some call this lack of innovation conservatism, but Lazarus knows it for what it is… stagnation.

Of all the classified reports he's read over the years, not one mentioned this advanced state of technology. The Lunarian computer system had to be crunching data at a tremendous rate to provide them with such high quality video, better than anything he had seen or heard about. Once again, the Federation must have purposefully kept this from him and the other Senior Analysts. He files the omission away with all the others.

Like a bird soaring high above the trees, Tempel takes them back the way they had come. Three adolescent boys are sitting at the same table they had so recently vacated. Tempel moves in close bringing Lazarus and Sam with him. It's as though they're standing right next to the table, listening to their horseplay, seeing every expression as clearly as if they were actually present. The boys are wearing visors and one of them turns, looking right at Tempel.

"Something wrong?" He asked.

Tempel shakes his head and said, "Nope. We just want to wish you boys a nice lunch." He nods to them and departs.

Back across the mall they soar, this time staying beneath the massive limbs, weaving around the tree trunks. Lazarus is starting to really enjoy the ride by the time they reach their destination, back at the flesh and blood versions of themselves standing patiently beside the picnic bench.

Tempel brings Lazarus to a standstill, centimeters from himself. It's like looking into a mirror. Lazarus can see every pore, every hair, every twitch of his mouth, more clearly then if he were in his luxury apartment back in Arizona staring into the bathroom mirror. He can't resist reaching out, watching his hand disappear into the chest of the image in front of him. He hears Sam's musical laugh, pulling him back to something real.

"Scanners throughout the city are available to anybody at any time but the malls are covered in greater detail. This is where we come to play," Sam said.

With a grand wave of his arm, Tempel sweeps their images away, scattering the millions of tiny pixels like dust in the wind.

Lazarus gathers his wits about him, leaning against Sam. He notices a man and a woman a short distance away, standing and watching.

"Who are those people?" Lazarus asks.

"They are the Lunarians monitoring our conversation," Sam replies. When Lazarus looks confused, Sam adds, "What you see is the result of morphing forty-seven men and women into a single couple."

"I don't understand," he said.

Sam said by walking over to the woman. She nods a greeting and asks, "Constance, do you mind?"

The image nods.

"I would like you to meet Mr. Lazarus Sheffield," Sam said.

The face and countenance of the figure before them changes smoothly into the features of a heavyset woman with shoulder length brown hair and a hawkish nose.

"Greetings… Constance Haig," she said tipping her head politely.

"Lazarus Sheffield," Lazarus nods in return.

"Constance works with Tempel and if I don't miss my guess, you are keeping tabs on him. Isn't that right?" Sam asks

"No, actually I find this Earthman fascinating. All this talk of nukes and terrorists."

"I'm surprised you have time," Sam said.

"Humph. You're right of course, I don't have time." With a curt nod, Constance melts back into the composite, removing herself from the conversation.

Lazarus abruptly reaches up and takes off his visor. Sam and Tempel exchange glances, keeping theirs on. "If you don't mind, I would like to see Aldrin Station with my own eyes."

"It's your choice," Tempel said. "It's stopped raining." Tempel leads them away from the picnic area.

Lazarus is starting to get the knack of walking in lunar gravity. It requires a completely different rhythm but he's learning.

"We're early," Sam said.

"Let's stop at the Plantation," Tempel suggests.

"Why not," Sam agrees.

Tempel leads them to a quaint French-style sidewalk café close by the mall's East entrance. There isn't an alcove here, just a few shops looking down upon the arboretum.

Weaving around tables, Tempel picks one close to a pool surrounded by ferns with a miniature waterfall. The air's damp and tall broadleaved plants shade the café. A thick Asian carpet softens the mall sounds. To Lazarus, it seems like he has entered yet another little world.

A tall lanky young man with broad shoulders comes over to take their order. He immediately notices that Lazarus is not wearing his visor.

"Mocha Sanani," Tempel said.

"Two ambrosia's with honey and a couple of Blackberry rolls," Sam orders.

"Ambrosia?" Lazarus asks.

"It's white tea originally from south China that we have grown on Luna for over fifty years. It's very good with honey," Sam said.

"Sounds wonderful," Lazarus said. Rachel had liked tea. He leans back in the chair and relaxes. The chair is soft and the sound of the water soothing. A yawn escapes before he can stop it.

"When are you due?" Tempel asks Lazarus.

"Due what?" Lazarus asks.

"Sleep... When was the last time you slept?" Tempel asks.

"On the shuttle. I'll be fine," Lazarus said.

Sam laughs and said, "Time lag."

Tempel nods knowingly, "It will take a while for your system to adjust to the lack of night and day."

"I don't understand why Lunarians don't use Universal Shiptime. Why not dim the lights half the day?" Lazarus asks.

"Only civilian spacecraft do that, mostly because it offers them a measure of control over their passengers. Military ships use the same twenty-four hour schedule that we do," Tempel pointed at the clock above the door of the café. "Twenty-four hours is divided up into three eight hour shifts, red for first, green for second, and blue for third. Some people still use morning, noon and night but it doesn't mean much. A long time ago, they tried dimming the lights at night but it turned out to be a colossal waste of effort. There is not one single reason why one shift should be singled out for sleeping and not another. We leave it up to the individual to decide when they should be sleeping."

"The words tomorrow or today or yesterday don't have much meaning here, do they?" Lazarus asks.

"Sure they do. A day is still twenty-four hours just like on Mother Earth. We just don't have a nice neat twelve-hour light and dark cycle here. Even if you're on the surface, a lunar cycle is fourteen days freezing darkness and fourteen days of blazing sunlight. It's simpler to have all of Luna work off the same time," Tempel said sipping his coffee.

"I think you like explaining things to Lazarus," Sam said grinning at Tempel.

Tempel blows her a kiss. Turning back to Lazarus, "Most people adjust their sleep cycle to fit those they work with. I only need about four hours sleep in every twenty-four."

Lazarus nods his thanks as the waiter deposits a steaming mug next to the prettiest pastry he had ever seen, a perfect spiral of dark purple set in piecrust. "That might take some getting used to," he said shaking his head. "I personally need at least six hours or I'm not worth much the next day."

Tempel grunts wondering if any shortimer is worth his O2, regardless of how much sleep they get.

Sam peels a layer from the side of her pastry and pops it into her mouth with obvious pleasure.

Lazarus nods and takes another sip. Sitting the cup down, he said, "I can't tell you how much I'm looking forward to meeting your grandmother. You may not realize how famous she is on Earth. In some circles she's spoken of with Einstein, Darwin and Hawking. Her white paper on Biotronic DNA manipulations is the definitive work on the subject," his voice betrays his excitement.

"You seem to know a lot about Abby. Where did you learn it?" Tempel asks.

"We routinely monitor your netsites and when something new is posted, it was my job to read it." Lazarus pauses and adds, "Right before I blocked everyone else from it."

Without Lazarus wearing his visor, Tempel doesn't have access to his polygraphic indicators, but he's sure something's bothering the shortimer.

Lazarus raises his hands in mock surrender, "I was young and idealistic and convinced myself I was working on the side of good." He drops his eyes and runs his fingers through his hair. "It's not something I'm proud of but Lindsey stressed honesty above all else. I will not hide or avoid the things I have done."

"Good advice," Tempel said.

"We're not here to judge you, Lazarus," Sam said.

"You seem to be doing a good job of that all by yourself," Tempel said.

Lazarus sighs and runs his fingers through his hair again, "I have told you about me and my family. Please, tell me something about yours."

Tempel is a product of an open society where the free flow of information defines freedom. Branded a liar is one of the worst things that can happen to somebody, their opinions, and they themselves, are rendered irrelevant. It never occurs to him to lie or avoid the truth.

"Grandma Abby was born in 1999 in Kansas City. She was educated in one of your universities and in 2024, she volunteered for the old US Space Command. She was the doctor on the mission that founded Aldrin Station. As one of the original settlers, she helped set up the city's first hospital and the first biotronic research program. She's still involved in biotronics and is an active professor at the University of Luna. Her lectures are always attended by thousands, sometimes millions."

"That's amazing, still teaching at ninety-three." Lazarus said. "What about your father and mother? Brothers and sisters?"

"My dad, Patrick Ryan Dugan, was Abby's youngest child. Everyone called him Duce. He married my mom, Elizabeth Anne Turner, a few months before my oldest brother Ben was born in 2060. Then they had Stone in '62, Patrick Ryan III or Tray in '64, Magie in '65, Krystin in 67, Skylor in '70 and Alex in '71. I was born Halloween 2072."

"In the Federation, families must pay for the privilege to have more than one child," Lazarus said. "The government calls them fines but the result is only the rich have large families."

"That's horrible," Sam said.

Lazarus is tired of seeing her visor and not her eyes. He slips his visor back on, noticing for the first time that his surroundings sharpen and colors appear more vibrant with the device. Staring at the little waterfall, he clearly hears every splash, but the sound reverts to background noise when he looks away. Turning his head, Lazarus stares at the waiter inside the café, being able to observe his interaction with another customer as if he were standing next to them. The man turns and looks inquisitively at Lazarus, who hastily breaks eye contact and concentrates on Tempel. Lazarus is not sure what just happened.

"My mother's family, the Turners, belong to Humboldt freehold over in Mission. When she married my pop she kept her maiden name and honored her new husband by accepting his as well, Elizabeth Anne Turner-Dugan. This seems to be catching on with my generation. It makes for some interesting names."

"Just the women? I thought Lunarians were all about equality?" Lazarus said.

"That's what I've been saying. The men should change their names too." Sam said.

"What about you Sam, what's your family like?"

She smiles, "Not nearly as interesting as Tempel's, I'm afraid." Turning to Tempel, she said, "We need to be going."

Tempel nods, gulping the last of his coffee.

They exit the mall and it isn't long before Lazarus is completely lost. The tunnels seem to curve and twist without rhyme or reason. Abruptly, they emerge into another enormous space dominated by trees.

At first, Lazarus thinks it's another mall. Overhead is the same blue sky, but this space is different, a huge tunnel cut into the stone where the mall was a bubble. It extends as far as he can see in both directions, foliage gently swaying in the breeze.

They are on a broad ledge at least twenty meters up one side. To his left and right ramps lead to the grassy floor below.

Instead of going down, Tempel leads them to the overview. Two wide paths wind their way through the forest. People are standing on small disks that move along the paths as if they had wheels. The trees here are not Ash like those in Brooklyn Mall. Lush grass carpets the ground and manicured flower gardens and shrubs add color. Across the way is a stand of cherry trees in full bloom.

"Is this a commonway?" Lazarus asks.

"Aye, this is Asimov Commonway. It extends about three kilometers in that direction and less than a half kilometer in the other." Sam said.

"This isn't the only commonway, is it?" Lazarus asks.

"Not hardly," Tempel said.

"Asimov is only a small loop that services the west end of Lincoln County. Our meeting with Abby is about twenty minutes away. We will take the slidewalk to Central then to Sherwood." Sam said. Following his gaze, "The trees here are Sycamore, Elm, Yew, some Chestnut and a variety of fruit trees."

"Do they also have a Norse legend attached to them?" Lazarus asks.

Sam smiles and said, "Maybe… but if they do, I don't know about it."

Movement attracts his eye and he looks up. Soaring silently far above the treetops at high speed is a long sleek train. When he continues to stare, the parallel lines of its rails come into focus stretching out of sight in both directions. Instead of riding on the rails, this train hangs from them. *Such technology.* Lazarus feels like a Neanderthal trying to make sense of a jumbo jet.

The train is gone an instant later leaving Lazarus to wonder if he imagined it. No… it never made a sound but the rails are still there if he looks hard enough.

"It seems like a lot of resources have gone into making and keeping things pretty. Who pays for all the extras?" Lazarus asks.

"What extras?" Sam asks, puzzled.

"Well… moving people from point A to point B doesn't require forests," he said nodding at the nearest tree, "or cherry trees," shifting his gaze to the colorful pink flowers in the distance. The longer he looks the more distinct the tiny flowers become. He begins to hear the bees buzz among the branches and catch a whiff of cherry blossoms.

Tempel frowns, "Are you saying you prefer staring at a wall whizzing by, or the person's head in front of you, like we see on vids of people riding the New York subway? The increase in size doesn't add much to the cost of excavation and Magi takes care of maintenance."

"Why wouldn't you welcome beauty into your home? Who wants to live in a dungeon?" Sam asks genuinely perplexed. "Luna didn't come with trees and green grass. We make every cubic meter of dirt and nurture every tree, shrub and blade of grass or they wouldn't exist at all."

"There are mechanical scrubbers to clean our air but nothing beats trees for doing the job right," Tempel said. "Biodiversity is very important to us."

"I think I just redefined what I consider extras," Lazarus grins. "You have created something unique and special here. You should be very proud," Lazarus said softly "You don't expect me to travel on this carnival ride do you?"

"Carnival ride? I'm not sure what a carnival ride is but slidewalk's are how we get around. Don't look so worried. If you can stand, then you can use a slidewalk," she points down to a collection of small octagonal disks, each about sixty centimeters across, strewn along the edge of the slidewalk below them. It reminds Lazarus of a disorganized little parking lot off the main highway. "Those are drifters. Just step on one and Magi will do the rest. To move forward, shift your center of mass forward, same with left and right. To move faster, shift more of your balance in the direction you want to go."

"How do you stop?" It's one thing to know how to get it going, but as far as Lazarus is concerned, it's much more important to know how to stop.

"Simply center your mass," Sam said.

"What about rules of the road?"

Sam grins, "Good questions. Traffic obeys the right hand rule. East bound traffic uses the south slidewalk and conversely, west bound uses the north slidewalk."

"How do you move larger goods around?" Lazarus asks.

"There's a network of tunnels below the city for truck convoys. The commonways are for people. Where you're from doesn't have slidewalks?" Sam asks.

"Nothing like this." Lazarus exclaims. "Some of the larger airports and spaceports have moving walkways but not slidewalks." Lazarus shakes his head. "The Federation can't seem to get past the automobile. Everyone still has to have one or two, even after the cost of hydrogen has gone through the roof."

"It angers me to think of America burning all the fossil fuel," Tempel growls. "Do you realize over eighty-five million barrels of crude oil was pumped out of the ground daily? 365 days a year? For almost a hundred years? It was all burned. What could they have been thinking? It wasn't about the future, that's certain. What a bloody waste."

"I personally have never even been inside a petroleum powered vehicle," Lazarus said defensively. "Besides, it wasn't a total waste. It allowed us to build the infrastructure we needed to get to space."

"I've heard the justifications, I just don't buy them." Tempel shot back, "It could have and should have happened much sooner. Too many people were making too much money to stop the burning. What I find particularly loathsome is you build shrines to the idiots who profited from the biggest rape of resources in the history of mankind."

"Politicians build shrines to each other. I didn't have anything to do with it," Lazarus said.

"Of course you didn't, but it was your government," Sam takes some of the sting from her words by patting his arm.

Lazarus looks up at her, "They did what they felt they had to."

"They made money, that's what they felt they had to do." Tempel retorts, "Corporations used that money to buy political power and make even more money while raping the planet. They didn't care that they were causing pain on another life or extinguishing a valuable resource for all time. They BURNED IT. All they cared about was short-term profit. They ran the world into a global meltdown, all because they wanted to make more money."

"Most of that happened before I was even born," Lazarus said.

Sam turns to Tempel, "You cannot blame the one for the sins of the many."

"Why not." Tempel said. "Who else is there to blame?"

"What would you have me do?" Lazarus asks. "I can't fight the Federation. I am but one citizen."

Tempel leans over bringing his face centimeters from Lazarus and looks him in the eyes. After a moment's pause, he said, "You do what you can."

Sam nudges her friend, "That's enough Tempel. It's time to go. We don't want to be late."

He heads towards the nearest down ramp letting his anger boil away. It's unreasonable to blame this one Earthman for the sins of a planet, but some things are easier felt than analyzed.

"Don't let Tempel's passion harm you. He realizes it's not your fault anymore than it's his," Sam takes Lazarus by the arm and follows.

Lazarus lets the young woman lead him down the ramp.

Already at the bottom, Tempel steps on a drifter and slides out about ten meters and circles back. He's angry but now is not the time or place.

Sensing the fear rise in Lazarus as they approach the edge of the slidewalk, Sam pats his arm and said, "Stop worrying. You can ride with me. Magi, pull together a double for us, will you?" Her reward was a grateful smile.

Two of the octagon plates rise off the surface and assemble into a single platform, the common edge almost disappearing. It slides over silently and stops right in front of Sam.

Sam steps confidently onto the arrangement, "Take my hand."

Lazarus obeys, expecting the assembly to wobble as he puts his weight on it. Sam slides her arm inside of his, steadying him until he can get his sense of balance on the moving platform.

"The first time might be a little tricky," she said squeezing his arm in a motherly fashion. "Let Magi control the drifter, you just let her know where you want to go."

Lazarus glances over at Tempel, wondering just how much animosity he will encounter within the Republic. Humanity continues to do many despicable things, preemptive wars, political assassinations, and torture, all in the name of national security or ideology, and he's right, the global environment is in shambles. The melting of the polar ice caps and the subsequent rise in the ocean levels has submerged the homes of a billion people. The terrible increase in storm intensity and massive shifts in climate have led to widespread starvation and food wars. How can he possibly defend such atrocities?

Sam eases them out onto the slidewalk with Tempel bringing up the rear, picking up speed until they are moving along at a leisurely ten kph, about the speed of a brisk run. As Lazarus gains confidence, Sam increases their speed. Magi smoothes out and prevents jerkiness when an arm swings or a head turns. Lazarus begins to enjoy the ride.

"This is exhilarating." Lazarus exclaims. "How fast can we go?"

Sam chuckles, "On a good day with no other traffic around you can achieve about thirty kph."

"If you want to go somewhere fast, take a maglev train. They top out above a hundred." Tempel adds from just behind Lazarus, a spot where he can catch the Earthman if he falls. He may not like it, but Lindsey gave the Earthman hospitality and he will not be the one to dishonor that.

"I can't wait to ride in one." Lazarus said.

As they move along the commonway, Lazarus lets his attention wander among the trees, glad to have the steadying influence of Sam's arm in his. The designers and architects of Aldrin Station knew the value of keeping mystery in the vistas presented to the inhabitants. Moving down the slidewalk, they pass through a variety of environments, each unique. Some are lit up in bright afternoon sunlight, others in the overcast of an impending storm. Some are crowded with hardwood trees while orchards dominate others. Many have roses and other flowering plants set in manicured gardens. Green grass carpets most of the commonway, highlighted with colorful shrubs and plants. A few are polished stone cathedrals devoid of plants and animals, glorious in their simplicity. One section contains strange twisted stonework that surrounds the passing traveler like something out of Dante's Hell.

More than once Lazarus observes squirrels running across the grass or frolicking in the high branches. Bird species from sparrows to macaws flicker about adding to the rich tapestry of the environment. Hummingbirds and beehives are especially plentiful.

"It's beautiful," Lazarus said. "I have never seen so many roses."

Sam nods, remembering something Abby once said, "We should always take the time to smell the roses."

"Very good advice," Lazarus said.

Sam has spent her entire twenty years in and around Aldrin Station and New London. She's at that age where she yearns to see more. She glances at Lazarus with just a touch of envy. At least he had the courage to leave Mother Earth and everything familiar. Did she?

Tempel and Sam maneuver out of the main flow of the slidewalk. The drifters settle to the floor.

"Well done." Sam smiles at Lazarus.

Tempel grunts. After all, Magi deserved praise if anyone did. She had done all the skilled work. This bozo had simply managed not to fall off.

Abigail Dugan

"The feminist agenda is not about equal rights for women.
It is about a socialist, anti-family political movement that
encourages women to leave their husbands, kill their children,
practice witchcraft, destroy capitalism and become lesbians."

Pat Robertson (1930-2011)

They lead Lazarus through a maze of corridors. On Earth, his sense of direction was impeccable. It's useless here in this subterranean labyrinth. He has no chance of retracing his steps even if his life depended on it. Most of his normal visual cues are absent and too many passages look the same. Lazarus is completely dependent on the two young Lunarians and that makes him uneasy.

Finally, they stop before an airlock off a small corridor deep in the heart of Aldrin Station. Tempel passes his left hand in front of the security panel and the heavy door slides open.

Sam smiles encouragement, "Relax, this is just a meeting between two citizens, that's all."

"He's not a citizen yet." Tempel's low opinion of shortimers is common among his age group.

Sam reserves her judgment, sensing something about the Earthman that warrants patience. Besides, she trusts Lindsey and if she thinks Lazarus is worth the trouble, then he must be.

The room is stark, utilitarian, and devoid of right angles. An oil painting of a full Earth hangs on the wall. The blues and browns of his home planet provide the only color in the room.

"You must wear your visor throughout the meeting with Abby. Do you have a problem with that?" Tempel asks watching for even the most subtle rejection. He detects only excitement and possibly a little apprehension.

Lazarus nervously runs his fingers through his hair, "No, of course not," he said. He had forgotten he was wearing one.

Satisfied, Tempel leads the way through the next door.

Three women and a man sit around a long conference table. They arise from their seats to greet Lazarus. One of them looks familiar… it's Lindsey but her beautiful hair is gone. All that's left is short black stubble, not much longer than a week old beard. She gives him a quick wave and smiles encouragement, which he returns nervously.

"Mr. Lazarus Sheffield," Tempel said stepping aside, "This is Doctor Abigail Dugan."

What. This beautiful woman is much too young. She couldn't be forty.

Abby nods in the Lunarian custom, "Greetings, Mr. Sheffield. Welcome to Dakota."

Lazarus nods awkwardly, "Ah… greetings, Dr. Dugan. It's my very great pleasure and honor to meet you. I appreciate you granting me this interview," Lazarus starts shaky but finishes strong.

Abigail Dugan exudes calmness and maturity that transcends her apparent age. Broad full lips and radiant smile enchants Lazarus just as it has many more worldly men than he.

Abby nods then draws his attention to the older woman standing on the other side of the table. She's the personification of a loving grandmother. Her caring brown eyes emanate a gentle kindness so thick he could cut it with a knife. "This is Magi. She's your AI. We assign a Magi to every Lunarian. It's how we put you in the system, so to speak. Don't worry. It's just a formality. Think of it as a Lunarian Social

Security Number. This one's yours."

Lazarus is stunned. Never in his wildest dreams did he think the Lunarians capable of projecting such a splendidly accurate image of someone who never existed, right down to wisps of hair wafting in the breeze and sweat glistening across her forehead.

"I don't understand. Isn't there just one Magi?"

Abby grins, "Do you know what Magi is?"

He looks across the table at Magi. "You just said she's an AI, right? The Federation has AIs. I know what they are. It's a program that imitates a human being."

"Magi is so much more than that."

"Ok… but this Magi right here is mine? Not yours?"

Abby looks amused. "In a way. Every Lunarian has a Magi and now you have yours."

"I didn't know I needed one," Lazarus looks across at Magi, not knowing what to say… "Hi."

Magi smiles, "Greetings young man. I'm sure we'll get along just fine."

"When you need something, ask Magi. She's there to help you," Abby said.

"Does she always look like this? Like someone's grandma?" He asked.

"No, of course not. We find it avoids confusion if she uses a single persona. She can appear to be anyone or anything." Abby motions to Magi, "Do Lindsey."

Magi is gone and Lindsey takes her place. Startled, Lazarus steps back. He turns and stares down the table at the real Lindsey then back at the AI. The only difference is that the Magi/Lindsey still has long black hair.

"That's enough," Abby said.

Magi morphs back in place of Lindsey. Lazarus gasps. The flawless three-dimensional fluidity of the demonstration makes his head spin.

"You will understand why we limit Magi to one persona after you've been here a while. You are free to explore other avenues but we ask that you respect our wishes while we do business." Abby said.

"Yes, of course," Lazarus said. Something bothers him about Magi. Has he met her before? He doesn't have time to dwell on it.

Abby presents the man standing next to her, "This is Aldrin Station's Security Chief, Corso Dugan."

Corso Dugan is ruggedly handsome. His dark skin reveals African heritage but his sharp features are European. Gray eyes burn with an inner fire and there's not a single hair on his head. Wrapped around each earlobe are loops in the shape of a viper eating his tail. Muscles ripple and bulge along his arms, his shoulders, and across his chest, stretching his shirt to the breaking point.

Lazarus guesses him to be in his mid thirties. The oldest son of a ninety-three year old that looks thirty-five. It drives the point home of just how different these people really are. Lazarus keeps a tight grip on his emotions.

"Tell us again, Mr. Sheffield, what brings you to Luna," Corso rumbles, never one to beat around the bush.

With a rush, Lazarus realizes what's going on. This meeting, these people, the entire event must be taking place in cyberspace. Vidcasting would explain everything. He reaches up to remove his visor, stopping just in time. Nonetheless, he relaxes, glancing at Magi as if her image represents proof.

"Corso. Where's your manners." Abby scolds gently. "Let's sit and have some tea. There's always time for tea, isn't there Mr. Sheffield?" she indicates with a flip of her hand which seat he was to take. Abby picks up the steaming teapot and fills two cups, placing each in a matching saucer. Sliding one to a spot in front of Lazarus She asked, "Do you take anything in your tea, Mr. Sheffield?"

"Ah… No… Please, call me Lazarus," he said, flashing back to a little restaurant over on Seventh Street, not far from his office at Homeland Security. It seems a lifetime ago. How did she know he liked tea? How could she serve him tea if this meeting is in cyberspace? Too many questions and not enough answers. His mind swirls.

"Then you must call me Abby," she said. "You don't mind if Lindsey joins us, do you?"

"No, of course not," he said, glancing at Lindsey. None of this makes any sense.

"Good. Let's get started," Abby said.

As everyone settles in, Magi said to Abby, "All those present have been identified and authenticated."

"Thank you Magi," Abby said and turns back to Lazarus, "I understand you're from Phoenix?"

Lazarus looks nervously over at Corso and back at Abby, "Yes. I've lived in Arizona my entire life. I was born and raised in Casa Grande, a suburb of South Phoenix."

"Fascinating," Corso rumbles deep in his throat.

Abby ignores him, "You've recently lost your wife and daughter. Please, let me express sorrow for your loss," she tips her head, never taking her eyes off Lazarus. "I've lost loved ones. Nothing ever fills the void they leave behind."

"Thank you… Abby," Lazarus said.

"Do you have other family?"

"Yes, two brothers and a sister. My mother lives in Portland, takes care of my youngest brother. I was ten when my father died in the line of duty. I think I have some cousins somewhere but I haven't kept track. I haven't seen any of my wife's family since the accident."

"Did your family help you when you lost your wife and daughter?" Abby asks.

Many strange and wonderful things have happened to him since he left Phoenix, but this was verging on the surreal. Lazarus takes a deep breath and continues to tell the truth, "My sister was the only one around and she did what she could, but she has her own family to worry about. My brother was in college and had to stay focused. I managed."

"I see," Abby nods. How typical it is for Earthmen to isolate themselves. It fills her with pride that Lunarian families are so tight. She feels pity for Lazarus and even more for the society that drove him out. What provokes a man to leave everything behind? "As an employee of Homeland Security, you must have attended a church. Did they help you through your grief?"

"Of course, they helped tremendously. I have many dear friends there," Lazarus admits. "They are good and decent people who stand firm in the laws of the land and Christianity."

It sounds mechanical, even to him, but to say otherwise would put these people at risk if the Federation ever managed to get their hands on this conversation. Guilt by association is what the Federal Prosecutor would call it when explaining to a Judge why they placed bugs and other monitoring devices among the members of the congregation. After all, the Freedom of Information act gave everyone the right to know if an individual was a true Christian.

"I'm sure they do," Abby said. "What church is that?"

"The only church is the American Church of the Trinity. I attended a neighborhood gathering. It's just a small group of families that get together to worship." Lazarus said growing alarmed by the nature of her questions. He's toyed with suspects in this manner. It's not reassuring.

Abby smiles and said, "Do they share your lack of faith?"

There it is. Even though he had been expecting it, the question chills him to the bone. Lazarus pauses for a moment gathering his wits about him before responding to the frontal assault. "I cannot speak for anyone but myself. I freely admit to many faults, a lack of faith is but one," Lazarus said stiffly.

"Are you an atheist?" Abby asks.

"Well… maybe I am." To those branded an atheist in the Federation, it meant the end of any hope of a good life. An atheist can't hold a decent job, attend a university, or run for office. If you owned a business, your customers stopped coming. If you went into a business, they could refuse to serve you. Even your family shunned you. Any way you looked at it, the label changed a person's life.

"Just like your father when he first arrived," Abby smiles.

"What do you know about my father?" Lazarus is stunned.

"I met Thom Sheffield in June 2065. He was a good man," Abby said kindly.

"He's here?" Lazarus can't believe his ears.

"Well, no, not exactly. He died in the Hampton Bay collapse in 2066. I knew him for less than a year but it was long enough to learn who he was," Abby said.

Lazarus is dumbfounded. "Why would he come here? I don't believe it."

Corso growls and starts to rise. Abby stops him. "Lazarus, I never lie and I never withhold information relevant to another person which is why I'm telling you about your father. To accuse me of lying is a very serious charge."

Lazarus stares at her wide-eyed then ducks his head in confusion, "Please forgive me," he mumbles.

She lets him stew for a few long seconds, "You're forgiven… Magi, provide Lazarus with the vids of his father's time with us."

"Aye," she replies.

"Did you know about this?" Lazarus asks Lindsey.

She shakes her head, "No."

Lazarus runs his fingers through his hair. It's hard for him to accept. Why would his father abandon him? A lifetime of hero worship teeters on the brink of the abyss. It takes a major effort to keep his mouth shut.

Abby watches Lazarus come to grips with the knowledge. Lindsey was right. There's something unusual about this man. "Between your mother and the Federation, Thom didn't have many options when he defected. He explained his reasons many times. You can relive every moment with him. You don't need to take my word for anything," Abby said.

Lazarus doesn't fully appreciate what Abby's telling him. The records will allow him to witness the events and conversations his father had in a way not found in the Federation, through visor recordings. Ignorance helps him set this aside and concentrate on Abby.

"However, that must wait…" Abby said. "We reviewed the relevant parts of your conversation with Lindsey. What interests us most is the rather large number of missing people. People don't just disappear, especially the followers of Minister bin Aunker and General Arif."

"Let me get this straight, you're afraid of the missing men more than a battlestation?" Lazarus asks.

"The Brotherhood's space fleet is a problem. Under the Treaty, we can't build any ship larger than 5000 tons. A battlestation is over 100,000 tons. Mother Earth has almost four hundred military ships and we have none. Mother Earth has over ten billion citizens and we have a little over a million. These are facts I can't change."

"What about a nuclear bomb?"

"Nothing moves in or around Luna that I don't know about. Uranium or plutonium will show up like a super nova on our sensors long before it's close enough to do any damage." Corso rumbles.

Now is as good a time as any to drop the last piece of supposition on them. "What if they had a way to fool your scanners?" Lazarus asks.

"Energy absorbent materials have been around for at least a century but they're not perfect. There's always some leakage… and even if the Brotherhood has come up with better materials, it will still leave a void in the data. That in and of itself, speaks volumes." Corso's voice is a deep rumble, hypnotic in its smoothness and complete in its certainty.

There's only one way to handle Corso and that's head on. "I'm not talking about EAM's. I'm talking about a shield that will actively portray itself as something other than what it is?"

Corso sits and thinks about that. Better than anyone, he knows how dependant Lunarian security is on the MRI scanners. During war games, fooling the scanners is the one development that consistently defeats the Lunarian defenses. All contingency plans become ineffective. He finally asks, "How could this be so?"

"Five weeks ago, a bomb was set off in an Israeli resort in the Sinai. A hundred and thirty three people died," Lazarus said.

Abby sadly shakes her head.

Corso growls, "What's so unusual? That's been happening since the 1960's and will undoubtedly continue."

"What's different is the bomb had to have passed through several MRI scanners, modern up-to-date equipment, not antiques. I grant you, the evidence is circumstantial, but it's the only explanation left when all others are eliminated." Lazarus said. "Homeland Security thinks it was a practice run for something bigger."

Lazarus believes this as absolute truth. Magi continuously monitors his critical biological and neurological functions making it virtually impossible for him to lie. She makes this data available to anyone. Lazarus is sweating bullets, but he's not lying.

"Magi, what can you tell me about the incident?" Abby asks.

"Sharm el Sheikh is situated on the Southern tip of the Sinai Peninsula with the Red Sea on one side and Mount Sinai on the other. On Saturday September 22, 2092, at four hours and fifty-one minutes after local sunrise, a rocket attack took the lives of one-hundred-thirty-three people; one-hundred-twenty-four Jews, five Egyptians and four Jordanians. A group calling itself the PRC claimed responsibility twenty-six minutes later. Seven minutes after that the Brotherhood denounced it and offered aid," Magi said.

"The rocket story is just cover. Nobody wants the public to get a whiff of the possibility that the scanners can be beaten," Lazarus said.

"The data is unusual," Magi admits. "Many authentications are completely absent and some of the normal reports that would grow out of an investigation are incomplete. There's just enough detail to get by. I agree with Lazarus. This incident report has been altered," Magi said.

"I know it's been altered. I helped alter it." Lazarus said irritably. He's not accustomed to talking to an AI like a person. His distrust runs deep.

"Thank you Magi," Abby said warmly.

"You're most welcome," Magi said.

"Do you have any idea how they're doing it?" Abby asks.

Taking a deep breath, he runs his fingers through his hair. "Logic dictates two things. Just as you pointed out, our scanners would see a void in the data and raise a warning, so it can't simply absorb the spy beam. The shield must actually send back a signal of something normal. We call it active camouflage. Second... even with active camouflage, they must have greatly improved the energy absorbent material, stopping and soaking up virtually 100 percent of the MRI beam. Because if they didn't, it wouldn't matter how many false signals were generated, the MRI would still excite the material they're trying to hide."

"We know about the improved EAM, but a way to transmit a false MRI signal is new." Corso admits.

"Let's revisit Corso's original question. Why are you here Lazarus?" Abby asks.

With sweat beading up on his brow, Lazarus takes a deep breath, never breaking eye contact with Abby. "Every Tuesday for the past three years my team has presented a weekly report to Director Dempsey. We have suspected for over a year that Iran or Afghanistan is hiding a bomb factory... ah... thermonuclear manufacturing facility. We think they're recycling old uranium, probably Russian. A couple months ago, we started getting hints of a mission. About two weeks ago, we came to the conclusion the mission was bringing one or more thermonuclear devices to Luna."

"Is there an answer to the question coming soon?" Corso growls.

Refusing to back down, Lazarus turns to Corso, "I don't believe the Federation will honor the Treaty of Independence. If the Brotherhood has active camouflage and a nuke, then you can be sure the Republic of Luna is in big trouble." Lazarus turns back to Abby. "Heaven help me, I can't stand by and watch hundreds of thousands of innocent people die, even if it means my life."

The room is silent until finally Abby breaks the tension. She calmly, without the slightest tremor, leans forward and picks up her tea, sips it without looking at anyone in particular.

"What would happen if your application for Lunarian citizenship were turned down?" Abby asks.

Staring at her, Lazarus seems to wilt a little. "The Federation would prosecute me for treason," he said.

"They would wipe your memory in one of those Canadian vacation spots." Corso said coldly.

"I'll die before that happens Chief Dugan, one way or the other," Lazarus declares. "My life's in your hands. I can't go back."

Abby looks at Corso who said with a shrug and rumbles, "He's sincere, I'll give him that much. It remains to be seen what value his information really has." Turning back to Lazarus, "Assuming you're right, do you have any other information concerning these nuclear devices? How will they get here? Who will transport them? When will they arrive?"

With a sense of relief Lazarus said, "No, I don't know anything definite. All I can say is the communications intercepted over the last three months paint a very ugly picture. You may think I'm jumping to conclusions using incomplete data but please realize, I've been studying the Brotherhood for many years. Hard data is something collected and analyzed after an incident. Trying to predict what these people will do next is the challenge. I deal with subtleties and suppositions most of the time. Occasionally we capture a talker or get some revealing electronic files, but not often."

"Educated guesswork," Abby said.

"Exactly." Lazarus said. He locks eyes with Corso. He runs his fingers through his hair and continues, "The only thing solid is a possible operational name. We intercepted a message from a confirmed moneyman. Inside was a reference to 'Allah's Cleansing Fire'. Cleansing has meant killing in the past. That's as close to a smoking gun as it gets in my line of work."

Corso raises his eyebrows thoughtfully, his eyes never leaving Lazarus. They too had run across references to Allah's Fire, but the social gulf between Islamic culture and the Lunarians is much wider than between Lazarus and the Brotherhood. Interpretation of data is difficult for Lunarians. They rely on Magi too much.

"Let's see what Jordan and Jamie make of Mr. Sheffield's evidence," Corso rumbles.

Abby nods, "It's not every day that we have a Senior Analyst defect Lazarus. For now, let's get you acquainted with two of our top researchers." Turning to Magi she said, "Get him fitted for a suit and start training ASAP. I don't like having someone not vacuum qualified. Oh… and find something appropriate for Lazarus to wear."

"Aye." Magi said. "He also needs some proper deck shoes."

"Fine. I like the flowered shirt but it makes you stand out," Abby said to Lazarus. "Also, I want you to stay close to Lindsey or Tempel for the next few weeks, just until you're accustomed to Luna. Are you ok with that?"

"Of course," Lazarus is in no position to argue. "I appreciate all you're doing for me," he looks down the table at Lindsey. She smiles.

Magi leans forward in her chair and said to Abby, "Pardon the interruption but Pellegrini said he must speak with you immediately. He's waiting outside with Constance and Weenie."

"Magi. His name is Winthrop, not Weenie." Abby scolds.

"I'll try and remember," Magi said with a noticeable lack of sincerity.

Lazarus has no experience with a sarcastic AI. In his world, he tells AIs what to do and they do it. Magi's different.

"Pellegrini is the Director of Operations at Falconhead and Weenie is his lackey," Tempel said to Lazarus.

"You know he doesn't appreciate that nickname," Abby said.

Tempel chuckles, "Aye... everyone knows."

Abby shakes her head, "Magi, please tell them I will be another moment."

"Aye," Magi said settling back, the seat cushion squeaking as it receives her weight. Lazarus is the only one to notice. There's something familiar about her that he can't seem to remember.

Rising and turning to Lazarus, Abby said, "Please accept the hospitality of the Dakota warren. Tempel will get you settled and show you around. I will expect to see you at dinner tonight."

"Yes, of course. Thank you Abby," Lazarus said rising with her and remembering not to extend his hand, tipping his head in the customary fashion.

"Tempel, introduce Lazarus to Jordan and Jamie. Have them report directly to me." Turning back to Lazarus, Abby said, "Lazarus, words cannot express the amazement I have for your willingness to risk so much for people you don't know. You give us all hope for our brethren on the home world."

"Thank you Abby, for taking the time to see me," Lazarus said, marveling at the unusual shade of her eyes, pale green like rare beryl gemstones. What would she look like without his visor? He hopes this is real and not some cyberspace illusion.

Nodding in return, Abby said, "If you will excuse me. I have another meeting."

"Oh. I almost forgot. Izzy said hello," Lazarus blurts.

Abby's brow furrows, "Izzy? Isaac Crenshaw?" She asked. When Lazarus nods she continues, "Where did you run into him?"

"He was on the shuttle," Lindsey said.

"That old reprobate is still kicking? Last I'd heard, he was out in the asteroids somewhere. He and I spent… time… together back in '24… when Patrick was still alive… Thank you Lazarus," Abby said. "I will review the vid." She nods and walks out the door.

Lindsey comes over to Lazarus, "I've got a lot to do, but I will see you later, if that's ok?"

"Sure." he said. "I'll count on it." He reaches out to touch her and is shocked when his hand goes right through.

Lindsey grins and Sam laughs. Tempel shakes his head at the stupid Earthman. To him, Lazarus is just another shortimer needing special handling. "Come on hero," he said heading for the door. "Let's go find the twins."

Lindsey nods and vanishes.

Having employed virtual reality throughout his career, Lazarus is utterly amazed at the quality of the Lunarian system. His visor can create the image of a person, real or imagined, so accurately that he cannot tell the difference. Before this meeting, Lazarus would have sworn that was impossible, but now he knows better.

"Come on Lazarus. Let's get you settled in." Sam takes his arm and they follow Tempel. "Was Abby what you expected?"

Lazarus shakes his head in wonder, "Not even close. She and Corso look so young," Lazarus observes. "Was that really them or just how they make themselves appear vidcasting?"

"Why can't it be both?" Sam asks.

"How's that possible?" Lazarus retorts. "Abby is ninety-three and her oldest son must be in his sixties or seventies."

"We have gene therapies that eliminate wrinkles and keep skin smooth," Sam said.

"Gene therapies?" Lazarus exclaims. Right now, gene therapy isn't what's on his mind, "Can you show me how to view my father's records?" Lazarus asks.

"Magi, how many summary hours on Thom Sheffield do you have?" Sam asks.

"Seventy-six hours," Magi replies.

"When can I start?" Lazarus asks.

"Later, when you have some free time, Magi can get you started. Don't be in such a hurry," Sam said.

"Magi, are Jordan and Jamie available?" Tempel asks.

"They suggest bringing Lazarus to their lab in a few minutes," Magi said.

"Excellent. That gives us time for a beer at the Commons." Tempel leads them down a long corridor and through another airtight door.

Lazarus is several steps past the threshold before he looks around. Nothing prepared him for this, not the towering cathedral these Lunarians call a mall, nor the underground forest they call a commonway. This room is everything good about a home multiplied a thousand times.

Lazarus can't believe this is a subterranean cavern carved from the heart of a lunar mountain. Richly upholstered furnishings divide the expanse into innumerable sitting areas, some sunken, others raised, each with its own lighting. No two are the same creating a mosaic of shadow and light. Columns are everywhere but do not seem to be in any particular pattern, or if there is one, it escapes Lazarus. Colors jump out at him from an endless assortment of rugs, tapestries, and pictures. Arches define a brightly lit focal point roughly in the center of the vast room. Tempel is already there.

"This is your home?" Lazarus asks.

"This is Dakota Commons," Sam said.

In the distance, Lazarus can see the lower sections of much larger columns. Beyond them, it opens out into a large grassy courtyard with more columns on the far side capped with high arches. He assumes the columns on his side match those he can see. They remind him of the Parthenon model he had handled back in Athens.

The courtyard's lit up like a sunny afternoon. Across the way, beyond the far row of columns, Lazarus can make out a room matching this one. Light and shadow dance in its heart as people move about. Above it is a balcony. Several people stand at its edge looking down. As he stares, his visor magnifies their image and he can hear their voices. He looks away, breaking the link.

Groups of kids loudly chase each other across the grass. Someone is strumming a guitar and singing. Several people are playing pool. Many more are sitting in the comfortable chairs and sofas vidcasting. A man emerges from between two columns on the far side of the courtyard yelling and waving to someone Lazarus cannot see. Children are throwing a Frisbee out on the lawn. Laughter resonates. The Commons is vibrant with life.

Sam smiles and tilts her head inquisitively, watching the amazement wash over his face with each new discovery. "It's funny how we take things for granted until someone new comes along and lets us see through virgin eyes once more."

Lazarus looks at her with a dazed expression, "My awe meter just bent its needle. I've never seen anything like this." The room welcomed him. "I don't know what I was expecting, but certainly not this."

She smiles, "I would like to visit Mother Earth someday." From the way she said it, Lazarus realizes she doesn't actually foresee that happening anytime soon.

Seeming to materialize from nowhere, a large black dog startles

Lazarus. He's glad Sam's between him and the apparition. He's never seen such a dog. It has a long narrow face, floppy ears, and a slender body reminiscent of a Greyhound. The muscles in the dog's shoulders ripple under the silky black hide.

Sam gets down on one knee to greet the dog, vigorously rubbing its chest. "Dueler." the dog lays a heavy wet kiss across her face. She giggles like a little girl.

"What a beautiful animal," Lazarus said.

"Don't say that too loud. Dueler he thinks he's human, and he's definitely a member of the family." Sam looks at Lazarus, "Come over here and let's get you properly acquainted."

Dueler tenses. "It's all right," Sam reassures him. The big dog glances at her and visibly relaxes. He moves forward sticking his nose out to sniff Lazarus. A moment later, Dueler pushes his nose under the Earthman's hand. Introduction complete.

"Good boy." the young woman gives him one last hug around the neck before standing.

"I'm unfamiliar with the breed. What is he?" Lazarus asks.

Puzzled She asked, "What do you mean, breed? What's a breed?"

They resume walking with Dueler between them. Sam lightly caresses the dogs head.

Taken aback, Lazarus thinks for a moment. "Within the canine species there are many breeds. Collie is a breed, shepherds, terriers, hundreds of others. You don't know what a breed is?"

"Oh, I see. A breed shares common features such as hair, color, size and shape. Right?" She asked.

"That's right." Lazarus said.

"We select the characteristics when we create new life. If you want a dog that looks just like your neighbors, that's your choice."

She said it so matter-of-factly that Lazarus has to think about it for a second. "The dog's a tuber?" He instantly regrets his choice of words, letting it slip out from long use within the Federation. Tuber is derogatory slang for any life created using genetic engineering. To a large degree, the word symbolizes the growing hate Earth has for Lunarians.

Lazarus feels ignorance descend upon him like a heavy cloak, "Please, accept my apology. I meant no disrespect," Lazarus speaks anxiously.

Instead of getting angry, Sam's eyes sparkle with amusement. "Please… no need to apologize. Each question is but a step in life's journey… that is how we learn and you obviously have a long path before you," she softens her words with a smile. "To answer your question, we apply the science we must in order to survive. We have eliminated all genetic defects and diseases. Does anyone talk about that?" She asked. To Sam and most of her generation, Lazarus is a backward, almost primitive human being. The care taken in selecting her genes is completely missing in this man. He's a role of evolution's dice with no idea as to the outcome.

"Not in the Federation," he said.

"I didn't think so."

Sam enters the kitchen with Dueler at her side, opens the refrigerator door and withdraws two cold beers. Sam twists open one and hands it to Lazarus.

Motioning for Lazarus to follow, she joins Tempel. Lazarus takes a seat and sips his beer. It's good. He watches Dueler wander out of the kitchen and disappear into the shadows.

"Mind if we join you?" Skylor asks as he and Krystin approach.

"Not at all. Lazarus, this is my brother Skylor and sister Krystin," Tempel introduces. They exchange nods.

"Greetings," Lazarus said, "Very pleased to make your acquaintance."

Skylor sits down next to Sam, and Krystin lays a pile of clothing on the table and takes the seat closest to Lazarus. Skylor is slender but broad shouldered. Tempel could have been his twin. Both of them wear military style clothing more out of convenience than as a fashion statement. Even though Skylor is six years older than Tempel, it's virtually impossible to tell by looking at him.

Krystin is also slender and a few centimeters shorter than Skylor, not as tall as Sam but close. Like Sam, her hair is short, and like Sam, she's quite beautiful. Her body is on display under a t-shirt open at her midriff and a pair of tight shorts.

Are all Lunarian women so strikingly beautiful? Krystin reminds Lazarus of an American Indian princess. Her dark eyes are brash and honest.

It hit him, like most epiphanies. Like Dueler, the parents of these young Lunarians conceived them from a shopping list of characteristics. He envisions them sitting down with the family geneticist deciding what little Johnny was going to look like.

"The clothes are for you Paul Revere," Krystin said looking intently at Lazarus.

"Thanks. Tell me, has everyone seen the vid of my conversation with Lindsey?" Lazarus asks.

"The British are coming. Sorry, the Brotherhood is coming. The Brotherhood is coming. What I want to know is, where's your horse and lantern?" Krystin asks.

Skylor laughs, "Jordan and Jamie certified the vid for inclusion in Public Records five minutes after Lindsey submitted it."

"Who are Jordan and Jamie?" Lazarus asks Sam.

"Jordan and Jamie are network programmers," she said.

"Excuse me, but they prefer AI designers," Krystin insists.

"If there's anyone better at handling software, I've never met them," Tempel said taking another drink.

Krystin heads for the refrigerator. "Who needs another beverage?" she calls over her shoulder. A chorus of "sure" and "I do" follow her to the kitchen.

166

"I thought you would be in with Abby and Pellegrini. I saw him come through here earlier with his two bozos." Skylor said.

"Abby spared me, but I'm sure I'll have to deal with Pellegrini soon enough." Tempel finishes his first beer.

Krystin comes back placing more beers on the stone table. Tempel grabs the nearest one, twisting it open.

Lazarus finishes his first beer in several big gulps and reaches for another. "Is Pellegrini another Dugan?"

"Shit no." Krystin snorts, "What makes you ask that?"

"I just figured Dugan's held all the high profile jobs in the freehold," Lazarus states.

Skylor laughs, "Dakota has over seventeen thousand citizens spread out in fifty seven habitats. The Dugan family is prominent in Dakota politics but the freehold encompasses many families."

"Pellegrini thinks he's going to start a new freehold. He lives in Piper warren and wants to break it free from Dakota, that and Falconhead refinery would make a fine nucleus to build a new freehold around." Krystin said, clearly annoyed with the idea.

"It wouldn't be the first freehold Dakota has spawned," Skylor said.

"I just don't like the mealy mouthed S O B." she said.

"Tony's my supervisor, sis. He's a good engineer and knows how to run the refinery," Tempel wonders how he had gotten into the position of defending the man, especially to his sister. Pellegrini dated her a few years back but dumped her for a younger woman. So… if anyone had an ax to grind, it would be Krystin.

"How do you make a new freehold?" Lazarus asks.

"A proposed new freehold must be laid out and voted on by the parent freehold. Financial restitution must accompany any transfer of habitats and other assets to the new freehold. I think it's similar to corporations divesting or spinning off a new company on Mother Earth." Sam said.

Lazarus nods, taking a drink, wondering how much of today he will remember. So much has happened and it continues to come at him. It's like trying to get a drink from a fire hydrant.

"I don't like the pressure he's putting on you. He wants you out of there but he's too gutless to just come out and say it." Krystin said to Tempel. "And don't try and tell me Pellegrini runs the refinery. He's never there. Constance and Weenie feed him what they want him to know. You solve the major production problems while those yahoos grab the headlines. When is the last time Weenie or Connie had an original thought?" She asked defiantly.

Tempel shakes his head, "That's not the point. Pellegrini deserves respect. He's been in charge of operations for over two years, and helped set up the new refractory purification process." He notices Lazarus looking past his shoulder.

"Greetings everyone," Constance said from the kitchen. She's opening cabinets looking for something. Finding it, she peels open a hi-nutrient cereal bar and takes a bite. Walking over to the table, she nods to Lazarus, "So we meet again."

Recognizing the woman from the mall, Lazarus returns the gesture, "Yes, so it seems," he said.

"You're from Phoenix," she said. "It's such a beautiful city although much too hot for me. I visited a few times mostly in the winter."

In person, Constance looks to be in her late forties with straight mousy brown hair cut shoulder length. She carries a heavy build and is below average height. Her most prominent feature is her nose. She's the first woman Lazarus has seen since his arrival that he would not classify as beautiful. She's not ugly, just plain. Even at his admittedly low level of understanding, Lazarus is instantly sure Constance is not part of the same genetic makeup as the other Lunarians sitting at the table. She's earthborn like him.

"I didn't think you could remember that far back." Kristin snarls at the woman who pointedly ignores her. Not getting a response she continues, "Where are the other two butt nuggets?"

"Is that how your mother taught you to talk?" Constance spit back. "If you must know, Tony and Winthrop are with Abby. They have legitimate concerns about the direction Dakota freehold is going." Looking back at Tempel, "What have you done about the Gravity Separator problem?"

"Come on Connie, you know I have other commitments and can't even start for another week. Pellegrini knew my schedule when he gave me the assignment," Tempel replies defensively.

"Falconhead will end up waiting for your analysis or someone else will have to do it for you." Constance said rather hatefully.

Tempel empathizes with Connie. It's hard for her to understand, but her attitude is getting to be a distraction. "Constance." Tempel said tersely, "If it's that important, why doesn't Pellegrini give it to someone else?"

"Because everyone is already working twenty hours a day. There isn't anybody else." She retorts angrily. "Now the rest of Falconhead must deal with it. But why should you care. You're a Dugan. Nothing touches you."

With a speed only a native Lunarian can achieve, Krystin moves across the room and confronts Constance, their faces only centimeters apart. "You have something against Dugan's?" She asked, the intensity flowing between them like an electric current. "Or maybe you think you can run the freehold better than Abby?"

"Ridiculous." Constance backs away, startled and frightened at the abrupt close encounter. "I don't have to take that from you."

"Fine. Leave. Go back to Alabama or wherever rock you crawled out from under." Kristin keeps her nose close as the smaller woman backpedals.

Fear contorts her face. "Monster." Constance turns and scurries away from this menacing creature.

Krystin watches the retreating figure with disgust.

"You were pretty hard on her," Tempel said.

"Not hard enough." Krystin replies.

"You say Constance came from Alabama? What part? When?" Lazarus asks Krystin.

Krystin shrugs, "I haven't the foggiest idea. Magi, what's her bio?"

"She was born in the village of Blacksher north of Mobile in 2046. Moved to the Atlanta area when she was ten," Magi reports. "Did her training in Atlanta and Massachusetts, she arrived on Luna March 2068 and applied for Dakota citizenship a month later."

"Interesting," Lazarus said looking thoughtfully at the retreating figure.

"Why's that interesting?" Sam asks.

"2068 puts her at the very end of the Exodus, a time when the Federation was actively discouraging citizens from leaving, and a time when agents were sent out to establish deep cover among the emigrants. Most of these undercover operatives turned out to be a bust, becoming just another part of the expansion and never reporting to their controllers. However, a few did and are still in place, their identities kept top secret. Not even the President knows who they are. It's something to keep in mind."

Tempel looks at the Earthman with a touch of disgust, "Such intrigue is unlikely here. You will learn that the Law of Full Disclosure is very hard to beat."

"You moron. I'm not an undercover operative." Constance said.

Lazarus looks surprised and the others laugh. It usually takes a few days for a new arrival to figure out there's no such thing as a private conversation anymore. Back room gossip is a thing of the past.

Lincoln County Hospital

As to those who disbelieve, neither their possessions, nor their children shall avail them at all against the punishment of Allah; and it is they that will be the fuel of the Fire.

Holy Qur'an 3:10

Not far from Dugan warren, located in a lower level of the Aldrin Station Security Administration, are some of the city's laboratory facilities. Their primary mission, as stated on the annual budget, is as a crime lab supporting all police investigations, but that was a smoke screen. The shortimers over in Little America would never tolerate Lunarians investigating or policing them and the extremely low crime rate among the Republic's citizens make this a standing joke among the techs who work in the lab. In reality, the lab is devoted to advanced research and the development of new technology. This lab specializes in Product Delivery Modules. Today, all the interesting toys are out of sight and it looks like an ordinary forensics lab, simple precautions until they learn more about this latest citizen.

Tempel leads Lazarus across the main floor to an office on the lower level. A soft chime sounds as they reach it and the door slides open.

"Come in. Come in." the person inside said, rising to greet them. "Greetings Tempel. This must be Lazarus." The person is wearing a blue shirt and gray pants.

"Greetings Jordan. Yes, this is Lazarus Sheffield," Tempel said. "Lazarus, this is Jordan Dugan."

"Very pleased to meet you," Lazarus returns the nod. He can't tell if Jordan is male or female.

"Greetings Tempel." It was the same voice but from behind.

"Greetings," Tempel said. "Lazarus, this is Jamie Dugan."

Lazarus turns and is confronted with an exact duplicate of the person he'd just met. Only this one's wearing a red shirt. Their voices are husky but not male, their build slender but not female. They could be either. He looks in confusion from one to the other.

They both laugh and say, "Just remember that Jordan is wearing blue," Jamie said. "I'm anxious to hear how you can help us understand what's going on." Jamie takes Lazarus by the arm and guides him towards a workstation in the back of the office.

"What do you make of Lazarus's story?" Tempel asks Jordan.

Looking across the office at Jamie and the stranger, "Rest assured, we're going to check every detail. Twice."

"I find Earthmen hard to understand. Some want to harm us, others, like this one…" Tempel shakes his head in puzzlement, "want to be us."

"Show me a Lunarian who hasn't had the same difficulty and I'll show you a fool. Mother Earth politics make my head spin, far too much intrigue. Enemies turn into friends and back again in the blink of an eye. They lie and exaggerate. No one trusts anyone. Who can make sense of it? Me? Born and raised on Luna? I think not. Abby is the only one I trust to interpret Earthly shenanigans, and she hasn't set foot on it for sixty-five years." Jordan exclaims. "Mark my words, this is a very dangerous position to be in. The Republic needs embassies physically located on Mother Earth. Relying on the business dealings of freeholds as our major political contact is making us easy targets."

"Then please explain how we can do that without breaking the Law of Full Disclosure. The United Nations has forbidden us recording their citizens. They claim it would infringe on their privacy in some way. The truth is their politics and the way they do business would not survive the visibility of Full Disclosure. They refuse to abide by our laws and we will not lower our standards to theirs. So here we are again at the same impasse," Tempel shrugs.

"We deal with it the same way we do business with them, we follow our laws, and they follow theirs with a firewall in between," Jordan said.

"That won't work and you know why," Tempel said.

"It's better than war," Jordan replies.

"What do you propose to do when our ambassador is called to a meeting? Suspend our Law? How can we tell our people to remove their visors and attend a meeting that produces no official record? That's in direct violation of Full Disclosure."

"There must be an answer," Jordan said.

Tempel shakes his head, "Talk to Lindsey. She spent six weeks down there. I can't imagine being without Magi that long... We can't let Mother Earth bring us down to their level. Secrecy is the evildoer's playground and absolute secrecy produces absolute evil."

"On that we agree," Jordan said.

Before the conversation can sink deeper into a subject beaten to death all across the Republic, Jamie catches Jordan's eye and motions to link with them.

"Lazarus seems to think we need to use a keyboard and a mouse to access the data we need," Jamie said.

Jordan raises his eyebrows inquisitively, "But why?" Tuning to Lazarus, "Why not use a simulation?"

"Because the netsite will recognize it's a simulation and not the real deal. The Brotherhood uses out-of-date protocols to hide behind, the older the better. For the last century, old hardware and software has been recycled to poor nations around the world. That has enabled them to construct a sub network inside Earthnet that's virtually invisible to anybody using VR. The protocols make it very secure, unless you know the secret handshake." Lazarus said grinning.

Jamie leaves the room with a determined look.

"Where are we going to get antique hardware that works? We stopped using keyboards and mice long before I was born. I've never even seen one used." Jordan can't believe it.

"What's a mice?" Tempel asks but before anyone can answer him, Jamie rushes back in triumphantly, an old-fashioned wireless keyboard with a built-in track ball.

"Will this do? I don't think we have a mouse," Jamie said, handing the ancient device to Lazarus.

Lazarus takes the plastic contraption and taps a few of the keys, which still seem to function. Turning it over, he looks intently at the faded identification label and makes out a model number, manufacturer, and date.

"2023, yes, I think I can make this work. I'm not accustomed to using a ball but that shouldn't be a major problem. We will need a power source for it. I doubt its batteries are still good."

"Not a problem," Jamie replies. She rummages around in a drawer and pulls out a small piece of equipment with several wires sticking out of it. Placing it on the table, she takes the keyboard from Lazarus and removes a small panel from its bottom. The battery space is empty. She solders the wires from the source to the small tabs inside.

Jordan frowns, "Even if it works, I'm sure we don't have drivers for it."

After looking closely at the label on the bottom of the keyboard, Jamie sets the power source to three volts. "There, that should do it. Magi, are you picking up anything?"

"Yes, at four point eight gigahertz," Magi replies.

"If you will allow me, I can download the drivers we need from the net," Lazarus looks from Jordan then back to Jamie.

The two exchange glances, "Nothing ventured, nothing gained." Jamie said. "Magi, isolate and firewall Lazarus. He's going to introduce some outside software and you're to take maximum precautions."

"Aye." Magi replies.

Sitting in his chair, the virtual workstation appears around him. Lazarus is gaining confidence every time he uses his visor. He arranges the relevant net-address symbols and calls up the netsite.

A 3D image of Jesus hanging on a cross set on top of a hill dominates the front page. The name of the netsite, Calgary Chapel, floats above Jesus in bold letters. Around the image are icons linking to other pages within the site. Lazarus touches the Ichthys icon. Jesus disappears and the page that takes its place contains a listing of names. He scrolls down until he finds the name '*Kenneth Whitaker*' and pulls it over to a clear portion of his desktop. At the instant of release, a 3D image of a middle-aged man appears in its place. His physical identification is alongside. Lazarus drags the man's DNA profile onto his desktop.

A standard DNA fingerprint appears. Lazarus picks one of the bright bars in the seventh column and double clicks on it. Instead of exposing the detailed description of that particular snippet of genetic code, it initiates a program Lazarus had modified several weeks earlier, a thirty-second audio file of a Pepsi jingle dating from the mid 20th century.

"Now we wait." Lazarus said.

Instead of playing the jingle, copies of the file distribute themselves on servers scattered across the Federation where they in turn, make more copies of the jingle sending them to even more servers. This process repeats until the chain has cascaded into hundreds of thousands of servers. At a predetermined point, all the files execute simultaneously, grabbing files at random from each server and sending them to other servers. From within this chaos, one program seeks out the file he needs and downloads it across the 385,000 kilometers of space to Lazarus.

By the time the massive downloading triggers Earthnet watchdogs, it's too late to backtrack any one occurrence to its origin. Their paths cross and re-cross millions of times in a pattern impossible to decipher in any reasonable amount of time. All they can do is stop the runaway process before it consumes more resources. Firefighters designed to combat this style of virus overtake and stop the programs. Within minutes, the attack is contained.

Pulling up the file, Lazarus commands, "Install this."

A pause of a few seconds, "Done" the AI said.

"I can't wait to see what you do for an encore," Jamie said.

Lazarus places the keyboard in his lap and begins typing, much to the amazement of those watching. "Magi, are you picking this up?"

"Aye, the signal's drifting but I can compensate," she said.

"No. Let it drift," Lazarus types in an old-style net address; *ubayd. allah.ibn.abd.allah.com.* He checks it twice for spelling and presses the enter key on the ancient keyboard.

"Ubayd-Allah ibn Abd-Allah was a companion of the prophet Muhammad. He spoke the Hadith of the pen and paper," Magi said. "It's the event that split Islam into Sunni and Shi'a."

A small box with its own input field pops up in the center of the workspace. He uses the trackball to move the tiny arrow to the field and presses the button. A small vertical bar begins blinking inside awaiting keyboard input. Lazarus carefully types, *sura24ayas5157.*

"Sura is the Arabic word for chapter and ayas is verse. Verses 51 through 57 in the Qur'an directs believers to either convert or kill nonbelievers," Magi said.

Thousands of pages of Arabic text overflow his workspace. Like a stack of papers on a table, the one on top is the only one he can see in its entirety.

"Magi, be a dear and translate for us?" Jamie asked.

"Certainly," she said.

To the utter amazement of Lazarus, word by word, the Arabic flips to English. This feat took his entire team, and their computers, several hours of hard work to accomplish.

"These are electronic communications generated within the Brotherhood's Ministry of Defense. The Federation isn't as efficient as Magi in translating so we've read only about ten percent of these, but it's enough to worry a lot of folks," Lazarus said.

"Pull up another," Jamie requests.

A second page of Arabic takes its place and Magi translates.

Jamie stares at the text for a second, absorbing the information it contains. "Magi, translate all of these and record," she directs.

"Aye," Magi replies.

"There are hundreds of thousands of documents here…" Lazarus warns.

One after another, Magi loads and translates the information. The process speeds up until it's a blur, giving Lazarus no opportunity to see a finished document before the next arrives.

Jamie monitors the progress, letting the information flow into her head without taking time for an in-depth analysis on her part. That will come later.

Lazarus looks at Jamie and realizes something strange is happening. It's as if she's reading the memos flashing by. *But that's impossible.*

Magi's incoming chime sounds softly in Tempel's ear and she said, "Pellegrini has asked if you can be spared. It seems he needs you at Falconhead."

Tempel turns away in disgust, "Abby and Corso ordered me to bring Lazarus to the lab and stay with him until Lindsey was back."

"I can do it," Jordan offers.

"Thanks Jordan," Tempel said. "Lazarus?" The Earthman looks up. "I need to go but Jamie and Jordan will take care of anything you might need."

"Yes, ok," Lazarus mumbles, much more interested in Jamie.

Jamie is sitting forward on the edge of her seat, eyes locked on the display. Tempel is genuinely astonished the Earthman commands such attention from his cousin. Live and learn.

ЯL

Lincoln County Hospital is one of the premiere facilities in Luna's continuing quest to improve medical science. It's also the birthplace of biotronics and home to Lunarian genetics and reconstitutional science. Constructed in 2024, before disrupter technology revolutionized excavations, it's one of Aldrin Station's first habitats. Some of its chambers still exhibit mechanical tool marks, left to remind Lunarians of their heritage.

Dr Haslett doesn't think anything amiss when he first notices the heavy gray case. Nothing about it stands out among the many crates and containers making up the shipment containing his Quantum Probe Microscope. Having waited impatiently for the scope for over a year, he's personally supervising each step in its unpacking and assembly. It's Japan's latest technology and cost a small fortune to buy and ship to Luna.

Maria Chapman has been Dr. Haslett's grad student for the last six months and is the only one among his staff he trusts to help him. She's almost as excited as he is about getting her hands on this magnificent machine. It has the ability to not only see an atom but focus on its nucleus. The two of them have been working steadily on the assembly for over four hours, and now, with the end in sight, they're anxious to get it finished. Picking up the touch panel, Maria stifles a yawn as she triggers the next step in the process.

Similar to other high-value crates in the shipment, this last one has an electronic lock. She's to enter a nine-digit code into the small keypad on the side of the case.

Maria kneels down in front of the case and enters in the first three digits just as Dr. Haslett torques down the final screw on the hood installation. He walks over to stand behind her. "What's this?" He asked.

178

"Quark detector," she said, entering the next three digits.

Dr. Haslett frowns, mentally tired and slow from the long assembly session, "This looks too big to be a detector."

Maria keys in the last three digits the same instant that Dr. Haslett said, "Stop."

The enormous release of energy vaporizes the laboratory. The thick walls contain the energy for the briefest fraction of a second before they too atomize. For many levels above and below, the energy destroys everything it touches. Expansion robs it of power and the thick stone floors that separate the different levels begin to hold the blast between them, focusing the energy horizontally. The blast pulverizes the corridors, rooms, and laboratories that lie between. Robbed of their support, many of the floors collapse crushing any that have managed to survive up to this point.

Seconds after it began, the beast spends itself in a thick cloud of dust that permeates the hospital and the surrounding city.

Airtight doors close in emergency lock down as Magi moves to contain the damage. Network communications fail cutting the AI off from the hospital.

ЯL

Magi exclaims sharply on all channels, "***Noooo.***"

At the same instant, the floor shakes violently and the air inside the lab reverberates with a heavy deep thump. Jamie jumps from her chair.

"What was that?" Jordan exclaims.

"There's been an explosion inside Lincoln County Hospital," Magi said.

Tempel's insides twist, "Explosion. What kind of explosion." he demands, fearing the worst even as he turns to look at Lazarus.

"Unknown, but it was big," Magi said.

Lazarus stares back blankly, his brain trying to get a handle on this turn of events. "Nuclear?" He asks.

"Negative. At least I am not picking up any radiation around the blast area," Magi said. "I'm not getting anything from the hospital itself."

"Attention. Emergency Response teams ER4 through ER16, report to Lincoln County Hospital. Everyone else sit tight. Stay off the net until further notice." Corso broadcast. His voice echoes from every corner of Aldrin Station for the benefit of those few not wearing visors.

Tempel links with Captain Osaka just in time to hear him say, "The highest priority is getting everybody out of the hospital safely. To do that, we'll need to know how badly damaged the habitat is. I'll lead a team in to mag the south periphery wall. Lieutenant Dugan," looking right at Tempel, "can lead the other team north. It shouldn't take more than thirty minutes to get a preliminary evaluation."

"Do it," Corso said. "We're already getting reports of massive damage, so take all appropriate precautions. We don't need more casualties."

"Aye." Keeping his eyes on Tempel, Kitajima said, "You're at the lab. Good. Grab two magnetometers from the storage room, ER packs, and whatever climbing gear you can find." Kitajima continues. "Magi, round up Quan Kiai and have them report outside the hospital."

"Aye." Magi said.

Tempel crosses the labs main floor heading for the storage room next to the big liquid helium Dewar. The magnetometers are on a broad shelf just inside the storeroom. He deposits them on a workbench outside. Returning, he rummages around in a metal locker, emerging with hard hats, climbing harness, and several ER packs. A little more effort nets Low Light Level flood lamps that clip onto the hard hats They cast a broader and less intense beam of light for use with the L3 sensors in their visors.

"Magi, where is the hemp rope kept?" Tempel asks.

"In the bottom cabinet to your left," she replies.

Tempel retrieves several coils of the strong rope, adding a bundle of carabiners and several ratcheting come-a-longs. Emerging from the storeroom, he finds Lazarus waiting by equipment.

"I understand you're headed for the hospital. I want to help. I'm no doctor but I do have emergency medical training."

Tempel tosses the Earthman a hard hat, "Looks like you've been promoted to field officer," Tempel said.

Lazarus feels a rush of adrenalin surge through his body like an electric shock. He expected Tempel to refuse him and was prepared to argue. Lunarians are full of surprises.

Jamie rolls up in a small electric cart, its cargo bed piled high with strap-on air tanks, enough for the entire platoon. They add Tempel's collection of gear to the load.

Lazarus climbs into the passenger seat. "Where are you going?" Jamie asks.

"He's with me," Tempel replies.

Jamie looks skeptical but remains quiet.

Tempel, with Lazarus beside him, drives away. It's been less than five minutes since the explosion.

Kitajima designated a location outside the hospital zone for the platoon's muster point to avoid the growing number of emergency vehicles coming and going. Tempel and Lazarus pull up and stop alongside the captain.

"What's he doing with you?" Kitajima growls when he sees Lazarus.

"Abby wanted him to stay with me. Besides, he said he has emergency medical training and we can use his help," Tempel replies.

"We don't have time to coddle a shortimer," Kitajima said.

"I don't need coddling," Lazarus said.

Kitajima gives him a long hard stare as several more members of Quan Kiai arrive. He turns back to Tempel, "Fine, but you're responsible for him."

Within ten minutes of the explosion, all but two members of Quan Kiai have gathered around the carts. Several look inquisitively at Lazarus as he passes the air tanks out. They strap on the tanks, leaving the breathing masks hanging by their flow tubes over their shoulders. A second mask clips to their belts. Lazarus looks at it puzzled.

"In case you need to share your O2," Tempel explains showing him how to use it.

After distributing the equipment, they all link with Kitajima. The captain pulls up a graphic display of Lincoln County Hospital. The hospital consists of two large habitats with fourteen entrances, including a maglev train station in nearby Sherwood Commonway. Hospitals should be centrally located and accessible, and Lincoln County is no exception.

Kitajima points at a glowing dot near the center of the habitat's north wing, "From all indications the bomb was here. Magi run the simulation."

"Aye," she said.

The blue lines of the habitat turn red as the blast consumes everything above and below it. Shock waves radiate outward weakening the habitats internal supports. Floors pancake downward. Even in the light lunar gravity, the weight of the collapsing structure is enormous, crushing everything.

No one speaks for a few seconds after the simulation finishes. Kitajima sighs, "Tempel, I want you to go through Central and descend the north ramp. Take it down four levels and proceed to the north periphery wall if you can. We need fracture data on the lower quadrant before we dare go any deeper. Got it?" Kitajima adds lines to the simulation that illustrate his instructions. His calmness reassures the men and women around him.

"Aye," Tempel said.

"The closer you get to the epicenter, the worse communications will get. We don't have any portable relays and I'm not waiting for them, so you guys will have to wing it without Magi," Kitajima explains. "You ok with that Tempel?" he looks intently at the young man looking for the slightest hesitation.

"No problem."

"Good." Kitajima said, "Magi, keep an eye on them and let me know when they're done. I want that mag data ASAP."

"Aye," she said.

"Is he coming with us?" Brice asks nodding at Lazarus.

"He's with me," Tempel said. "Anymore questions?"

Brice shrugs. He knows that tone.

"Let's roll." Kitajima leads the way.

Smaller than a commonway, Commonwealth Avenue looks more like an inner city neighborhood back on Mother Earth than a subterranean passage. Two and three story buildings line both sides of the street. Shops dominate the ground floor and residences the uppers.

Moving rapidly, Quan Kiai joins with the people converging on the hospital.

Commonwealth Avenue outside the hospital's entrance is organized pandemonium. It's become the outer triage for those able to walk out of the hospital. Blood and bandages are everywhere. ER personnel move among the victims trying to ease their suffering. Rivulets of blood make the stone floor slippery. The voices of the medics intertwine with the victim's moans in a strangely muted soundtrack to the horror. A loud cry of a child for its mother rips the quiet desperation.

Quan Kiai enters the hospital through a corridor that opens into a large central hall where the inner triage is still being set up. Dust is everywhere, making it hard to see the people moving about caring for the wounded. Without power, the only light comes from portables the rescuers have brought. Some lights remain stable. Others dart about sending shadows dancing across walls and ceiling. It's an eerie scene.

Kitajima approaches an officer directing traffic near the center of the chaos and asks, "Marty, what can you tell me?"

The figure turns and said, "Kitajima. I've been expecting you. It's bad down there and I don't have much faith the integrity will hold. The dust is thick as mud, so be damn sure your people have plenty of air."

Kitajima nods and asks, "Have you gotten everybody out?"

"Are you kidding? We're just getting started. The only ones who are out are those who could walk out. We haven't even started searching the lower floors. Below level eight, the bomb shredded the water and electricity so it's wet down there. Be careful what you touch. The electricity might still be hot in places," Marty said.

"There are portable transponders on the way so we should have emergency communications very soon." Kitajima said, "I would appreciate it if you could personally see they are deployed and fresh air tanks sent down. We have air for only an hour."

Marty nods, "Sure, you can count on it Kitajima." Marty said.

Kitajima turns and speaks to his platoon, "Listen up. I want everyone to switch to L3 sensors augmented by infrared," he orders.

Tempel notices that Lazarus is having problems. He links visors with the Earthman, showing him where his sensor controls are and adjusting them to his liking.

Lazarus is grateful for the help. The world inside the hospital transforms from a shadowy dust-filled vision into a strangely vivid monochromatic image unlike anything Lazarus has ever seen.

"This is where we part company. Make some good luck." Kitajima said.

"You do the same." Tempel said watching Kitajima and his squad disappear towards the south ramp.

Tempel leads them across the hall towards the north ramp. Lined up along one wall are a number of draped bodies, those people beyond medical help.

"Magi, can you access the hospitals network?" Tempel said.

"Negative, this habitat is completely down. At this point, I'm receiving only your audio signal," she informs him. "And even that is weak."

The mineralized rock of Rim Mountain dampens energy. It doesn't take many twists and turns within a Luna habitat to render long-range communications virtually useless.

"Great." Marcel exclaims, a touch of nervousness in his voice.

"Relax and keep your eyes open. We'll be fine," Zoey said patting her comrade on the shoulder.

Entering the ramp, their lamps flood the enclosed space casting long shadows on the walls. They descend three levels uneventfully. The first sign of damage is a section of wall collapsed across their path. They climb over the debris trying not to add more dust to the air around them. It's unnaturally quiet. The only sounds are their own muffled footfalls and the occasional grunt.

Stopping before a partially open airlock, "I think this is the right level," Tempel said. His voice is loud and harsh after the silence.

"The panel should tell us," Corazon mumbles. Getting down on one knee, he wipes the dust off and reads, "A310 South."

"That's it," Magi sounds grainy and distant. They were losing her as they move down the ramp. "Kitajima wants the outside wall magged first. We need as much information concerning the surrounding rock as possible."

Tempel wedges into the half open door and pushes hard with no result. Karl comes to help and the two of them combine their muscle. The door moves a few centimeters then stops.

"That's far enough," Tempel steps into the dark hallway. His hardhat is the only illumination. Dust hangs motionless limiting visibility even further. Chunks of stone litter the corridor floor. This had been the main access for this floor. The wall opposite the ramp is broken and open to blackness. His lamp reaches only a short way down what remains of the hallway before encountering a large pile of debris. Closer, he can make out tracks in the thick layer of dust. He wonders if they are from a rescuer or a victim.

In the blurry outer reaches of visibility, something moves. "We have someone," Tempel said. He heads towards the person who sinks to the floor before he gets there.

"Save my baby. Please save my little boy." the voice is definitely female.

Zoey follows and kneels beside the figure. "Take it easy. We're here to help."

"Magi, get someone down here with a litter." Tempel commands, routing his transmission through Marcel still on the ramp.

"Sorry. All crews are busy in the levels above you. They can't break anyone free for at least ten minutes," Magi said.

Tempel can barely hear her even with Marcel's help. Once they move away from the ramp, they'll lose communication with Magi.

Lazarus slides the ER pack off his shoulder and squeezes through the opening pulling it behind him. Moving up, he sets the pack beside the woman, retrieves a sterile wipe from its pocket, kneels and clears away the worst of the dust and blood from around her eyes.

"Where's my baby." she cries weakly.

Opening an inner pouch, Lazarus gets the med bracelet and snaps it on her wrist, adjusting it to fit snuggly. Turning back to the pack, he looks for a screen. Then, to his amazement, the woman's vital signs appear in his visor. It doesn't take him long to decide this is much better than comparable Federation medical equipment using screens and flat panel displays. "Low blood pressure, barely conscious, shallow breathing. She's suffering from shock. She needs immediate medical treatment." Lazarus removes the secondary mask from his belt and puts it on the woman.

"Can she be moved?" Karl asks.

"I didn't find any serious external wounds but she could have internal damage or a head injury," Lazarus said.

"Then I will carry her out of here," Karl said.

Tempel nods, "Do it then get back here ASAP. Marcel, I want you to stay in the ramp to relay messages to Magi."

"Aye," Marcel said.

Lazarus removes the bracelet and returns it to the pack. Karl replaces Lazarus's mask with his own secondary. Lazarus helps Marcel and Karl get the stricken woman through the jammed airlock door and into the ramp.

"My baby," she moans as Karl cradles her in his arms.

"We will find him," Lazarus said.

Lazarus hesitates watching the young man disappear, his light casting eerie shadows on the curved walls of the ramp.

"You shouldn't promise what you can't deliver," Marcel said.

Lazarus looks at him, "One way or the other, we'll find him." He slings the ER pack onto his back. Tempel and the others have already gone. He can faintly see the infrared glow of their bodies down the corridor and moves to catch up. It tests his meager but growing abilities to navigate in the lunar environment. He feels a touch of pride that he can do it at all. It reminds him of something his dad had told him long ago; *if you want to teach someone how to swim, toss them into the deep end.*

The dust hangs thick, making him thankful for the air on his back. Shadows play tricks on his mind. No one speaks and the only sounds are muffled footfalls and breathing.

As they move further away from the ramp, what remains of the wall disappears entirely and the void eats into the floor until they are walking on a ledge less than thirty centimeters wide. The stone is cut clean, as if a giant surgeon had removed the heart of the habitat. The Lunarians move across the narrow span and stop, looking back at Lazarus.

"Come on, let's go," Tempel said.

Lazarus puts his back to the wall, grits his teeth, and shuffles sideways, trying not to think about it. He can hear a rumble of settling debris from below. Glancing out into the void, his visors L3 sensors can't penetrate the dust and distance. All he sees is a swirling gray-green mass. Lower down, small flashes cut through the fog like fireflies on a foggy night.

He's only about half way across when they hear the moaning. It's almost directly below him. The others lights dart across the debris, searching. A massive piece of rock, probably the floor of the corridor, is slumped against the wall. Perched upon it is the head of a child. The rest of the body is invisible, perfectly camouflaged by a thick layer of dust. The eyes staring back at him are alive.

"Tempel, I see someone. A child," Lazarus said.

"Can you deal with it? My job is to mag this habitat. If it goes we all die." Tempel said.

"Go do what you must do. I'm taking this child to a doctor."

"I won't be long," Tempel said.

"Neither will I," Lazarus replies.

"Zoey, make sure he doesn't kill himself," Tempel said. "Corazon, you're with me." The two men head down the corridor.

"There's a slab about twenty meters back where you can climb down," Zoey said as she sits on the floor dangling her legs off the edge. "I will guide you from here."

"Ok," Lazarus said.

A moment later, she said, "Right below you."

The slab is a section of floor. It's very steep. Laying the ER pack aside, Lazarus starts down backwards, digging his toes into the smooth surface, expecting to slip and fall any second, but to his surprise, his new shoes grip the stone and he's able to descend without any problems.

The dust is thick at the bottom. It rises with each footfall behaving more like a liquid than a solid. The pile is unstable, ready to slide further into the pit at the slightest provocation.

Lazarus precariously crosses the distance and picks up the little broken body. Cradling the child in his arms, Lazarus looks down. There is a chunk of stone sticking out of its head and one arm is shattered and crushed, bent in far too many places. Yet the child's eyes stare at him from behind the mask of dirt and grime with burning intensity, not letting go of life without a fight.

Lazarus scrambles back across the debris towards the makeshift ramp, the child almost weightless in his arms. He's careful to support the head, cupping it with his right hand while immobilizing the broken arm between their bodies. He steadies himself with one hand and climbs upward.

"I got you," Zoey said reaching down to help him up. Together they retreat the way they'd come. "Marcel, call ahead and let Magi know Lazarus is coming up with a child."

"Aye," he said.

With help from Marcel and Zoey, Lazarus manages to squeeze through the jammed door without disturbing his young passenger.

It seems to take forever to retrace his steps back up the ramp. "You have only a few more meters to go," Magi informs him.

Emerging from the ramp Lazarus pauses and looks around. The chaos of a major triage is nearly complete. Cries of pain echo strangely in the shadowy chamber.

Magi is beside him, "Please follow me," she said and leads him through the mayhem. They pass people with missing arms and legs, blood is everywhere, some cry out in pain and despair. Others sit in shock not uttering a sound.

Lazarus stumbles and would have fallen if not for a man stepping forward, using his body and one good arm to catch him.

"Steady lad" the man said.

Lazarus looks at him and sees a bloody stump where his other arm should be. The two stare at each other for a moment.

"Lazarus please, you must hurry," Magi said.

"Go," the man pushes him in Magi's direction.

She leads him to an enclosed ER vehicle, the rear doors wide open. Two people are laying side-by-side inside. Several more sit in the forward section wearing dazed expressions and bloody bandages. A woman is under a blood soaked sheet apparently unconscious. Beside her is a man. He looks up at Lazarus.

"Give me the child," he said holding one arm out.

Lazarus lays the broken body on the man's chest, rolling it over gently, cradling it in the valley between the two people. The woman moans and looks down at the child, then up at Lazarus.

"You found my baby," she said.

"Step back," Magi said to Lazarus.

Obeying, Lazarus watches the ER pull away, the rear doors shutting as it gains speed. He stands motionless until it disappears down the corridor towards Commonwealth Avenue.

"Lazarus, are you able to continue?" Magi asks.

He turns back, facing the horror.

"Yes… I'm fine," Lazarus said and starts back the way he had come. He couldn't care less about lying at that moment.

ЯL

Tempel calls out, "Marcel? Can you hear me?"

"Aye," he replies.

"Stand by…" Routing through Marcel's visor Tempel calls, "Magi?"

"Yes Tempel," Magi sounds far away.

"I'm downloading the data." Tempel places the magnetometer on the floor and kneels down in front of it, keying the control panel.

190

A few moments later, "Transmission successful. I'm starting the analysis."

Tempel can see the lights of the others as he and Corazon approach the ramp. They squirm through the opening just as they hear the sounds of someone coming down.

"Welcome back Lazarus," Tempel said.

"What do we do now?" Marcel asks.

"Isn't that obvious? We go down and begin rescue operations," Zoey said matter-of-factly.

Marcel gives a nervous laugh, "Zoey, are you nuts?" He looks at her then at Tempel. "It's too dangerous. Let's wait until Magi clears the hab."

"I will not complete the safety analysis for another thirteen minutes," Magi said.

"We've already waited too long. If anybody is alive down there we need to get them out now," Zoey retorts. "It really doesn't matter what shape the hab is in. Someone will need to go down there and get them out."

"She's right," Tempel said, noticing Lazarus nodding in agreement. "Kitajima has the data he needs to determine the risk to a large scale rescue. We, on the other hand, are already here. Let's move down the ramp and see what we find." Tempel looks at each in turn, receiving approval from everyone, including Marcel.

"Why not lash a rope to me and I'll explore the ramp below us? That way if it collapses you have a chance of pulling me back up," Lazarus suggests.

"Or at least finding you under the rubble," Marcel said.

"Not you, me," Tempel said ignoring Marcel.

"It's my idea. Let me do it," Lazarus retorts. He's the oldest and stuck in the assumption that it means something.

Tempel simply shakes his head, unwilling to give this shortimer that responsibility. Besides, he knows this building like the back of his hand, as if this knowledge does him any good with the hospital in such a state of ruin.

"From the frying pan into the fire," Lazarus mutters, hoping this brash young Lunarian can handle the assignment.

"What was that?" Zoey asks with a frown. She doesn't think it appropriate for this shortimer to question her Lieutenant and is fully prepared to take him down a notch.

"He said, from the frying pan into the fire," Tempel repeats unnecessarily. "Magi, inform Kitajima we're doing reconnaissance down the north ramp."

"Aye. He knows. His team is already moving down the south ramp. It appears to be intact all the way down but they are magging it thoroughly. Perhaps you should as well."

"Negative. These cracks make that a waste of time." Tempel said.

"Please be careful Tempel. I don't want to report your death to Abby and Liz," Magi pleads.

"I will not take any unnecessary risks, I assure you," Tempel said. Looking at Karl, he said, "Set up an anchor here. If short range communications break down, I will tug three times when I need you to pull the line up and two times for some slack."

"Aye," Karl nods and gruffly adds "I'm with Magi, don't do anything crazy down there." He's comfortable with his role. This is not the first time he's anchored a rope for his comrades and he sets to work.

Karl drives a lost arrow into a large crack in the wall. The tight space inside the ramp rings with each hammer blow, the pitch rising as the metal spike runs home. Clipping a carabiner to it, he ties Tempel's rope using a Munter hitch. Taking up the slack, Karl gives the belay an experimental tug and nods at Tempel.

Tempel steps into a climbing harness and attaches the rope. He nods and starts down the ramp, picking his path carefully. The ramps outer wall is gone below level four, a vast darkness taking its place. Dust is thick, limiting visibility. The inner core of the ramp is the only thing holding the floor, a cantilevered corkscrew extending downward.

Tempel moves down until confronted with empty space where the floor should be. "Hold," he yells.

"Aye, holding," Karl said from above.

"The ramp is gone about thirty meters below you," Tempel reports.

Lazarus looks at his companions and involuntarily his body trembles as a cold shiver runs down his spine and goose bumps roughen his arm. He's never felt so alive.

Tempel gets down on his belly and worms forward until he can see over the edge, acutely aware of the vibrations he's creating. The single light source in his hard hat weakly illuminates the void forcing him to maximize the sensitivity in his visor's L3 sensors in order to see the jumbled mess less than thirty meters below. The stone that had been the hospital's walls and floors is heaped in broken piles, furniture and equipment lay upon them in a chaotic tangle as far as he can see. Dust covers everything creating a sameness of color that goes beyond the monochromatic image presented by his visor.

"Can anyone hear me?" Tempel calls out loudly. Maximizing his visor's audio inputs, he pulls his air mask away from his mouth and shouts, "Hey. Can anyone hear me?"

He is instantly aware of the smell and replaces his mask. With the gain turned up to maximum, his own heart beat and other bodily functions are filtered out letting him hear the slightest sound from below. Otherwise motionless, he slowly turns his head straining for the faintest whisper, hearing the tap… tap… tap… of unknown fluids dripping into puddles, the rustle of a small avalanche as the debris settles, and the distant thump of something larger falling. Then he hears it. A faint moan floats up from somewhere down in that dusty grave.

"Magi." Tempel said.

"Yes," her signal strength is very weak.

"I'm looking at the remains of the bottom levels. Floors and walls have collapsed. The ramp ends at level five and I'm approximately thirty meters over the rubble. But I heard someone. We are initiating rescue operations. Please inform Kitajima," Tempel said.

"Tempel, I think you should wait," Magi said.

Lazarus can hardly believe his ears. AI's do not argue with humans where he comes from.

"No, we can't wait any longer. Those people need our help right now," Tempel said.

"I agree, we need to get them out or this will turn into a recovery operation real quick," Zoey adds.

"Do it," Kitajima said, "I will send people as soon as Magi gets finished with the safety analysis. Right now, you are free to proceed as you see fit."

"Thanks Kitajima," Tempel said, "I'll be going down."

Taking his spare lamp, Tempel attaches it to the bottom of the broken ramp, a beacon in the dark. Replaying the few seconds of sound, he determines its approximate location below him. Adjusting the sensitivity in his visor's infrared sensors, the debris field below him takes on a mottled greenish glow with regions of intensity that varies from point to point. His eyes seek a human shape in the midst of the chaos, finding several possibilities.

He retreats, worming back from the edge and moving up the ramp as fast as he dares.

"I'm going with you," Corazon said as Tempel reaches them.

"The more people searching the faster it will go," Lazarus adds. The Earthman's intentions are clear. He's going as well.

"Fine." Tempel doesn't have time to argue. He removes the climbing harness and picks up an ER pack, handing it to Lazarus. He slings the pack next to it onto his own back. Corazon hoists a third pack. Tempel turns to Karl, "I will set up a second belay close to the edge. Let's keep things simple."

"Aye." Karl nods.

Turning to Marcel and Zoey, Tempel said, "The ramp is in bad shape but I think it will hold. You two will need to get the survivors to safety. Can you do that?" Tempel asks looking hard at Marcel.

"Of course." Zoey said.

Marcel nods.

"Good." Tempel slaps Marcel on the shoulder causing a cloud of dust to billow from his clothes. Ducking away from it, Tempel continues, "Always have a rope tied around you, just in case the ramp collapses." Marcel's eyes grow wide but he nods again.

"Zoey, make sure he doesn't forget. You either." Tempel said.

"Take some of your own advice. Liz would kill me if anything happened to you. You too Corazon." Zoey said.

"We can handle this," Tempel said before leading the way back down the ramp. They stop a safe distance from the drop off.

Tempel drives another lost arrow into a crack in the wall, attaches a carabiner to it, and ties off a second rope. Worming forward once again, he swings his legs off the edge and looks down into the void.

Leaning out, he can make out the rubble thirty meters below. He lets himself drop over the edge, easily descending hand over hand, even with the weight of the ER pack.

Tempel anchors the rope as Corazon and Lazarus descend.

"Oh my God." Lazarus exclaims, his adrenaline pumping from the climb down. For a distance of perhaps thirty meters, he can see good detail. Beyond that, the image succumbs to the dust.

Tempel leads, "Come on, this way."

Lazarus follows, cautiously making his way across the mangled remains of the hospital. Only the rattle of settling rubble and the occasional gasp of breath as they scramble through the ruined habitat break the deathly stillness.

Tempel and Corazon begin digging frantically, pulling stones and a broken chair from the wreckage. Lazarus reaches them just as they clear enough away to see the victim, legs pinned under a block of stone. Body shape identifies the victim as female but dust and grime create a uniform grayness making it impossible to tell anything else.

Her visor is gone but her eyes are open and confused. Tears streak her gray dust-covered face.

Lazarus removes the ER pack and sets it beside her while Corazon continues to pull debris off the pile. Tempel motions for Corazon to step back. He sets his feet and lifts the thick stone that pins her down, managing only a few millimeters but it's enough. Corazon and Lazarus quickly, but gently, slide the victim out.

"Don't say anything," Lazarus tells her when she tries to speak, a trickle of fresh blood runs from the corner of her mouth. He slides the med bracelet over her left wrist. Information begins to flow to their visors. She's suffering from multiple fractures to both legs, a punctured lung and shock. Lazarus stabilizes her while Tempel finds a stainless steel tabletop. They gently place the woman on the makeshift stretcher and move her below the ramp.

"Marcel." Tempel calls up. Light beams jump around erratically, silhouetting the ramp above them.

"Yo." Is the immediate response. "I rigged a pulley. Should make it easier getting people out."

"Good boy." Lazarus mutters.

"You and Zoey will need to carry her out and get back here ASAP," Tempel yells upward.

"Aye. We're ready." Zoey yells down.

After securing the woman to the tabletop with lengths of rope, they watch as Karl hoists her upward, the makeshift stretcher rotating as it rises. Hanging dust reflects Marcel's light slashing through this dark place as he swings the woman to safety.

The men work steadily, finding two more people in the space of thirty minutes, both alive but badly injured. Soon, other rescuers begin arriving. Tempel sends word up that they could use dogs in the search. Dueler and several others show up sometime later. Portable network relays are deployed putting everyone back on line and giving Magi a view of the devastation. More and more equipment descends into the hole to look for survivors and collect data. They must soon answer the question of long-term habitat stability, a very practical question when living on an airless world.

Lazarus strains his medical training to the breaking point. He's soon lost count of the number of tourniquets he applied. One person had both legs crushed beyond saving; another had her arm sheared off above the elbow. Many hours later, Lazarus finds the cluster of preschool children. They had been on a field trip to the hospital. Now their little bodies are shattered beyond any semblance of humanity. He sobs uncontrollably as he puts the tiny remains into body bags.

The scope of the devastation becomes increasingly apparent as more lights arrive and the dust vented away. For Lazarus, life becomes an endless parade of death. As the hours roll past, the dead blur into a horrible collage. Stress and exhaustion distort time until his mind discards the concept entirely, leaving him with only the present. In his world, he has been doing this forever and would continue past infinity. Life outside of this bloody hole recedes into a dream. Reality becomes an endless cycle of digging and pulling smashed bodies from the rubble.

Thirty-three hours after they had first entered the hospital, Tempel is close to total collapse. He finds Lazarus sitting on a chunk of broken stone staring blankly into the distance. Without uttering a word, Tempel pulls the exhausted man to his feet, and they make their way back to Dakota freehold, each leaning heavily on the other like a pair of drunken sailors.

Lazarus will not remember the walk or seeing Lindsey or her pulling him into the shower before removing his blood and filth-encrusted clothing. He will have no memory of getting into bed and her holding him until his trembling stops. His mind shut down hours ago. It simply stopped processing data.

He slips into a coma-like sleep that worries Lindsey. She asks a doctor to check on him. Following a hurried examination conducted over the network by an MD who has herself been awake for over forty hours, Lindsey's told there's nothing physically wrong with Lazarus. The best thing is let him sleep until he awakens on his own, however long that may be. Lindsey stays with Lazarus for many hours before finally slipping away.

Evolution's Child

Nell Goddard rechecked her calculations one last time before submitting them to Luna Central. She didn't want to spoil her perfect record, proud that LC has never corrected her figures in the years she's been piloting Evolution's Child.

"Course received. Awaiting verification. Stand by." The unsmiling face of the uniformed flight controller is someone she'd never seen before. Not that Nell cared who granted authorization, but the uniforms were starting to bother her.

When the man disappeared, Nell found herself looking at the tiny snapshot of her two girls. Don't let anyone tell you that time will heal all wounds. It doesn't. Her heart hurt every bit as much today as it did when she lost her two little angels.

Nell had rejected most of what human society had to offer on that day seven years ago. That was when her two girls, ages six and eight, were killed in a school bus bombing in London, England. She found out when a special bulletin announced the tragedy complete with video from an unmanned helicopter showing the smoldering remains in 3D high definition. It turned out to be Middle Eastern terrorists thinking they were somehow hurting the European Union by this senseless act of violence. Interpol tracked them down, one by one, extracted whatever information they possessed and executed them.

That didn't do Nell any good. Her life ended that day and a new person gradually emerged from the ashes of her former self. It wasn't the first time she had rebuilt her life, but it was the most painful.

In her youth, Nell danced in the bars along Stanwell Moor Road just outside Heathrow International Spaceport, back when it was filled with strip clubs and drug dens catering to business travelers. She had made excellent money flashing her green eyes up at the johns. At only 165 centimeters, most of them towered over her, bringing out either the protector or the dominator in every man. That was before she met James and fell in love, before the girls and that terrible afternoon when she lost them all.

Her marriage didn't last. James blamed her for what happened to the kids or maybe she blamed herself. She could have home-schooled them as so many of their friends had done, but Nell wanted her kids to experience what a real school was like, with real children interacting with real teachers on a daily basis. After James left her, Nell had a decision to make; go back to dancing or find something new.

She had played with drugs and alcohol off and on her entire adult life. Everybody did and she was no exception. It would have been easy to fall for their empty promise of absolution, but Nell had seen too many friends disappear down that rat hole and knew only oblivion was to be found there. To tell the truth, oblivion held a certain appeal but something inside wouldn't let her give in. Instead, she went a different direction. Nell walked into the local Space Recruitment Office and signed up for training.

The official who had administered the entrance exam never thought the disheveled, thin, malnourished young woman would pass but she did, with a very high score. Over the next twelve months, Nell quietly amazed a host of teachers and instructors in the program and graduated at the head of her class. The grand prize for being the best was first choice of the jobs being offered. She picked piloting Evolution's Child because of its splendid isolation, far away from the evening news.

That was years ago and millions of miles, yet the pain remained.

"You are free to burn for orbital insertion." The uniformed controller broke into Nell's thoughts.

"Roger, Luna Central. Initiating sequence." Nell responded.

Without another word, the flight controller disappeared leaving Nell wondering what was going on. Lunarians were usually friendly.

Some Things About Chuck

Autobiography

Let me tell you just a little about myself. My folks were divorced before I was three back when divorce was unheard of. Guess they just couldn't take my incessant howling. No matter. They both loved me and that was all I really cared about at that age. I grew up bouncing between Colorado and Southern California and loving every minute of it. By the time I started high school, I had visited every state west of the Mississippi.

Speaking of high school, mine was in a small town on the Mojave Desert. Counting the occasional tourist, Boron topped out at about 5000 souls, but it wasn't boring. The main part of the town is nestled at the feet of a high-desert volcano-looking mountain with a rocket engine test facility built into its summit. Edwards Air Force Base is just on the other side of it from Boron. You could always tell who was new in town; they flinched every time a sonic boom rattled the windows. The mountain we simply called the Rocket Site and ignored the loud noises. They tested the Saturn 5 engines at the Rocket Site, the ones that took our boys to the moon. Once in a while they would fire them up at night. What a sight. What a noise. Those babies would shake the world in a way impossible to describe. It's something that must be felt and then you will never forget it.

Long story short, after four years in the army mostly in Baumholder, Germany, I went to college and earned a BS in Engineering Mechanics-Aerospace from the University of Wisconsin-Madison and a Masters in Materials Science from Arizona State University. For a while I worked at Space Data/Orbital Sciences Corporation designing, building, and launching rockets and high altitude weather balloons. I launched rockets from Mexican, Canadian, and American soil. My sounding rockets even launched from the deck of a French frigate. Later, I was the Quality Assurance Manager for Hybrid Design Associates in Tempe. HDA is a small manufacturing company that specializes in harsh-environment electronic assemblies. Among a host of other customers, we built electronic boards for the oil logging industry, Halliburton, Baker Atlas, Pathfinder, etc.

A couple decades ago I was lucky enough to marry the most wonderful woman in the world. We have three kids and six grand-kids. I run a small publishing company, Writers Cramp Publishing, and write under my full name, Charles Lee Lesher. My debut novel, Evolution's Child, was selected as 2007's Best of the Moon Fiction by the Lunar Library. You can still buy it, but now it is part of the Republic of Luna series. Evolution's Child has morphed into two Kindle novels, **Evolution's Child - Earthman** and **Evolution's Child - Lunarian**. I know, its weird but what can I say. The creative process is not always as neat as we would like. The third book, **Evolution's Child - Thread,** makes this a trilogy. You can also buy all three novels in one big bathroom reader, Shadow on the Moon is 500 pages of science fiction excitement.

I used the research obtained writing the Republic of Luna series to write a nonfiction titled **Out of the Cradle** on sale as a conventional hardcover, a gorgeous Kindle Fire, and now as a Full Color 8.5 x 11 Paperback. The first half of the book will bum you out but the second half will lift you up giving hope to our future. The world is changing and we had better be ready. The biggest change will be energy. Electricity is a key component holding our technological civilization together. What happens when we finally run out of oil and the coal is gone? Don't sweet it. There is an answer and nuclear is not involved, at least, not in your backyard. Buy my book and see how we are doing the impossible.

My latest book is a western set in the Verde Valley before Arizona was a state. The story takes place in the Arizona Territory at a time when the only law enforcement outside the capital city of Prescott was a few men wearing a star. When one of them goes bad, all hell breaks loose.

Chuck's Other Books

Bad Day on the Verde

WESTERN FICTION

Lying awake on the floor, Tom cried out and made a weak play for his Winchester. He was stopped abruptly by the butt of Kingsley's heavy shotgun. Tom slumped back, dazed and bleeding. Kingsley relieved Tom of the rifle.

"I could of killed you, but I didn't. But I will if you give me any trouble." Kingsley gave Tom a real close look at the gaping muzzles of the Baker 10 gauge.

Kingsley rolled Tom onto his stomach tying his hands behind his back, relishing the moans this caused. He pulled Tom's boots off throwing them across the small cabin. Standing, he lashed out and kicked the man savagely in the ass. "Get the hell up, boy."

Bad Day is a western story of violence and brutality, of sudden frontier justice, but also of courage and enduring love. The story takes place in the Arizona Territory at a time when the only law enforcement outside the capital city of Prescott was a few men wearing a star. When one of them goes bad, all hell breaks loose..

ISBN 978-1-938586-72-9 Paperback
ISBN 978-1-938586-73-6 eBook

Shadow on the Moon

SCIENCE FICTION

The Republic of Luna is humanities first extraterrestrial nation. Science, genetics and a humanistic society mark it as a target for the powerful Islamic Brotherhood, a global empire with billions of believers. Luna is a world created by pioneers whose only religion is the humane treatment of one another in their common struggle to survive the ultimate hostile environment, space. The heroes that conquered the moon must now defend it.

Shadow on the Moon combines *Evolution's Child - Earthman, Evolution's Child - Lunarian, Evolution's Child - Thread*, and *Science of the Republic* into one 500 page Anniversary Print Edition.

ISBN: 978-0-977723-56-0 Paperback

Aldrin Station - Rise of Luna

Aldrin Station is a collection of short stories illuminating Lunarian history from the dawn of mankind to its expansion into space and colonizing the moon. These are stories of the families and individuals that play a role in the Republic of Luna.

ISBN 978-1-938586-00-2 eBook

Evolution's Child - Earthman

SCIENCE FICTION

Book One: Lazarus Sheffield is a man without a planet by the time he meets Lindsey on his way to Heaven's Gate Space Station. Lindsey quickly determines that the nervous guy sitting next to her is a high ranking government official on the run from one of history's most repressive governments, the totalitarian theocracy otherwise known as the North American Federation. She decides to help him and introduces Lazarus to some of Luna's finest citizens. So begins Book One of Shadow on the Moon.

ISBN 978-1-938586-06-4 Paperback
ISBN 978-1-938586-01-9 eBook

Evolution's Child - Lunarian

SCIENCE FICTION

Book Two: Tempel Dugan leads a group of Lunarians against impossible odds. They call themselves Quan Kiai. These young warriors, and a few more like them, are all that stands between the Republic of Luna and total annihilation but things are not always as they seem.

ISBN 978-1-938586-07-1 Paperback
ISBN 978-1-938586-02-6 eBook

Evolution's Child - Thread

SCIENCE FICTION

Book Three: The Republic of Luna is teetering at the point of collapse when the Lunarian General Council commits their last hope. They send Quan Kaia and the remaining Lunarian warriors against the Brotherhood. Fight or die. They fight in their great underground cities, they fight cross the surface of the moon, and they fight in orbital space. Earth and Luna become locked in humanities first interplanetary war, the Shadow War.

ISBN 978-1-938586-08-8 Paperback
ISBN 978-1-938586-03-3 eBook

Science of the Republic

A collection of articles, maps, and tables that help the reader understand the science and technology of the Republic.

ISBN 978-1-938586-04-0 eBook

Out of the Cradle

SCIENCE FACT

Where will we get our electricity when the oil and coal are gone? Why should I care? Abundant cheap electricity a key element in getting and maintaining high human living standards around the globe. Stated another way, electricity is the foundation of modern technology. Without it, we go back to sailing ships and the horse. Out the Cradle summarizes the major issues facing the world today and lays out a solution to our global energy needs.

ISBN: 978-0-983750-64-2 Hard Cover
ISBN: 978-0-983750-68-0 eBook

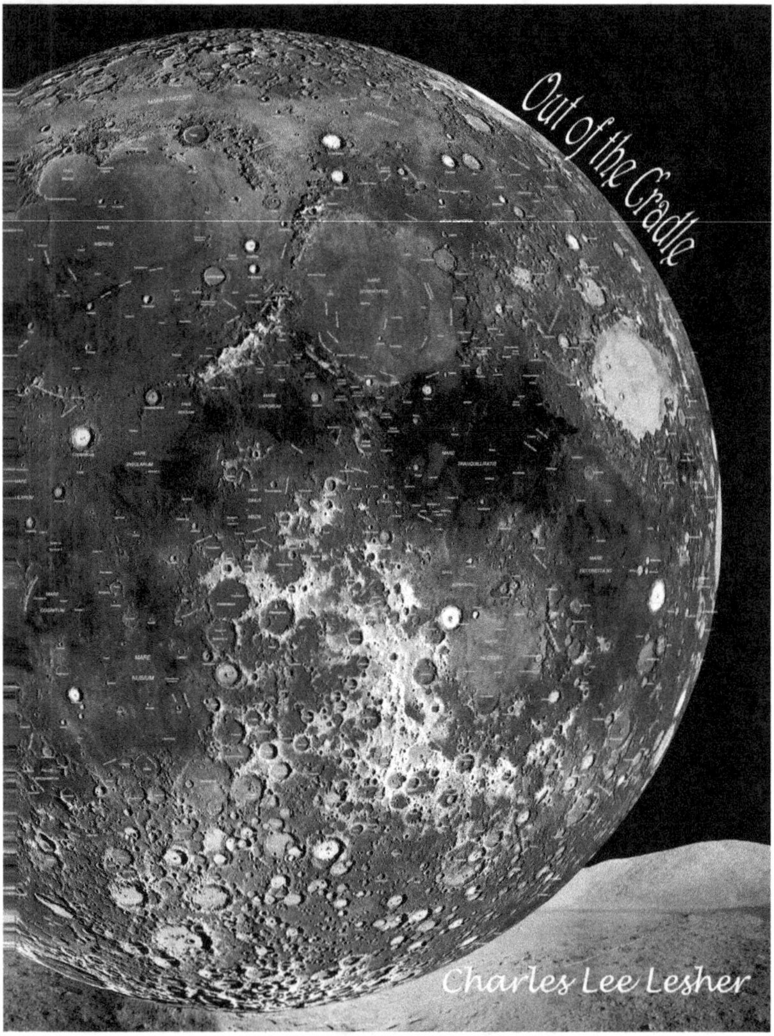

8.5 x 11 Color Version
ISBN: 978-1-938586-71-2 Paperback

Writers Cramp Publishing

http://www.writerscramp.us

editor@writerscramp.us

Amazon, Barnes&Noble, Google, Espresso

www.ingramcontent.com/pod-product-compliance
Lightning Source LLC
Chambersburg PA
CBHW070823180626
46818CB00001B/376